The Holiday Inn

FARRAH ROCHON
"Rochon presents a stellar story that
thoroughly entertains."
—*Romantic Times BOOKreviews* on *Release Me*

STEFANIE WORTH
"Worth has masterfully written a paranormal
adventure with superbly developed characters."
—Real Page Turners on *Where Souls Collide*

PHYLLIS BOURNE WILLIAMS
"*A Moment on the Lips* is refreshing...the subtle
romance is sweet and enjoyable."
—*Romantic Times BOOKreviews*

THE *Holiday* INN

PHYLLIS BOURNE WILLIAMS
FARRAH ROCHON
STEFANIE WORTH

LEISURE BOOKS NEW YORK CITY

A LEISURE BOOK®

October 2008

Published by

Dorchester Publishing Co., Inc.
200 Madison Avenue
New York, NY 10016

ISBN 10: 0-8439-6157-0
ISBN 13: 978-0-8439-6157-7

The name "Leisure Books" and the stylized "L" with design are trademarks of Dorchester Publishing Co., Inc.

Printed in the United States of America.

10 9 8 7 6 5 4 3 2 1

Visit us on the web at www.dorchesterpub.com.

THE *Holiday* INN

TABLE OF CONTENTS

A Change of Heart

by Farrah Rochon

Chapter One

Pillow-soft snow flurries flitted from the sky in a gentle shower, kissing the edge of Chandra Stovall's nose with the tenderness of a holiday angel.

"Here's the snow you wanted," came the call from the trunk of the yellow taxi from which Derek, her husband of twenty years, retrieved their bags.

"Yes, here it is," Chandra murmured, the disappointment settling in as the elation she'd hope to feel at the first sight of the snow she rarely saw back home in Dallas failed to materialize. She chewed the edge of her lip, and swallowed her sigh. It was naïve to think a simple change in the weather would instantly alter her mood.

Chandra wrapped her hands around her upper arms and sucked in a lungful of the crisp, pungent, pine-scented air. She had the entire weekend ahead of her, ample time for the Christmas card–worthy scene before her to work its magic, if there indeed was any magic nestled under the branches of these towering pines.

Chandra clung to the thread of hope that had surfaced when she'd first thought up the idea to spend Christmas in the Rocky Mountains. As her eyes took in the cabin, with its welcoming double-pitched entryway fashioned out of thick logs and shielded from the falling snow by a wide canopy, she was cautiously optimistic about the weekend. She wanted her children to have at least one more perfect holiday *just in case* this was their last together as a family.

Chandra thanked the cab driver with a generous tip. As she stared at the filthy tracks the car made in the pristine snow as it backed down the driveway, a disquieting thought settled into her bones. Would her plans for a picture-perfect holiday turn into a dirty, mucked-up mess like the one the tires had created in the unblemished snow? With the way she and Derek were getting along these days, this entire getaway could turn out to be disastrous.

No. She would not allow petty bickering to mar this trip. For the sake of her son and daughter, Chandra would make sure this Christmas was everything she'd envisioned. They deserved one last happy memory.

She glanced over at her husband. Derek stood at the base of the stone steps leading up to the cabin's large wooden porch. He was surrounded by their bags, his arms crossed over his chest. Naturally, Derek had overcompensated for the cold, the two sweaters and leather coat making his massive shoulders appear even wider. He wore a wool cap over his clean-shaven head. His neatly trimmed goatee twitched as his mouth twisted in a grim smile. Chandra followed his gaze to the side yard; saw his eyes had zeroed in on the stacks of logs resting against a thick tree stump with a red-handled ax wedged dead center.

With a derisive laugh, he shook his head. "I guess I have to spend my vacation chopping firewood." His eyes settled on her. "Tell me, Chandra, was that by design?"

Chandra flinched at his accusation, but she refused to rise to the bait. She was in no mood to fight.

Instead, she turned her attention back to the log home nestled under the shady, snow-laden pines of Boreas Pass Mountain in the quaint ski town of Breckenridge, Colorado. When she'd found the two-story cabin on a vacation rental home website a couple of weeks ago, Chandra had instantly fallen in love. By sheer luck, the ski party who had rented out the cabin had cancelled the same morning she'd called the leasing office.

For the past few weeks, she'd dreamed of sitting before the inviting fireplace while her children, Anika and Derek, Jr., filled her in on what they'd accomplished during the fall semester at school. She envisioned her family preparing Christmas Eve dinner together while Donny Hathaway's "This Christmas" streamed from the surround-sound system the website had boasted. When the kids were young, they'd helped with the preparations for Christmas Eve dinner. Even though their *helping* usually meant more work for her, Chandra cherished the closeness the ritual created. She missed that part of their past.

There was a lot she missed about the way life used to be, like the way she used to laugh with her husband. The way they would enjoy a glass of wine in the evening while discussing the events of the day. The way Derek used to sneak up behind her and plant tiny kisses along her neck while she folded laundry or washed dishes. She couldn't remember the last time she'd experienced any of those things that used to make her smile.

Chandra shook off the morose recollections and motioned to the two full-size suitcases and two carry-on bags at Derek's feet. "Do you need a hand with those?" she asked him.

Derek's eyes fell to the bags. "No," he said. He stooped and drew the strap of one carry-on over his shoulder. He looked back up at her. "Chandra, I'm sorry," he said, contriteness clouding his eyes. "What I said before about the firewood? That was uncalled for."

Burrowing deeper into the collar of her down-filled jacket, she accepted his apology with a nod of her head. "I don't want to fight, Derek. This weekend is supposed to be peaceful."

"I agree," he said. "But let's be honest, Chandra. I'm not the one who starts the fights."

Squelching the response that would undoubtedly lead to the argument they'd both just claimed not to want, Chandra took a step toward the footpath leading to the house. She refused to stand idle while he placed the blame for the state of their marriage on her shoulders again. She owned a portion of it, but this fog of indifference that had settled over their relationship was not solely her doing. It took two to make a marriage work, and neither one of them was pulling their weight these days.

Scary thing was, Chandra wasn't sure it was even worth the effort anymore.

Her cell phone's serenade of Beethoven's Fifth Symphony saved her from the bother of evading Derek's censure. She retrieved the phone from her jacket's front pocket. Her daughter's cell number illuminated the tiny screen.

"It's Anika," Chandra provided as she flipped the cell phone open. "Hello, baby, are you getting ready to board?"

"Nope," her daughter replied. "My flight's been delayed."

Chandra's shoulders slumped. The unreliability of the airlines was the only thing that could put a wrinkle in her family reunion. "Is there bad weather in New Orleans?" she asked Anika, who had just completed her first semester as a freshman at Xavier University.

"No, they said it's the weather out there in Colorado," Anika answered.

Chandra looked overhead at the sky. It was a ceiling of gunmetal-gray clouds. The snowflakes had indeed begun to fall in greater numbers. "Let's hope it clears up soon."

"Have you heard from D. J.? When I call, I get his stupid voice mail message."

Her eyes still trained on the increasingly darkening sky, Chandra shook her head. "No," she answered. "He should be in the air already."

"We're supposed to ride together from the airport," Anika pointed out. "You know he won't wait for me if his plane gets in before mine does."

"Yes, he will, Anika. You don't have to worry. His flight from Atlanta had a layover in Kansas City. You should still get in before he does. Did they say how long your delay is?"

"Forty-five minutes. Hold on," Anika paused. Chandra heard her groan. "They just pushed it back to an hour and fifteen minutes. When you talk to D. J. remind him that his flight was scheduled to get in a half hour after mine, and I was willing to wait for him."

"I'll tell him." Chandra smiled. "Let me give him a call. I'll tell him to call you when we're done."

"Alright. Love you, Mom."

"I love you, too. I can't wait for you to get here. You're going to love this place."

Chandra hung up the phone, but before she could locate her son's number in her cell phone's address book, Derek said, "I just got a text message from D. J. His flight's been delayed."

Great. Well, at least Anika didn't have to worry about her brother leaving her at the airport. Hopefully their delayed flights would sync and they would still arrive close together.

"So has Anika's," Chandra told him. "We should go in and find a weather report on television. I want to get an idea of how fast this bad weather is moving."

Despite her husband's insistence that he did not need

help, Chandra picked up the remaining carry-on bag and followed Derek into the blessed warmth of the house. The rental company's manager had left a message on her cell phone saying that she had turned the heat on earlier this morning.

Chandra's breath caught in her throat as they entered through the frosted-glass and wood door. The pictures on the renter's website did not do the cabin justice. Rich, glossy, maple brown logs encompassed the walls and vaulted two-story ceiling. A staircase led from just past the entryway up to the second floor, which included a bridge that overlooked the first level. A breathtaking display of snowcapped mountains was visible through the wall of floor-to-ceiling windows; two comfy recliners faced it to afford their occupants the stellar view.

"I'm happy I didn't complain about the cost," Derek said. "I'd have to eat my words. This is worth every penny."

"It is beautiful," Chandra agreed, unzipping the shoulder bag that held her photography equipment. "I have to take pictures of it untouched before D. J. gets here and it ends up looking like his room."

She wanted to capture the peace that resided in the stillness of this home. The inviting space before the massive two-story stone-laid fireplace screamed for a happy family sipping mugs of hot chocolate and telling stories of Christmases past.

The holidays had always been a reason for celebration in their household, but as the kids grew older, interest in the season had dwindled. Anika had spent last Christmas in her bedroom downloading music onto the new iPod Derek had bought her, and Derek, Jr. had accepted an invitation to spend the holidays at his college roommate's family home in the Hamptons.

"God, please," Chandra whispered to herself. Divine

intervention may be the only way to get the Christmas her heart was yearning for.

Derek Stovall deposited the suitcases at the base of the wooden stairs that led to the second floor of the log cabin. As his eyes roamed the rich wood interior and comfortable-looking furniture, Derek regretted the grief he gave Chandra for suggesting they spend Christmas in the mountains. He hated the cold, but he had to admit the prospect of a few days kicking back in a place like this held definite appeal. If he were able to pull off having a civil weekend with his wife, he was looking at the perfect Christmas.

They'd gotten through the flight from Dallas and the hour and a half cab ride from the Denver airport without arguing. That was a start. If he could, Derek would take back that crack about having to chop firewood all weekend. It was the cheapest kind of shot, and he'd be lucky if she didn't make him regret it the rest of their time here. Maybe she would let it slide. After all, Chandra had been the one to propose an argument-free holiday before they left Dallas. For the sake of the kids, of course. Derek mentally tacked on "for the sake of his sanity" to the list.

This constant conflict with her was driving him out of his mind. Things had been running as smoothly as ever, and then wham! Just like that, a few months ago she started picking and poking at every little thing he did. He had been forgetting to pick up the dry cleaning for twenty years, why did it all of a sudden warrant a fight?

Derek followed a fair distance behind Chandra as she scoped out the cabin's main floor through the eye of her camera lens. She'd removed the knit ski cap from her head, leaving her short, cropped hair to stick out at awkward angles. Of course, it didn't detract one bit from her attractiveness. Chandra was like a fine bottle of wine—she became more exquisite with age. Her creamy, toffee-colored skin was as flawless today as it had been twenty years ago. Her petite frame, fit and trim.

She stopped at the wall of windows that provided the perfect view of the mountains. Derek stopped about a foot behind her. He had an overwhelming urge to put his hands on her shoulders, but knew the gesture would not be well received, and he was in no mood for another rebuff.

"Breathtaking, isn't it?" Chandra said, lowering the camera and looking from one side of the landscape to the other.

Derek took a step up and stopped right beside her. "In my thirty-nine years, I've never seen the mountains with my own eyes," he said. "They're amazing."

"The kids are going to love this."

"Yeah," Derek agreed, shoving his hands in his pockets. "Maybe we should let them enjoy it before dropping the separation bomb on them."

She sucked in a deep breath and turned to him. She had yet to remove the bulky ski jacket. It seemed to serve as tangible evidence of the invisible wall she'd built around herself over the past few months.

"I don't want to mention the separation to the kids at all. The whole point of this vacation is to create a happy memory for them, Derek."

"We can't *not* tell them."

"I know that." She hunched her shoulders. "I just figured we'd wait until the time was right."

Derek ran a hand over his head and down his face. "When is the time ever right to find out your parents are going to start living apart?"

"I don't know. I just . . ."

"What, Chandra?"

A voice in his head told Derek to back off. Bringing

this up would not serve to make this the peaceful holiday weekend they were striving for, but dammit, when *would* they talk about it? Over the past couple of weeks—ever since she'd brought up the idea of a separation—Derek had been trying to get her to sit down and talk to him. They had yet to do so.

Chandra cradled the camera against her chest, and hunched her shoulder again. "I don't know, Derek. Telling the kids makes it so real."

He crossed his arms over his chest. "You're the one who suggested the separation."

"I know that."

"So, what? You don't want to go through with it?" *Please say yes.*

"It's not that," she said quietly. "We already decided a separation is for the best."

Derek's heart constricted as his brain railed against her words. *She* had decided a separation was for the best. She hadn't given him a chance to say anything about it.

Chandra had blindsided him Sunday afternoon three weeks ago when she'd come to him during halftime of the Steelers/Packers game and told him she thought it would be a good idea if they spent some time apart.

At first, Derek didn't grasp what she was saying. Certainly she wasn't talking about moving out, separating in the *breaking up their marriage, living in two separate homes* sense of the word.

After dropping that initial bomb, she went an entire week without mentioning the separation, and Derek figured it had all been just a knee-jerk reaction to some infraction he hadn't realized he'd made against her. Soon after, she'd jumped on this perfect-holiday bandwagon, and Derek assumed that was the end of the separation talk. When he'd discovered Chandra's motivation behind this trip—to give the kids one last perfect Christmas as a family—it sent a shock of pain rioting throughout his brain.

"Chandra," he prodded.

"Derek, please." She held up one hand.

Derek stopped. Despite his questions, he held off for their promised holiday peace. Hopefully, his fears will disappear like melted snow.

"I want to take a few shots outside," Chandra said, un-hooking the clasp on one of the French doors that led to the wraparound veranda. Derek followed her, bunching the collar of his leather coat around his jaw. The snow was coming down in earnest now, the light flurries of just a half hour ago making way for thick, fat snowflakes.

"This is crazy," Derek said, stretching his hand out and marveling at the precipitation that held its form even when faced with the warmth of his palm. "The few times it's snowed in Dallas has nothing on this."

Chandra laughed. It was that laugh he hadn't heard in months. True, natural, noncondescending.

"What's so funny?" he asked, returning her smile.

"You," she said, gesturing to him. "You look like a little boy on Christmas morning."

"Just excited." He shrugged, wiping his hand on his jeans.

"All of this snow does put you in the spirit, doesn't it?" she said, stretching her hand out and catching a few snowflakes.

"A lot more than the seventy-degree weather they're having back in Dallas," he agreed.

The shrill of the classical music from Chandra's cell phone came from just inside the house.

"That must be Anika," she said before shouldering past him and heading into the cabin.

Derek stood on the deck a minute longer, taking in the clean, fresh air. He squinted, trying to see if he could spot skiers on the mountains ahead, but the snow was coming down too fast and too thick. If it kept up this pace, they were probably looking at three or four inches of snowfall overnight.

Derek went back into the house and, not finding Chandra in the great room, walked to the kitchen. It was a decent-size kitchen, with plenty of counter space and stainless steel appliances Chandra was sure to love. In the center there was an island with a single sink and a tall, gooseneck faucet. At the far end of the room was a dining area with a round table accompanied by four chairs and a sideboard. A bowl of pinecones sat in the center of the table.

Chandra was standing next to the island with her cell phone to her ear, the intense look on her face squishing the faint scar at her temple, courtesy of D. J.'s toy sword years ago.

"Well, what did the ticketing agent say, Anika?" A pause. "That's it? She didn't give you an idea of when flights would resume?"

That didn't sound good.

Chandra rubbed her temple. "I know, baby. I know." She noticed him and shook her head, an agitated frown creasing her mouth. "Call me as soon as you hear anything, no matter what time." Another pause. "Okay. Yes. I love you too, baby. I'm sorry about this."

Chandra expelled a deep breath as she snapped the phone shut and placed it on the counter. She shoved both hands through her hair.

"Her flight's not just delayed anymore, is it?" Derek guessed.

"Cancelled. Along with all of the other flights to the Denver area on every other airline."

"Have you heard from D. J.?"

"I was just about to call him." She flipped the phone open and put it to her ear. From what Derek could gather from her one-sided conversation, D. J.'s flight had been cancelled, too. "Cancelled," Chandra confirmed when she closed the phone. "He's already back at his dorm. You would think he'd have the consideration to call and let us know."

Derek could only shake his head. Knowing D. J., it didn't surprise him that his son wouldn't think to give them a call.

"So what? It's just wait-and-see?" Derek asked.

"I guess. Let's hope this weather clears up so they can catch the earliest flights out in the morning."

"It's coming down pretty hard out there." Derek motioned to the window behind her as he took the few steps that would bring him alongside her.

"Great," Chandra said, disappointment clouding her face.

"They'll get here," Derek assured her. He took a chance at putting his arm around her shoulders, and thought he caught a slight flinch. But then her muscles relaxed, and he wondered if he'd just imagined her recoil. When did such a nonchalant gesture become an oddity between them?

"You hungry?" Derek asked, even though he had no idea if there was any food in the house. He hadn't even thought about how they would eat while they were here, and he didn't think to look for a grocery store on the cab ride up the mountainside.

"I could use a little something," Chandra said. "There should be a quart of potato soup in the refrigerator."

He gave her shoulders a final squeeze before strolling

over to the refrigerator. He opened the right door of the double-door stainless steel fridge and found it well stocked. Milk, eggs, cheese, a spiral-cut ham sealed in clear plastic, and over a dozen cartons of different sizes. Derek reached in and pulled them out one by one. Cornbread dressing, candied yams, giblet gravy, potato soup.

"How did all this food get here?" he asked.

"I ordered it to be delivered before we left Dallas," Chandra answered.

"So we're not cooking Christmas Eve dinner tomorrow?"

"There should be a turkey in the freezer, and we've still got to make the mashed potatoes, greens and dessert."

"I didn't know they had places that delivered your Christmas dinner." He closed the fridge and carried the container of soup to the island. "Makes sense, though. Gives you more time to enjoy the holidays without spending your entire day in the kitchen. Maybe coming out here *was* a good idea."

Chandra snorted. "Don't sound so surprised. I am capable of coming up with one of those every now and then."

Derek turned at the cynicism he heard in her voice. "Oh, c'mon, Chandra, you know what I meant." This was the type of crap she'd been pulling lately, harping on any little thing he said and finding a way to twist his words around. "Are you doing this on purpose?"

"Doing what?"

"Picking these petty fights with me?"

"I haven't been picking fights with you," she said defensively.

"Are you kidding me? I can't say two words to you without you taking my head off, or even worse, walking out on me."

"Like I'm about to do right now, you mean?" She pushed away from the island and headed out of the kitchen.

"Chandra!"

"Forget the soup," she said. "I'm going to bed."

Chapter Two

Chandra woke to the sound of heavy thumping coming from just below her window. She stared at the wooden slats of the vaulted ceiling and contemplated all the reasons to stay cocooned in the seductive warmth of the plush bedding. But if she stayed in bed her mind would continually conjure up the look on Derek's face when she'd left him standing in the middle of the kitchen last night.

A sick, sad feeling pitted itself in Chandra's stomach. What had happened to her vow to keep this weekend hostility-free?

Was Derek right? Had she purposely picked a fight with him? Did she harp on him at home?

No, she did not harp. If anything she'd gone too long without voicing her discontent, and after twenty years of being underappreciated, Chandra had had just about enough. She was tired of Derek's dismissal of every single thing she did for this family; as if her contribution didn't count simply because he was the one who brought in the money and she didn't.

But none of that was supposed to matter this weekend. She'd made the decision to leave all of the hurt and frustration back in Dallas. For the sake of her children, she was going to make sure this holiday was perfect.

"But the kids are not even here," Chandra said to the empty room.

They would be soon, though, and she did not want

them to walk into a house filled with tension. Which meant she needed to clear the air with Derek before Anika and D. J. arrived.

She didn't want to face him this morning. She was not in the mood to hear the accusations, or deal with his questions about why she had not slept in the master suite's bed with him last night. She'd asked herself the same question, but the answer continued to elude her.

Back at home, she'd fallen asleep on the chaise lounge in the study for three nights before this trip, but Derek hadn't questioned her. She'd done the same thing often enough over the past twenty years when wrapped up in a good book; this time, though, it felt different. Chandra wondered if the past three nights in the study had been her subconscious way of pulling away from him.

To be honest, she had started pulling away a lot longer than three days ago. She and Derek hardly talked anymore. They had not been intimate in nearly six months. It was only a matter of time before separate beds became a reality in their existence.

Chandra untwisted herself from the straightjacket she'd created with the bedsheet and searched the floor for her slippers. She washed up in the connected bathroom and threaded her arms through the sleeves of her bathrobe as she headed down the stairs. The rich aroma of freshly brewed coffee met her halfway to the kitchen. Chandra pulled in a lungful of the heady scent.

She spotted the coffeemaker, its carafe full. She searched the cabinet for mugs, finding them, along with plates, saucers, and glasses behind the second door she opened. She pulled out two mugs and filled both with coffee. She added two teaspoons of sugar and a splash of cream from the fridge to one of the mugs, then wrapped a hand around each handle and headed for the front door.

Derek was at the wooden stump. A respectable pile of quartered fire logs lay haphazardly just to the right of him. He brought the ax down on another log, splitting it in two before throwing the pieces to join the others.

"Is it time for a break yet?" She gestured with the mug from the edge of the wraparound porch, then took a couple of steps back and sat on the wooden bench just to the right of the door.

Derek wedged the ax in the center of the stump. He walked over to the pile, grabbed an armful of firewood and started toward her, a handsome smile gracing his face.

Chandra's heart lifted in appreciation. By his generous smile, she surmised Derek was willing to hold true to their truce, despite her abrupt exit last night.

"Good morning," he said, dumping his load into the meshed iron crate next to the bench.

"Morning," Chandra returned. She scooted to the side of the bench to make room for him. "For somebody who doesn't like the cold, you're sure out here early."

"The cold is the reason I'm out here. Did you catch the weather last night?" *While you were in your separate room* were the words that were not said, but definitely implied. He didn't voice them, so she wouldn't mention it either.

"I didn't even turn on the television," she answered.

"We're in for some serious weather," Derek said. He used his teeth to pull the glove from his right hand and wrapped his palm around the mug. "It's gonna fall down into the single digits before the day is out, and they're expecting at least eight inches of snow."

"Just today?"

Derek nodded.

"Ouch," Chandra said as she sipped from her mug. That was a bit more than she'd anticipated when she said she wanted Anika and D. J. to experience a white Christmas. "I hope the kids can get here before the snow starts falling again. I'd hate for them to be on the road in all of that."

"I talked to Derek, Jr. right before I put the coffee on. He's getting updates from the airline, but so far all flights into Denver are still grounded."

"Did Anika call?"

"You really expect that girl to be up this early in the morning?"

"You're right," she blew into her coffee mug before taking a sip. She'd hoped she could go without addressing last night's incident, but the space between them sizzled with uncomfortable tension. If she didn't clear the air now, Chandra knew it would fester. She didn't want this unease to infect the entire weekend.

"Derek, about last night."

He didn't say anything, just stared out into the wooded area ahead and sipped his coffee. Chandra's hackles rose at the air of self-righteousness she sensed in his calm, blasé stance. That was just one of the things that had started to irritate her more and more. She was always the irrational one, while he was the sensible one who was there to add reason to the situation.

Chandra tamped down the urge to get up from the bench and leave him out here; that would only serve to bring more tension between them.

"I'm sorry," she said.

Derek continued to stare into the woods.

"You could at least acknowledge my apology," she said when he remained silent.

He shifted from his rigged stance and fixed her with a confounded gaze. "I don't know how to talk to you anymore, Chandra." There was genuine confusion in his softly spoken words.

"So you just don't say anything at all?" Chandra asked. He nodded. "That seems like the safest bet these days."

"That's not fair, Derek."

"If I'd said 'Fine, I accept your apology,' you would have accused me of being patronizing. If I'd asked you to explain why you all of a sudden turned on me last night, you would have said I was trying to goad you into a fight."

Chandra was set to dispute his argument on pure principle, but stopped. Before she'd even voiced her apology she had been going over in her mind how to refute his response, whatever it may be. To actually listen to anything he had to say hadn't even occurred to her.

The picture his allegation painted didn't sit well with Chandra, especially since she could see truth in his claim. Still, the cloud of discontent shrouding their marriage was not entirely her fault. That Derek would try to lay the blame at her feet was so typical.

"You said you didn't want to fight," came his response. "I didn't say anything because I wanted to honor your wish."

"I also said I wanted peace between us. Do you really think the kids wouldn't sense the strain in the air? They're not stupid, Derek."

"Exactly. They're *not* stupid. They will see through this pretense, Chandra."

"Not if we vow to bury this right here, right now. Can we make a pact to leave the hostility out of this weekend?"

"I thought we already did that?"

"For real this time. I'm serious, Derek. I want to enjoy this holiday."

"That's all I want too, Chandra."

He switched his coffee mug to his right hand and stretched out his left hand to her. Chandra placed her palm in his, mixed emotions flooding her brain at the sensations touching him created within her. When was the last time she'd held his hand, for any reason at all? She gave his hand a squeeze. It felt like the right thing to do.

He returned the gesture, and a margin of the peace Chandra had hoped for seeped into her bones.

"I want to chop a few more logs, just in case," Derek said before letting go of her hand.

"Have you had breakfast yet?" Chandra asked.

"Just the coffee."

"I was going to make some pancakes. Want some?"

"I won't turn down your famous pancakes," he smiled. He rose from the bench and headed back down the steps. He stopped at the last step and turned back to her. "Thank you, Chandra."

"For what?" she asked.

"For all of this. All the planning you did. Finding this place, ordering groceries. For wanting to give our kids a perfect Christmas. All of it. Thank you. That's what I didn't get the chance to say last night."

Chandra's chest constricted at the sincerity in his eyes. She hadn't given him a chance to say anything before storming out of the kitchen.

"I'm sorry, Derek," she said. She owed him at least that much.

He hunched his shoulder. "It's buried, remember?" He touched two fingers to his head as if tipping an imaginary hat to her. "To a perfect Christmas."

The unmistakable aroma and sizzling hiss of bacon frying in a cast-iron skillet greeted Derek when he entered the cabin. He walked over to the fireplace and deposited the stack of chopped wood in the brass bucket, then headed straight for the kitchen.

Chandra was at the stove, pushing the bacon around

with a fork. She'd changed into a pink fleece jumpsuit, and had turned on a holiday CD. She was humming along with an old Jackson Five Christmas carol and shaking her hips.

Derek stood back for a minute and just looked at her. It had been a long time since he'd seen her like this. Carefree. Unreserved. She looked like the old Chandra for a change. His heart twisted. He had not realized how much he missed that person until this very moment.

What would it take to get them back to the way they used to be, when she stood at the stove of their home back in Dallas and sang with the radio while she cooked breakfast? These days, barely a word was spoken between them during the few minutes they saw each other before he headed to check on the operation of the twelve car detailing shops he owned in the Dallas/Fort Worth area. It had actually become commonplace not to talk to his wife for days at a time.

God, how had they allowed that to happen? And why had it just occurred to him that he and Chandra had floated so far apart?

Taking a step forward, Derek said, "Something smells good in here."

"Derek!" Chandra screeched. Her free hand flew to her chest. "I didn't even hear you come in. I'd been watching to see when you were done chopping wood. I didn't want to start the pancakes too soon. I know you—"

"Don't like them rubbery—"

"—don't like them rubbery—"

They spoke in unison.

"Yeah," Chandra said, dropping spoonfuls of batter on the sizzling griddle.

Chandra always knew what he liked and just how he liked it. She'd spent the past twenty years taking care of him, and he'd spent the same twenty doing the same for her. So why had she all of a sudden started treating him as if he was a bother?

Derek kept his mouth shut. They'd made a vow of civility, and he'd be damned if he broke it.

He strolled over to the stove where Chandra was flipping disc-size pancakes on the built-in griddle. Derek grabbed two plates and two glasses from the cabinet.

"Juice or milk?" he asked Chandra, since she'd already had her one cup of coffee this morning.

"Juice," she answered. She took the plates from him. "You want two or three pancakes?"

"Two is fine."

"You sure? I used real butter and real buttermilk." Derek's mouth started watering. "And, there is real maple syrup," Chandra finished. She laughed. "I think you'll take three."

She brought the plates to the table and they settled in to eat.

"I think we should go to the ski lodge," she said halfway through their meal.

"What's at the lodge?"

She shrugged. "It looked really nice on the website. I'd like to browse around for a bit, maybe buy the kids a little something extra for Christmas."

"That's not a bad idea," Derek mused. "I only bought one gift for Anika."

"What'd you get her?" Chandra asked, and Derek had to wonder when they'd started buying separate gifts for the kids. It was a decision they always used to make together.

"I got her a pair of amethyst earrings."

"Amethyst, like my grandmother's wedding ring?"

He nodded, taking a sip from his mug.

"I still can't find it." Chandra sighed. "I don't even remember losing the ring. It was there one day and gone the next. I keep hoping it will turn up someday."

"It will," Derek said with an inward smile.

"I'm sure Anika will love her earrings. She's always loved Nana's wedding ring."

"With Anika, you can never go wrong with jewelry."

"She does take after her mother." Chandra laughed.

"That's not a bad thing." Derek smiled over the rim of his mug.

"Is that compliment *my* Christmas present?"

"C'mon now. When have you ever known me to be cheap?"

Her laughter faded as she eyed him across the table. "Derek, you did not buy me a gift."

"I'm guessing you didn't buy me one." He couldn't help but laugh at the scowl she shot him.

"Well, no."

He waved her off. "Don't worry about it."

"But why would you get me a gift?"

"It's the holidays. That's what people do."

"But—"

"Don't worry about the gift," Derek said. He pushed his empty plate away and rose from the table. "How do we get to the lodge? You mentioned there's a shuttle?"

Chandra nodded. "At the base of the lane that leads up to the house. It runs every twenty minutes."

"How about we head out in another half hour. It won't take me long to wash up."

Derek was true to his word, grabbing a quick shower and changing into fresh jeans and a sweater in less than twenty minutes. He was waiting outside the door to the bedroom where Chandra had slept the night before. Derek wasn't sure why it had come as such a shock to him that she'd chosen to sleep in one of the spare rooms. They had not shared the same bed for days; why would it change simply because they were away from home? But what about when the kids got here? Would she still insist they sleep in separate beds?

Derek knocked lightly on the door. "Chandra?"

The door opened. "You're done already? That was quick." She closed the bedroom door behind her.

"Actually, I'm wondering if I should have gone out and chopped a few more logs. I want to give us a bit of a cushion with the wood supply." He shrugged. "Maybe when we get back."

"As long as you don't accuse me of making you spend your Christmas doing manual labor," she said with a rueful grin.

"I'm sorry about that," he apologized again.

"I was only teasing," she said.

Teasing? The concept wasn't foreign, but it had been a while since she'd teased him about anything.

Derek helped her with her coat and locked up the cabin behind them. As she was walking down the stairs, Chandra slipped on a patch of ice and stumbled back.

"Whoa, there." Derek caught her under the arms. Her back fell against his chest, and in that instant it occurred to him just how long it had been since he'd felt the sensation of his wife's body against his. God, it felt good. She worked out on a regular basis, but still managed to remain completely feminine, soft and warm and perfect.

Derek's blood started to stir, but he tamped down his awareness, admitting that it was more than likely one-sided.

"You okay?" he asked.

Chandra nodded, righting herself and grabbing onto the railing. "That's all I need—to fall and break my neck.

With the way this snow is falling, it would be nearly impossible for an ambulance to get here."

"Yeah, we'd better head out so we can get back to the cabin before it gets much worse."

The shuttle stop was only about twenty yards down the winding lane, but with the steadily falling snow and undetectable patches of ice, it felt more like twenty miles. Derek used the opportunity to get closer to Chandra. It felt good to hold her close, to feel her body heat melding with his. It occurred to him that he had not availed himself of the joy of just being close to her for months.

"There's the shuttle," Chandra said as they approached the stop.

"Just in time."

The doors to the shuttle bus opened and Derek held a hand to her lower back as she climbed the steps ahead of him. The bus was empty save for another couple who snuggled so close together they were almost fused as one.

Judging by how young they both looked, they probably hadn't been married more than a couple of years. Derek found himself envying the husband, who caressed his wife's reddened cheek without much thought, while he was still relishing the rush he experienced over just being able to hold his wife's hand.

"This is beautiful, isn't it?" Chandra's eyes were glued to the scene outside the shuttle's smoked-glass windows. "It looks like the winter wonderland you hear about in Christmas songs. Look at those street lamps." She pointed to the wrought-iron structures straight out of a Norman Rockwell painting.

The town did have that fairy-tale look to it. Old-fashioned shops, cobblestone roads, the snow dusting it all in a bit of magic.

"It's all so quaint." Chandra's eyes were lit up like the decorated Christmas trees visible through the shop windows.

God, she was beautiful.

Derek couldn't help himself. He reached over and covered her hand with his. He could feel her heat through the leather glove she wore. It seeped into his bones and warmed him from the inside out. Instead of pushing his hand away as he first thought she would, Chandra covered it with her other hand. A ball of emotion the size of a goose egg welled in Derek's throat. He missed this. The sensations evoked by simply holding her hand were so profound; he could hardly understand how he'd gone so long without her touch.

The shuttle driver parked at the slot closest to the entrance to the ski lodge. Before exiting the shuttle, Chandra stopped and addressed the driver. "Have you heard anything about how long this storm is supposed to last?"

He shook his head. "Not sure. From what I hear, as soon as one storm passes, another forms to the north of us. It's not unusual for this time of the year."

"Will flights be able to get in?"

He shrugged. "I have no idea." Before they could get off the bus, the driver stopped them. "If you want to make it back up the mountain, you need to hurry. When it gets like this, the authorities usually shut the roads down."

"Our children haven't arrived yet. Will they allow an airport shuttle or a cab to get through?" Chandra asked.

"They might," was all he said before closing the doors of the shuttle.

Derek could see the worry etched on her face. He was worried, too. The airport in Denver was over an hour and a half away. If the skies cleared up enough for Anika and

D. J. to fly in, the roads might still prevent them from being able to reach Breckenridge.

Derek looked over at Chandra. The delight he'd seen in her eyes as she'd looked out at the town had been replaced with worry.

"Hey, there." Derek gave her shoulder a squeeze. "Why don't we get to doing what we came to do? You need to start shopping. You've got to find me a gift, remember?" he teased, hoping to lighten her mood.

The smile she returned wasn't nearly as genuine as Derek had hoped. He couldn't blame her after the shuttle driver's ominous prediction. Still, there wasn't much they could do other than wait out the approaching storm and pray that another would not follow.

Taking Chandra's hand, Derek led her into the ski lodge.

Chapter Three

"Don't think it."

Chandra jumped. She hadn't heard Derek enter the bedroom. Her mind was too occupied with thoughts of Anika and D. J. What if they didn't make it here for Christmas Eve dinner? D. J.'s flight had a layover. What if he spent his Christmas Eve sitting around in some airport?

Chandra swiped at invisible dirt on the handsome armoire that stood catty-corner to the shorter wardrobe.

"Chandra, stop." Derek was right behind her. He reached around and stayed her hand. He took the pillowcase she'd been using as a dusting rag and, with his hands on her shoulders, turned her around to face him.

"The kids will be fine," he said, his astute brown eyes filled with understanding. "Stop worrying about them."

"I'm not worried."

The quirk to his brow reminded Chandra that this man knew everything about her, including her tendency for excessive cleaning when she was anxious about something.

"Any more of you not being worried and you're going to start washing the clean towels in the linen closet."

Chandra opened her mouth to retort, then noticed the makings of a grin edging up the left corner of Derek's mouth. A burst of laughter came out, despite her attempt to keep it bottled.

"I can't help but worry," she admitted, wiping a tear that had managed to escape. "Spending Christmas in the mountains was my idea. If the kids' holiday is ruined over this, I'll never forgive myself."

"First of all, whether or not the kids make it in time for Christmas will not have that much of an effect on their holiday. They both have friends who will take them in. And secondly"—he gave her shoulders another reassuring squeeze—"the only thing anyone can blame you for is trying to give your family the perfect Christmas. You couldn't plan for the weather, Chandra."

"Yes, I could have," she said. "I'll bet there's no snowstorm in Hawaii."

Derek's head tilted back with his crack of laughter. "We can do Christmas in Hawaii next year."

Derek instantly sobered. The camaraderie that had surfaced between them in the last few moments died a swift death at the thought of next Christmas. If they continued on the course she'd set before they left Dallas, they would not be together this time next year.

The significance of that thought hit Chandra squarely in the chest, causing her breath to hitch in her throat. She had never truly thought about what life would be like without Derek. Since she was nineteen, he had been irrevocably intertwined with every part of her existence. How different her life was going to be when they separated.

The faraway look in Derek's eyes told her he was thinking the same thing.

Was she making the biggest mistake of her life?

"I was thinking, maybe I should go out to that wooded area behind the cabin and find us a Christmas tree," Derek suggested.

"Really?"

"Why not?" Derek shrugged. "May not be as nice as the one you put up back home, but it'll be something. What's Christmas without the Christmas tree?"

"But we don't have any ornaments," Chandra pointed out.

"We can be creative. Come on, let's go find us a tree." His voice was so full of fake cheer that it had raised half an octave.

It didn't take a genius to see what he was trying to do, and Chandra's heart melted at his thoughtfulness. That he would care enough to try to get her mind off the kids—by bearing time in the cold to find them a Christmas tree, no less—caused Chandra's chest to tighten with emotions she had not felt in a very long time.

"I think I'll take some pictures while you're chopping down the tree," she said. "I heard a woodpecker yesterday. I don't get to see those often. Just let me change out the memory card in my camera."

"I'll meet you downstairs," he said. He grabbed her makeshift dust rag. "I'll take this just in case you spot more dirt."

"Get out of here," she laughed, pushing him on the arm. Chandra leaned against the armoire and shook her head as he retreated. She'd forgotten how sweet Derek could be when he put in just a bit of effort.

Just a few weeks ago, Chandra had come to the conclusion that a large part of their problem was that neither of them were putting in much effort these past few years. They'd been going through the motions, projecting the image of a happy, successful couple without actually living the life. It wasn't until the kids left the house—D. J. to start his freshman year of college at Morehouse, and Anika to study in Italy during her senior year of high school—that

Chandra had been forced to acknowledge the chasm in their relationship.

The kids had been a great distraction, her reason for not examining the state of her marriage. After Anika and D. J. left, the silence in the house had been deafening. Other than a quick word over coffee in the morning, or the occasional call asking him what he'd like for dinner—a dinner he usually ate long after she'd gone to bed—she and Derek hardly spoke at all.

The most disappointing realization came when Chandra acknowledged that her husband saw nothing wrong with the way things were between them. He could go the next fifty years just existing.

She didn't want to just exist. She wanted to *live*. She wanted to feel again; to experience the excitement she'd known when they were first married. Was that asking too much?

Chandra caught movement out of the corner of her eye and moved to the bedroom's second-story window. Derek was zipping up his coat as he walked toward the tree stump.

"At least he's trying," she said. She grabbed her camera from where she'd placed it on the nightstand. "Time to go find a tree."

When she joined Derek outside, he was holding the ax Paul Bunyan style, gripping the hilt with one hand and the neck with his other.

"You look like you're ready to chop down a ten-footer."

"Nah," he said with a smile. "Nine and a half, tops."

Derek motioned for her to go ahead of him, but Chandra shook her head. "You go first." Self-preservation dictated that she follow a couple of steps behind. She wasn't sure what type of mountain animals lurked out here.

They had only walked a few yards into the wooded area when Chandra spotted two rabbits traipsing in the snow. She raised the camera and zeroed in on them through the lens, snapping off over a dozen shots with the high-powered, rapid-shutter camera Derek had surprised her with for their anniversary back in February.

Memories of the awful fight they'd had that night invaded her mind, but as she settled on the scene before her, Chandra stopped short, another thought coming clear. She'd been eyeing the Nikon D300 Professional Series camera since the moment it hit the market nearly four months prior to their anniversary. She'd just bought a new camera during the Day-After-Thanksgiving sales, so even though they could certainly afford it, Chandra couldn't justify spending the money for something that was still, essentially, a hobby.

Derek must have been paying attention, because the camera had arrived elaborately gift wrapped the morning of their anniversary. But her elation over his thoughtfulness had been tainted when he'd chosen to go to the Dallas Mavericks basketball game with a group of supervisors from the body shops instead of coming home to enjoy the steak dinner Chandra had prepared as a surprise.

Chandra had been so angry she'd left the camera in the box for a month. As she thought back on that day, and the subsequent argument, she realized Derek was not the only one at fault. When he'd asked if she wanted to go out for dinner on their anniversary she'd told him no. In fact, she'd told him she'd had a photography class that night. During their argument, Derek had pointed that out, and said he'd called the camera store and had them move up the delivery time so she would get her gift before her photography class.

How could she blame him for not being there for dinner when she'd told him she wouldn't be there herself?

An unease similar to what she'd felt when Derek accused her of picking a fight with him settled over her. How much of her discontent was of her own doing?

She shook off the depressing thought and focused on the rabbits as they scampered over a fallen log. She captured shots of the landscape. Snow-laden pine needles just moments from falling under the weight of their burden. A lone squirrel rummaging through a mixture of dead leaves, needles, and fallen tree bark, moving from pile to pile and coming up empty. Poor little thing. Would he survive the impending storm?

Chandra heard a thwack and turned around, the camera still to her eye. She spotted Derek through the lens. He swung the ax and connected with a tree. Chandra depressed the button, catching him in progressive stages of chopping down their Christmas tree.

He looked oddly familiar through the eye of her lens. Like the husband who used to spend his Saturday mornings doing yard work around the tiny two-bedroom house they'd started out in when they were first married. So different from the man who'd had to hire a private gardener to maintain the extravagant landscaping that was required in the gated community where they now lived.

Derek gave the tree another whack and stepped back as it keeled over onto the snowy ground.

Chandra snapped one final picture of the tree in motion before securing the lens cap.

Derek picked the tree up from its pointed top. "What do you think?" he asked. "Not a ten footer, but it'll do, right?"

The tree looked a little under five feet tall. Without

Christmas lights or ornaments to adorn it, Chandra surmised they would have been just fine with a two-foot shrub, but the look of pride on Derek's face as he hoisted the tree stopped her from voicing that opinion.

"You need any help carrying it?" she asked.

He shook his head. "I'm good. Why don't you go ahead of me and see if you can find something to put it in."

Chandra followed the path they'd taken. The footprints they'd made were already being refilled with freshly fallen snow. It was coming down even harder.

When she reached the cabin, she went around to the side just to the right of where the wraparound porch ended, but didn't see anything there that would hold the tree. Chandra sloughed through the snow that had become ankle deep to the other side of the house, but again, came up empty.

She came back to the front yard and found that Derek had made it back to the cabin.

"Found anything?"

Chandra shook her head. "What about the wastepaper basket in the guest bathroom?"

"Not sure the plastic will hold up," Derek said.

"Wait." Chandra climbed the steps, unlocked the cabin's front door and headed to the fireplace. She unloaded the seven pieces of firewood Derek had sat in the round, brass bucket and carried it back outside.

"What about this?" she called from the porch. Chandra navigated her way down the steps, taking care not to slip. "Maybe we can loosen up enough ground to pack the base with dirt."

"Sounds like a plan." Derek took the bucket from her and used it to shovel away a patch of snow. He kicked away the remaining snow with his boot, and hammered at the ground with the ax. "This baby sure has come in handy," he said. It didn't take him long to break up a good portion of the dirt.

"I hope they don't charge us for mutilating the ground," Chandra said.

"It'll be worth it to have a Christmas tree for the kids."

At the mention of the kids, Chandra unzipped the side pocket of her parka and pulled out her cell. She hoped the kids had some news about their flights, but when she checked for missed messages on her phone, there were none.

"Nothing?" Derek asked.

Chandra looked up at him, noticing the concern that was probably reflected on her own face. She shook her head.

"Check mine." He stuck his hip forward where his phone was clipped to his belt. "D. J. may have left a message on my phone."

Chandra slid the phone from the holster at his waist. Despite the cold, the phone still held his body heat and a faint trace of the scent that was uniquely Derek. She loved that smell.

Chandra stared at the phone that resembled a pocket computer with its full keyboard and numerous buttons. She was completely lost.

"How do you even work this thing?"

Derek looked over at her and grinned. He laid the tree down and walked over to her, slipped the device from her fingers and pressed a couple of buttons.

"You need to take a step into the twenty-first century, Sweet Pea."

His use of her old nickname, combined with the handsome grin that still tipped up the corner of his mouth, caused a heady sensation to course through her veins. She took a deep breath.

"No missed calls or messages," Derek said, clipping the

phone back at his hip. "You know how those two are. They're probably both in the air by now, and didn't even bother to call."

"Probably," Chandra murmured as the comfortable ease of being with Derek filled her mind. "Yes, of course," she said, shaking off the haze of sensual awareness that had suffused the air around her. "I'm fine." She nodded at the pile of dirt he'd been able to break loose from the ground. "You need some help with that?"

"If you don't mind getting your hands dirty."

"When have I ever minded a little dirt," Chandra huffed. She stooped down and was about to scoop up a handful of dirt before Derek stopped her.

"On second thought, how about you hold the tree up and I pack the dirt around it."

"I can do that," she said. She didn't mind getting her hands dirty, but didn't relish the thought of handling frozen dirt one bit.

Chandra stuck her arm between the branches and wrapped her hand around the tree's inner shaft while Derek scooped dirt around the base. He packed it down, and all Chandra could think about was the scrubbing she would have to give that brass pot before they headed back home to Dallas.

"Let it go," Derek said.

She did. The tree tilted to the side.

"Maybe a little bit more," Chandra suggested. Derek nodded his agreement and scooped in more dirt. Chandra stuck her hand between the branches again, and at least four of them fell right off the tree.

"Umm . . . oops," she said.

Derek looked up at her, then down at the branches at her feet. "What did you do?"

"Nothing," Chandra said defensively. "I was just trying to hold it in place."

"Then what happened to the branches?"

"I don't know. You're the one who picked this baby tree to chop down. This tree probably had a long life ahead of it."

Derek's expression became mournful, almost guilty, as if he was genuinely sorry for the pain he'd cause the scraggly pine tree.

Chandra tried to keep a straight face, but couldn't hold it. Derek's eyes flashed to her after the giggle escaped.

The makings of a smile edged his lips. "That was a low blow," he said. "You know ever since I accidentally sat on Bingo I've had this hang-up about taking out living creatures."

Chandra burst out laughing at his reference to the gerbil Anika had received for her eighth birthday. Derek had probably spent a thousand dollars on gifts to make up for squashing Bingo. It wasn't until Chandra reminded him that Anika should have had the pet in its cage that he realized Anika was in the wrong, and had been milking his guilt for all it was worth.

"And now you're laughing at me," Derek said.

"No." Chandra shook her head, but couldn't get out another word for all the giggling. "Oh, gosh," she said, wiping at the tears that nearly froze as they streaked down her cheeks. "I'm sorry."

Derek stood up from where he'd crouched in the snow. His arms were crossed over his broad chest, and the thoughtful look on his face had Chandra stifling her laughter.

"What?" she asked.

He stared at her for a long moment before saying in a

soft voice, "It's been a long time since I heard you laugh like that."

She tucked in some of the hair that had escaped the confines of her suede-lined ski cap, inwardly cringing at the self-conscious gesture. She was out here with her husband of twenty years, but all of a sudden felt as insecure as the nineteen-year-old freshman at the University of Texas in Arlington who had dented his front fender while backing out of a parking spot.

"Where has that laugh been, Chandra?"

"It's been there," she automatically answered, though she couldn't remember the last time she'd heard herself laugh either. "I guess I just haven't had much to laugh about."

They stood there in the snow, the flakes falling around them.

After what seemed like forever, Derek broke the tension with a smile. "At least I'm still good at giving you something to smile about," he said. He turned back to the tree. "Though I'm not sure how you can still smile after committing Christmas tree homicide."

Chandra gasped. She stooped down, scooped up a fistful of snow, and hurled it at the back of his head, catching him at the collar of his jacket.

Derek turned, humorous surprise etched across his face. "I can't believe you just did that."

"That's for calling me a tree killer."

"After you called me one."

"Yeah, but *you* really *are* one."

Before she knew what he was doing, Derek had a ball of snow in his hand and was threatening to throw it at her.

"No!" Chandra screeched. She took off, trying to get away. The ankle-high snow was not making it easy, especially with the snow boots weighing her down.

"Why run?" she heard Derek call. "I'm going to catch you no matter what."

"Leave me alone!" she yelled, giggling. "Go find another baby tree to murder!"

Chandra ran to the edge of the yard where the snowdrifts had begun to build even higher. She tried to step over one, but when her foot sank shin deep in snow, she knew she was caught.

She twisted around, finding Derek right behind her.

"No," she squealed. He lunged at her and they went flailing back into the puffy snowdrift.

"Ouch," Derek breathed next to her. Chandra was so overcome by a fit of giggles, she was barely able to catch her breath. Or maybe it was having the wind knocked out of her that had stolen the air from her lungs.

Or maybe it was the feel of her husband against her after all this time, the weight of him so familiar as it pressed upon the parts of her body she hadn't realized felt so neglected.

"I'm sorry," Derek said, rolling off her and collapsing in the snow. Her body instantly mourned the loss of his, both for the heat it provided and the reminder of long-forgotten feelings.

"I was supposed to stop right before I got to you, but my momentum got the better of me," Derek continued. He sat up and leaned over her. "Did I hurt you?"

Chandra looked up at him, unable to bury the desire his proximity had stirred up in her. She shook her head slowly from right to left, unconcerned about the snow wetting her face.

"No," she whispered. "Actually, it felt really good."

Chandra saw the instant her meaning registered. Derek's eyes went from concerned to heated, his intense gaze zeroing in on her mouth. His head lowered. He asked permission with his eyes, which Chandra gave with a slight nod before he leaned in and covered her lips with his.

The pleasure was instantaneous, the remembered sensations so powerful it was as if she'd been catapulted back in time. Back to a place when her husband kissed her for no reason other than because he wanted to. When they snatched stolen moments to touch each other. When he would come home in the middle of the day to make love to her.

It all seemed so long ago. But one thing had not changed. Derek's kiss could still set her on fire. Despite the bed of wet snow, or the flakes falling from the sky, heat suffused her body as Derek's tongue took the first tentative dip into her mouth.

Chandra welcomed his slow, sweet kiss, her body burning from the inside out as he explored her mouth. She returned his kiss with matched ardor, sucking his tongue into her mouth and feeding him her own.

The whirl of a police siren jolted her and Derek apart. He rolled off her and quickly stood. Chandra accepted his proffered hand as he pulled her from the snowy ground.

The patrol car pulled up to them.

"Good morning, Officer," Derek said, shaking the snow from his pant leg and wiping it from his sleeves.

The officer tipped his hand to his hat, his mouth quirked in a knowing smile. "Sorry to disturb you," he said. "We're letting everybody know that we're shutting down the mountain in anticipation of the big storm. Slopes and roads are officially closed."

"I thought the storm passed through last night," Chandra said, moving to the driver's side of the police cruiser.

"That was nothing," the officer said. He looked up at the sky through the car's windshield. "We're expecting upwards of two feet of snow and forty-mile-an-hour winds. It's going to get ugly out here. Make sure you have a reserve of firewood. This can go on for at least thirty-six hours."

"Wait!" Chandra put her hand on the car door, halting the window's upward motion. "What about people flying into town?"

The officer shook his head. "Denver International shut down a half hour ago. Take care, it's going to be a rough Christmas." The officer tipped his hat again and drove off.

Chandra looked over at Derek. They went for their phones at the same time. As Derek pulled his phone from its holder, it rang.

"It's D. J.," he said.

Chandra wrestled her cell from the pocket of her parka. The screen was black. Her battery must have died.

"Okay," Derek was saying. "Thank Mrs. Miller for us. Yeah, your mom's calling Anika right now." Chandra shook her head, but Derek wasn't paying attention. "Okay, D. J. We'll call you later. Be safe, son," he finished.

Chandra held up her phone. "My battery's dead."

"I had eight missed calls," Derek said as he pressed more buttons on his phone.

"What did D. J. say?"

"Both their flights have been cancelled. D. J. had just talked to Anika. Here." He handed her his phone. "Call her while I get the tree."

"You know I can't work that thing," Chandra said.

Pulling the tree from the pot of loosely packed dirt, Derek chuckled. "Wait until we get inside. I'll give her a call."

"Just leave the tree," Chandra said.

"I've already cut it. Besides"—he stopped to peer up at the sky—"we might need it for firewood."

Chandra grabbed the brass pot she'd taken from the

fireplace, dumped the remaining dirt, and followed Derek toward the house. She went ahead of him up the front steps and held the door open as he dragged the tree up and pulled it into the house, leaning it against the wall just inside.

He took out his cell phone and called Anika's number. From where she stood more than a foot away, Chandra heard her daughter squawking.

Derek listened for a moment, then said, "Talk to your mother." He handed the phone to Chandra. When she was done convincing Anika that they were okay and were well stocked to spend the night in a snowstorm, Chandra hung up the phone and turned toward the great room.

"Is she okay?" Derek asked.

"Just worried about us," Chandra answered.

"Like mother, like daughter."

She gave him a wan smile, but didn't deny that she was worried, too.

"I've stocked up on firewood, and we have a fridge full of food. All we can do is wait it out. Doesn't make sense to work yourself up about it."

"You're right," Chandra said.

Though, after what had happened minutes before the patrol car pulled up, Chandra wasn't worried about the storm nearly as much as she worried about spending the night alone with Derek in this cozy cabin.

Chapter Four

Derek stoked the fire one last time before returning the poker to its holder. He walked over to the expanse of windows. The snow had started falling hard again. The empty chairs of the immobilized ski lift dangled haplessly in midair. It created a sad picture. The lifts had only one job, to bring happy skiers to the top of the mountain. Without the skiers, their purpose was meaningless. Sort of like a picture-perfect family Christmas with only half the family present.

For no good reason, his mind jumped to the young couple who'd been snuggled up together on the shuttle this morning. How different they must feel about this snowstorm that would keep them sequestered in a cozy mountainside cabin. They probably hadn't made plans to leave their cabin that often to begin with, but Mother Nature had provided a better excuse not to venture out into the cold.

Derek wasn't sure what to think of the situation he'd landed in at the hands of Mother Nature. Sure, he and Chandra were alone in their house in Dallas all the time, but there was over six thousand eight hundred square feet for them to roam about, and the routine they'd fallen into, especially over the past few months, kept them apart. While this cabin was big enough, it was still pretty close quarters compared to what he and Chandra were both used to. Close quarters could be a dangerous thing, especially when the thoughts swirling through his head at the moment had him ready to revisit their tumble in the snow.

His gut clenched at the remembered feel of her body pressed against his.

What would Chandra's reaction be if he kissed her again? Would her lips part for him the way they'd parted this morning—timidly at first, but still accepting? Derek's eyelids slid shut as he imagined running his hands down her backside while he thrust his tongue in her soft, warm mouth.

"Lord, help me," he groaned. He was seriously jonesing for his wife.

He turned to find her back in the great room, fluffing the throw pillows on the sofa. She pulled the blanket that was draped over the back of the sofa and started running her fingernails through the fringe, smoothing them out until they were precisely the same width apart.

She was still worried about the kids. At home, whenever he'd find perfectly spaced fringes on the crocheted throw she kept on her grandmother's old rocking chair, Derek would know there was something weighing heavily on her mind.

He walked over to the hearth and shoved two additional logs under those already smoldering in the fireplace, then he moved to the sofa and gently pried the blanket from Chandra's fingers.

"You've got to stop this, Chandra. The kids will be fine," Derek reassured her, bringing her hand up to place a soft kiss in the center of her palm. He wanted to kiss away the troubled look in her luminous brown eyes. He just wanted to kiss her, period.

"They won't make Christmas Eve dinner," she said in a small voice. "Anika said the earliest flight she could possibly get won't leave until seven tomorrow morning, and D. J. still isn't sure when he will be able to get out."

"So, we'll save the big meal for tomorrow," Derek suggested.

After the kiss they'd shared, the idea of the kids not making it to Colorado until tomorrow didn't seem like such a bad thing. The prospect of spending time in a secluded cabin with his wife suddenly had all kinds of appeal.

He put his hands on Chandra's shoulders and squeezed. "It's not as if the kids are spending Christmas Eve stuck in the airport. They're both staying with friends we trust."

"I know." Chandra pulled her lower lip between her teeth. She lifted her head and Derek was rendered breathless by the vulnerability in her gaze.

He brought her hands up to his lips again. "Why don't we just enjoy today?"

After a deep breath, she said, "Okay." She set those dark-colored eyes on him again. "What did you have in mind?"

"Oh, baby," he murmured. "That's not even a question." Derek felt a twinge of guilt for attacking while her defenses were down, but it was not enough guilt to stop him. He lowered his head and captured her lips in a slow, sweet-tasting kiss that sent chills running along his skin.

It was like coming home after a long, arduous absence. Her full lips were soft and warm, and they relinquished with heart-stopping ease to the insistence of his mouth. Derek parted her lips with his tongue and found what he was seeking within the depths of her mouth—a hot, inviting cavern of remembered tastes; that unique flavor that was unmistakably Chandra.

The sense of familiarity pummeled him, catapulting Derek back to a time when he used to avail himself of

Chandra's kiss whenever the mood struck him. It was the most natural feeling in the world, remembering the supple give of her lips as she invited him in.

Why had he gone so long without this? Why had he deprived himself of the magic of Chandra's delicious mouth?

He didn't want to question it any longer. Not right now. All he wanted was more. So much more of her lips and tongue and sweet, sweet flavor. Derek ran his hands along her sides, then over her butt where he cupped and pulled her into full contact with his increasingly aroused body.

Chandra moaned into his mouth. He drew his hands up the small of her back, lifting her shirt, and bringing his fingers to the front to span her smooth, flat stomach. God, she was still as sexy as ever.

Derek cupped her breasts, and felt her instantly stiffen.

"No . . . wait," she said, tearing her mouth away.

"What's wrong?" he murmured against the column of her throat.

"I . . . we." She took a step back.

"What is it?" Derek soughed between deep breaths.

"We can't just lose ourselves in a kiss and pretend everything is okay, Derek."

He ran his hands down his face in frustration. Unleashed desire rang in his ears. "What in the hell is the matter with you?"

She took another step back, wrapping her arms around her waist. "I just don't want you to think this changes anything."

"Change from what, Chandra? I missed the big change the *first* time. When did we go from being man and wife to being these two people who can't even share a kiss without it being a big deal?" She turned from him, but Derek grabbed her arm and turned her to face him. "No. I'm tired of you brushing me off."

"Let go of me," she growled and jerked her arm, but he didn't let up his hold. The look she shot him was deadly.

"You're not going anywhere until we settle this, Chandra."

"Let go of me!"

"Dammit, woman, talk to me!" Derek roared.

"I *tried* to talk." She flung the words at him, ripping herself away from his grasp. "That's the problem, Derek! Whenever I tried to talk, you were too busy to sit and listen."

"Don't pull that stuff with me, Chandra. There's not a minute of the day that you don't know where to find me."

She cut him with a scathing glare. "As if you would ever tear yourself away from work long enough to talk to me."

"That's no excuse. It might be hard to get a hold of me during the day, but I come home to you every night. If you really wanted to talk, you know where to find me."

"Where? Locked up in your home office? Entertaining friends in the fancy entertainment room you just had to have?"

Not this again.

Derek plopped down on the sofa, and folded his hands between his spread knees. He hung his head, trying to figure out a way to get through to this woman.

"How many times have I told you, that's the way you get things done in this business. There are no boardrooms. Business deals are made over a game of pool. Potential investors listen to your pitch during halftime of the Super Bowl! The people I entertain are the same people who help keep a roof over our heads!"

Derek raked his hands down his face, the frustration and lingering sexual arousal making him edgy as hell. "You know, the wives of most of my friends would love to have your problems, a husband who's concerned about providing for you. Do you even realize how lucky you are, Chandra? You want me to list the names of all of the guys I know who constantly sleep around on their wives?"

She speared him with a cynical glare. "And you don't have a mistress?" she asked.

Derek saw red. He shot up from the sofa, blood rushing to his brain like hot lava. He'd be damned if he sat here while his wife accused him of being unfaithful.

He stepped up to her; got right in her face.

"Don't you ever try to pin that label on me, Chandra. I have never once even *thought* of cheating on you with another woman, and you know it. I can't believe you would try to play that game with me."

"I didn't say anything about another woman, Derek," she said. "You don't have time for another woman, but you've been cheating on me with your other love since the very first location opened." She wrapped her arms around her waist. When she looked up at him, her eyes were filled with hurtful resignation. "The way I see it, those other wives are lucky. They only have one mistress to compete with. I'm up against twelve, with two more coming up in the Richland Hills area."

Derek jabbed a finger at her. "That's not fair, Chandra. I've busted my tail building that business."

"And I appreciate everything it has provided for our family."

"So why are you blaming the business for what's going on between us?"

She shook her head, a remorseful grin edging the corner of her mouth. "You just don't get it, Derek."

"What?" He held his hands out. "What don't I get, Chandra? I get that I've worked day and night to put a roof over your head, and food on the table. I've done everything I could to provide my children with a good education. Do you know how much it cost a year to send Anika and D. J. to school?"

"Of course I do." She lifted her chin in the air. "I'm the one who writes the checks."

"Yes, with the money my *other lover* provides!"

"And if we didn't have that money, Anika and D. J. would have done the same thing I did in order to pay for school: scholarships and student loans."

"Yeah, and they would be paying off those loans for the next twenty years, just as you would have had to if not for Stovall's Body Shop. Is that what you want for your children?"

"That's not what I'm saying, Derek." She shoved her fingers through her short hair. "Can we please just let this rest?"

"No, Chandra. It's rested long enough. I deserve to know why my wife is so ungrateful for the lifestyle I've given her. While all your old friends have had to get up and go to work every day, you got to stay at home and raise your kids. But I guess that wasn't good enough for you."

"Don't you even try that with me," she spat. "I never said I wasn't grateful. I've always been right there with you, Derek, supporting you while you busted your butt building that business. But remember it was *you* who chose this path. You're the one who decided one shop just wasn't enough. No, you had to build an empire."

His anger cooled a bit. "That's what everyone strives for, Chandra. The American dream."

"Working like a maniac is not my version of the American dream."

Derek crossed his arms over his chest, disbelief jockeying with annoyance for the chief spot in his brain. Annoyance was winning.

"I can't believe you can stand here acting so self-righteous, as if you haven't been enjoying the fruits of my labor all these years."

Chandra's eyes were swamped with regret. "Derek, it isn't all about the money. I would have given up all of that stuff a long time ago if it meant I'd have my best friend back."

He heard her speak, but her words could not penetrate the part of his brain that focused on the fact that after all the sacrifices he'd made, Chandra had the gall to blame him and his business for the rift in their marriage.

"I can't believe you're putting all of this on me. Forget this," he said, then stomped out of the great room and headed out the front door.

Chandra plopped back onto the sofa. She grabbed one of the throw pillows and tucked it underneath her chin. She wanted to cry. Lord, did she crave to just let the tears roll down her face. But they would not come. She'd cried all the tears she would cry over the state of their marriage long before they boarded that plane and headed for the mountains.

Chandra half sobbed, half snorted, and realized maybe there were still a few tears left to be shed. She thought back on all the planning she'd done for this weekend, fussing over every little detail to make this Christmas one her family would always remember. Yeah, she wasn't likely to forget the shouting match that had just sent Derek storming out into the cold without a jacket.

"I should let him freeze," she sniffed.

But she knew she wouldn't. She would give Derek the benefit of the doubt, since he hadn't had much time to digest all of this.

She'd toiled over the situation in her own mind already,

making the same arguments Derek had made. Yes, he was a great provider. Even in those lean days when he had been just another mechanic working out of his uncle's garage, their family never went without a meal, or received so much as a single notice from the electric company. Derek did everything he could to take care of them. It's when the fancy cars, private schools, and lavish vacations fell under his definition of "taking care of his family" that things had changed.

He'd gone out and made a million without ever consulting her. He just thought it was what she'd wanted.

"And did you ever once tell him you didn't?" Chandra asked out loud.

She knew her part in all of this. She could have spoken up back when he'd opened the shop in Arlington, Stovall's sixth location. Chandra knew then that with every new shop, Derek's time at home dwindled, but instead of approaching him with her concerns, she'd sat back and allowed her frustration to fester.

No, this definitely was not all Derek's fault.

A part of her wanted to head upstairs and sleep away the rest of this weekend, but the grown-up in her knew she needed to smooth things over with her husband. If she was going to maintain a semblance of the peaceful holiday she'd planned, she and Derek could not spend the rest of their time here in combat mode.

The first step was to bring a peace offering.

Chandra went into the kitchen and whipped up two cups of hot chocolate. She walked over to the front door and placed them on the small table next to the entry. Donning her coat, she unhooked Derek's jacket and threw it over her arm. Chandra opened the door, picked up the mugs, and went out into the cold in search of her husband.

She found him standing just a few feet beyond the door

with his shoulders hunched up to his ears. The sky had turned a more ominous gray. The snow fell in earnest now. It came down so hard Chandra could hardly make out the tree stump for chopping firewood.

It was a good thing the kids' flights were cancelled. The thought of them traveling in this weather would have driven her out of her mind.

"Derek?" Chandra called. He didn't turn, didn't acknowledge her one bit. "I whipped up a quick batch of hot chocolate. It's instant, but it'll keep you warm."

He gripped the rail, but still didn't turn. The snow fell upon his bare knuckles.

"Derek," Chandra tried again.

"Go back inside," he said.

"Will you come with me?" she asked.

He didn't answer.

"Derek?"

His head fell forward. "What do you want from me, Chandra?" he asked, his voice a rough whisper.

"I want you to come inside the cabin before you freeze," she answered.

"I'm fine," he said, the ice dripping from his words colder than the snow swirling around them.

Chandra ventured farther onto the veranda. Her body registered the drop in temperature, and she shivered despite her coat. She stopped a few inches from Derek.

"I brought your jacket," she said. She held out the arm with the jacket. Finally, he turned. He slid the jacket from where she'd draped it over her arm, and reluctantly accepted one of the mugs.

"Can we sit?" Chandra gestured to the bench.

He looked over his shoulder then backed up a few steps and sat. Chandra took a seat beside him and sipped her drink. In just those few minutes it had cooled considerably.

Derek sat with his elbows on his thighs, his bare hands clutching the ceramic mug. He looked out at the patch of woods where they'd gone to find the Christmas tree. He looked as immovable as a block of ice.

Chandra shivered. As unapproachable as he appeared, she couldn't help herself. She scooted a couple of inches and huddled to Derek's side. After a beat, he let go of his rigid stance, opening up his right arm and allowing her to slip in. Chandra burrowed into his side.

The silence between them was as thick as the snow falling in fat clumps just beyond the covered veranda. Chandra didn't want to bring it up, even though it was the reason she'd followed him out here in the first place.

"Okay, Derek, we need to talk, but I can't do it out here."

He remained silent. Chandra's teeth started to chatter. "Derek."

"I'm not ready to go back inside," he stated.

"You're going to get sick if you stay out here. You don't even have on your gloves."

"I can handle it."

Chandra rolled her eyes. He, who abhorred the cold, could handle sitting out here in the snow, but he couldn't handle being in the cabin with her. This was so far past ridiculous Chandra questioned whether they could find their way back to sanity.

"I can understand why you're upset," she started. "There's a lot I haven't shared with you that I should have told you a long time ago."

He twisted the mug around and around. Finally, he said, "I'm more hurt than upset, Chandra. And confused. Yeah, I'm pretty damned confused at the moment." He looked over at her, disbelief making his voice rough. "All this time you've been resenting Stovall's, while I've been doing everything I can to make it bigger and better."

Chandra was about to tell him she didn't resent the business, but suddenly realized that she did. Not only did she resent it, she was jealous of the miniconglomerate that was Stovall's Body and Detailing Shop.

"You're right," she admitted. "I do resent it."

She felt the air escape Derek's lungs as his chest heaved. "Do you have any idea how that makes me feel? I've spent my life building this business from a two-man operation in my uncle's garage to the largest chain of body and detailing shops in the Dallas/Fort Worth area." He sounded like one of his commercials, but Chandra understood his hurt. "Other than my children, Stovall's is my proudest achievement. It's what makes me *me*, and my own wife resents it."

"I'm sorry," she said, but she couldn't deny what she felt.

Derek huffed out a frustrated laugh.

"Do you want to know *why* I resent it?" Chandra asked.

"That would be nice."

"Okay," she said. "But first, can we please go inside the cabin? I can't take much more of this cold."

He didn't say anything. After several long, uncomfortable, *freezing* moments he took the now equally cold mug of hot chocolate from her hand and stood up. Chandra popped up as fast as she could from the freezing bench and led the way into the cabin. Her entire body sighed in contentment at the first rush of warm air.

Derek walked to the kitchen, where he poured the hot chocolate down the drain and deposited the mugs in the sink. He turned, leaned against the counter, crossed his arms over his chest and said, "Okay, what's the reason? Why do you resent my business?"

"You just pointed out one of them," Chandra said with a sad smile. When he just continued to stare, she said, "It has always been 'my' business to you."

"What are you talking about?" His caustic tone raised her hackles, but she refused to let this turn into another shouting match.

"Exactly what I just said," she returned softly. "In twenty years, you've never tried to make me feel like I had any stake in the business at all. It has always been *your* business. Look what Derek built from the ground up."

"Do you know how to fix cars?" he asked derisively.

Chandra tamped down the urge to retort with her own sarcasm. She knew this was the reaction she would get from Derek, but he needed to hear this.

"You haven't been under the hood of a car in ten years, Derek. You know that has nothing to do with this."

"So what's your problem? You're feeling left out?"

Chandra held her hands out, the need to get her point across burning in her gut.

"Have you ever once thought about my contribution, Derek? Do you think Stovall's would be where it is today if I wasn't there taking care of the house, getting the kids cleaned and ready for bed when they were young, helping with their homework, taking do-it-yourself plumbing classes at the Home Depot because you weren't home to fix the leaky faucets?"

"I was working!" he erupted, his nostrils flaring.

"So was I!" Chandra returned with just as much heat. "That's my point! Those things had to be done, but you never had to worry about how it happened because I was there to take care of it while you built your business." Chandra slammed her hand on the countertop. "I'm tired of being taken for granted, Derek!"

He didn't say anything, just stood there like a wall of stone, his arms crossed over his chest as he stared at her from across the kitchen island.

Chandra's heart tightened in her chest. She wasn't sure

what she'd expected. An apology maybe? Remorse? A request for forgiveness for years of dismissing her loyalty?

From the look on his face, she would not get so much as an "I'm sorry." Chandra accepted that knowledge with a sinking heart, but refused to allow regret to overshadow the relief she felt at finally voicing the disgruntlement she'd kept bottled up for so long.

Coming clean had a cathartic effect. The secret had finally been revealed. She felt free, relieved. Whether she'd just dealt the final blow to her marriage, she didn't know, but at least she'd said her piece. The ball was now in Derek's court.

Chandra searched his unyielding countenance one last time for any sign of remorse. Not finding any, she turned and started for the great room.

"You're right."

Chandra whipped around at the softly spoken words.

Derek's stare was intense, his jaw rigid, but Chandra caught the hint of regret in the way the corners of his mouth dipped. He uncrossed his arms and pushed away from the counter, coming to rest his arms on the island in the center of the kitchen.

"Actually, no, you're not right," he said. "Not entirely." She opened her mouth to speak, but Derek stayed her with his hand. "I've never come right out and thanked you for everything you've done for the family, but—"

"It's not just the family," Chandra cut him off. "I'm talking about the business."

"It's all the same, Chandra. The family, the business; it's one big unit."

"No, it's not. The Stovall Family, with its two stellar children and big house in the suburbs is one thing, but Stovall's Body and Detailing Shops is an entirely different entity." She motioned between them. "*We* built the family, but in your eyes, *you* built the business."

He braced his hands against the island and leaned forward. "Okay, you're right," he admitted.

Hope blossomed in her chest at the sincerity in his voice. She was hesitant to test the bounds of this tremulous balance they'd discovered, but they'd started this conversation. They needed to see it through.

"That's not all," she said.

He ran his hands down his face in exasperation. "Great. What else have I done wrong?"

At his disgruntled growl, Chandra's hope that she'd finally gotten through to him took another blow. "Have you heard a word I've said, Derek?"

"Yes, I have. But do you want to know what I honestly think? I think this is a lousy reason to throw away twenty years, Chandra." He shrugged dismissively. "So you feel unappreciated. Fine, tell me that. But don't just decide the fate of my marriage without even talking to me about it."

God, had this man always been so blind? She dragged her fingers through her cropped hair in frustration.

Stretching her arms out, Chandra said, "Put yourself in my place for just a minute, Derek. Let's say I decided to go on to medical school as I'd first planned before turning to nursing. I go through med school, my internship, and residency. Then I decide to open up my own practice. You stay at home with the kids, still working off and on at your uncle's garage the same way I did a couple of days at the nursing home when we were first married.

"At night, I bring home the books from my practice. And after you've fed the kids, washed them and put them to bed, you then stay up and help me figure out how much capital it will take to expand my practice. For years you help brainstorm potential investors, figure out pay-roll, liability insurance, and OSHA regulations until I'm able to afford to pay an office manager."

Chandra matched his posture against the kitchen is-land. She leaned forward and looked him dead in the eye. "Now, imagine that when I talk about my practice to oth-ers, it's all about me and how I single-handedly built it from the ground up."

Her meaning was beginning to sink in; she could tell by the way his shoulders sagged.

"I was wrong in what I said before. I don't resent the business. Not entirely, anyway." Chandra stared into his eyes, pleading with him to understand. "Derek, I am so proud of what you've been able to accomplish. I would just like a little credit for my contribution."

Derek shook his head and raised his hands in earnest apology. "I'm sorry," he said. "I know how much you mean to Stovall's. Chandra, we both know I never could have done this without you."

Her heart lifted. Just that small recognition was enough to chip away a bit of the wall she'd erected around her heart. She reached across the island and covered Derek's hand. "Thank you," she said.

"Thank *you*," he returned.

Finally, Chandra experienced a bit of the magic she'd hoped to feel on Christmas Eve.

Chapter Five

The clock may have read just after three o'clock in the afternoon, but the sky was dark, with steely clouds, bringing with them snow that fell so hard Derek could barely make out the cabin from where he stood just at the edges of the wooded area.

"This is pretty stupid," he said to himself as he stooped down for another pinecone.

He'd given Chandra the story of going to find a few decorations for their pitiful little Christmas tree as his excuse for leaving the cabin, but truth was he'd needed to be by himself after that loaded discussion they'd had over the body shops. Moving to another room in the cabin wouldn't cut it. He'd needed to separate himself completely from Chandra in order to wrap his mind around all she'd laid on him.

Was he really that blind and self-absorbed?

The idea that he had unconsciously dismissed Chandra's role in helping to build their business caused a sick feeling to settle in Derek's stomach. In his mind he'd always given her credit for her part in getting Stovall's off the ground. Not just in the early days, but even now. He couldn't devote the time he did to the business if not for Chandra holding things down on the home front.

"You took her for granted," Derek admitted aloud.

As hard as it was to stomach the thought, as he reflected

on everything Chandra had said, Derek had to admit that she had been right.

But why was she just saying it now?

She certainly had been thinking about it for a lot longer than a few weeks ago when she'd first brought up the idea of a separation. Why hadn't she said anything when she'd first started feeling underappreciated?

Or, maybe the question Derek should ask is why hadn't he seen it? He knew her so well. He always knew the ideal gift to buy for her birthday, or the perfect words to say to wring a smile out of her when she was feeling down. How had he not noticed his wife's antipathy all these years?

One thing Derek did know, he wasn't giving up on his marriage over this. He'd find a way to make this up to Chandra, but it would not be by granting her the separation she was seeking. They would get past this.

Derek gathered the pinecones in the pouch he'd made with his sweater and headed back for the house. He found Chandra in the great room.

He pointed to the Christmas tree she'd propped against the wall. "Looks like you found a way to decorate the tree." A rainbow-striped scarf was draped around the branches like Christmas garland.

"Yeah," she said with a nod. "I also found some paper and crayons in a dresser drawer upstairs. I was just about to draw a few candy canes. You want to help?"

"That's one way to make myself useful," he said.

Chandra retrieved the supplies from upstairs and together they drew candy canes and snowflakes and took turns using the scissors from the first-aid kit to cut them out. Chandra cut lengths of thread from a miniature spool in a sewing kit she'd packed and used them to tie their paper ornaments to the tree.

"This reminds me of when I was growing up," Derek commented. "We couldn't afford to buy ornaments for the tree. It was a rare occasion my dad was able to find one somewhere. Usually, we didn't get our tree until after Christmas when Dad could drag in one our neighbors had already thrown away."

"You've come a long way from those days," Chandra said, a hint of pride in her voice. "He would be so proud of you."

"I don't know about that," Derek said. "He never took my mom for granted."

Chandra's hand arrested halfway to the tree, a red-and-white-striped candy cane dangling from her finger. "Derek."

He waved her off.

"No," Chandra said. "Look, Derek, we've allowed this to ruin enough of our Christmas Eve. Can we just make a promise not to mention it again until we get home?"

"If you promise to give us a chance to work through this," he said.

She shook her head. "Derek, I don't know."

"Come on, Chandra. You have to at least give me a chance. I'm just finding out what the problem is."

"I promise to think about it," she conceded.

"Okay," Derek decided, holding his hands up. "So, here's our tree, huh?" he said, gesturing to the lopsided tree. They stood back and surveyed their work.

"All it needs is a few presents," Chandra said. "I'll get the ones I brought from home." A couple of minutes later she came walking down the stairs, tearing the ice-blue foil wrapping from a rectangular box.

"What's that?"

"Anika's gift," she answered.

"You're opening Anika's Christmas present?"

"I'll rewrap it before she gets here." She balled the paper up and tossed it on the leather recliner.

Derek smiled to himself. Whatever it was in that box, it had curbed her anxiety if she was now making a mess instead of doing her frantic cleaning routine.

"Besides," Chandra continued. "I think this gift would serve us better down here, out of the wrapping."

"What is it?" Derek walked back over to the middle of the great room.

"Just wait." Chandra placed a picture frame on the square coffee table, flipped a switch, and a picture of Anika and D. J. playing in a mud puddle appeared. It faded to black and was followed by a formal picture the four of them had taken for the family Christmas card back in the early nineties, if Derek recalled correctly.

"It's a digital picture frame," Chandra explained as the screen jumped to a shot of Derek holding Anika as a baby. He remembered when Chandra had taken the picture. "The last time she was in Dallas, Anika complained about not having enough things in her dorm room to remind her of home. I figured she would appreciate this. I uploaded close to four hundred pictures."

"I didn't even know they made these. Are the pictures saved on a CD?"

Chandra shook her head. "On a Smart Card, like the ones I use in my digital camera. I scanned a bunch of pictures from the old photo albums and transferred them to the Smart Card. I plan to take a weekend to scan all the old pictures. It's safer to have them in electronic format, just in case something happens."

"I remember that," Derek laughed as he took a seat on the sofa, chuckling at the picture of D. J. with his diaper on his head instead of on his behind.

Chandra settled back on the sofa and smiled. "I couldn't

get that boy to keep a diaper on his butt for anything in the world. I think he started the trend with boys wearing their jeans hanging halfway off their behinds."

"Anika's Teenage Mutant Ninja Turtle birthday party. Remember how all of her friends' parents thought we'd mixed up the kids' birthdays."

"Nobody believed prissy little Anika wanted a Ninja Turtle birthday party. Remember the fights she and D. J. used to have over those action figures?"

Derek wasn't sure how long they sat on the couch laughing over picture after picture. Chandra had compiled a collection that spanned from when their kids were babies up until when they'd both come home for Thanksgiving just a month ago. Derek felt a swift kick of disappointment when the electronic picture frame returned to the shot of a muddy D. J. and Anika.

"That's all of them," Chandra yawned. She stretched her hands over her head and kicked her legs out from where she'd tucked them under her on the sofa. "Think Anika's going to like it?"

"If she doesn't, I'll take it," Derek said. "I'd forgotten just how much fun we used to have." He let the words slip without realizing how they may sound. But it was true; they didn't have that kind of fun anymore. When was the last time he'd seen that look of delight on Chandra's face?

Just a few hours ago, when she was playing around in the snow and his mouth had connected with hers. Just like that, the remembered kiss brought with it a rush of longing that was hard to fight.

"We did have some good times, didn't we?" Chandra mused.

"We can have them again," Derek reminded her in a soft voice.

Her eyes flashed to his face, and Derek made sure all the lust and desire their kiss had stirred was evident in the intense look he returned. There was too much history between them to let go of it. The fire was still there. It may have been smoldering for a while, but that kiss in the snow had stoked the flames, and every drop of blood in his body was burning for more.

Derek trailed his hand down her cheek and leaned in. He kissed the edge of her lips, below her ear, the top of her shoulder.

"You remember how good it used to be?" he asked huskily, trailing his tongue up the column of her neck.

"*Used* to be," Chandra stressed, putting a hand on his chest.

"We can have that again," Derek murmured.

Chandra turned her head. Why was she so determined to toss away everything they had together?

"Chandra, listen to me. Do you realize we've never really talked about it? This whole separation business? You just all of a sudden decided you wanted out."

"It was not all of a sudden, Derek. This problem between us has been building for some time now. I just didn't realize how bad it had gotten until Anika and D. J. left for school."

"Nothing changed when they left the house," he said.

"I know." She looked up at him. "That's the problem. I was hoping something *would* change to get us out of this rut we've been in."

"You think we've been in a rut?"

"You don't? Think about it, Derek. We hardly talk anymore."

He couldn't argue with her on that point. Just a few weeks ago he'd been sitting in his home office, working on the inventory for the Los Colinas location. He'd looked up and noticed the chair where Chandra used to sit and talk to him whenever he was working at home. It had occurred to him that he had not spoken to his wife in over twenty-four hours. Derek had thought about taking a walk around the house to find her, but he'd waved off the thought. He'd had too much work to do. With two new body shops opening in the next few months, nearly every waking hour was consumed by work.

A thought occurred to Derek. "Wait, are you saying this rut you think we've been in is my fault?"

Chandra hunched her shoulders. "I don't know if it's anyone's fault. It just happened. The kids took up a lot of time with their school activities, but I thought once they were gone we would find that friendship we used to share. It's just not there."

He shook his head. "I don't know what else to say to you. You said you didn't feel appreciated, and I apologized for taking you for granted. Now you're saying you want a separation because you don't think we're friends anymore?"

"Stop trying to downplay this, Derek. It's not that simple. Tell me something; are you even happy with me?"

His head reared back. "What kind of question is that? Are you saying I make you unhappy, Chandra?"

She closed her eyes and leaned her head back against the sofa, covering her eyes with her arm. She opened her eyes, and they brightened. "There," she said, pointing to the picture frame that was still playing their family memories over and over like a movie. She reached over and pressed a button, causing the picture of them at the Grand Canyon to freeze on the screen. "Do you remember that trip?"

"Grand Canyon, the summer of ninety-nine," Derek answered automatically.

"Do you remember how we would put the kids to bed every night, then go walking along the trails around the campgrounds? I can't remember what we talked about, Derek, I just remember how good it felt to hold your hand while we walked under the stars. I haven't felt that way in years," Chandra admitted. "And if you're honest with yourself, you can admit that you haven't either."

"So you want me to take you on long walks?"

"It's not about the walks," Chandra sighed. She pushed her fingers through her hair, leaving it spiky in some places. "It's about what happened during those walks. I want us to talk to each other. I want you to come home and tell me how your day went and then have you sit and listen while I discuss mine."

"It's not like my day changes all that much," he said.

"Have you heard a single thing I've said?" Chandra asked with a frustration that confused him.

"I hear you," Derek answered. "I just don't understand . . ."

"Derek, we've grown apart." Chandra sat her elbows on her thighs and folded her hands together. "You asked if you make me unhappy, and the answer is no, you don't make me unhappy." She looked Derek in the eyes. "The problem is you don't make me feel anything anymore."

The mixture of shock and hurt clouding Derek's face elicited a pang of regret that, for a moment, caused Chandra to question the words she'd just uttered. She couldn't decide which emotion she should feel—relief that she'd finally said the words, or sorrow that she'd had to say them at all.

"I know it's hard to hear," Chandra said. "I felt the same way when I came to the realization, but it's the truth, Derek. If you think about it, you'd agree. These past couple of years we've just been going through the motions."

"Are you saying you don't love me anymore?" he asked, his voice rough.

Chandra's throat tightened with emotion, and the tears she knew would surface did not disappoint. She wiped at her cheek with the back of her hand, and, taking a deep breath, told him the truth.

"I've loved you most of my life, Derek. I can't imagine going through life not loving you." She ran her hands through her hair again. "But I'm starting to wonder if I'm still *in love* with you. My heart tells me that I am, but what if that's just the memories talking?"

He shook his head. "I'm not even sure what to say to that," Derek said. "Can't we fix this?"

She pulled a pillow under her chin, and shook her head. "I don't know. Maybe."

"I know I still love you," Derek said. "What I want to know is when did you stop loving me?"

"It's not that I don't love you. God, I'm not even sure what I'm feeling." She sighed, her voice filled with regret. "I just know there's something missing between us."

He turned her face to his.

"Tell me something, Chandra. Do you want to make it work, or are you looking for a way out?"

His question, so direct and to the point, left no room for misinterpretation. What was she really seeking? Did she really want to end her marriage?

No, Chandra realized. She didn't.

"If there is a way to save our marriage, I want to find it," she answered honestly.

"Then why don't we work toward doing that?" He took her hand in his. "I don't want to lose you, Chandra. Whatever it takes." Derek had a desperate, sincere look in his eyes. "You are everything that's good in my life. I can't lose you. Promise you'll give us another chance."

Chandra looked down at their clasped hands, her heart full to the point of bursting. She'd missed him so much. This is what she'd been hoping for, that Derek would, at the very least, acknowledge what she's meant to him.

"What do you say?" The apprehensive lilt to his voice seemed to match the hesitancy she was experiencing. She couldn't help but question whether this was real, or just the magic of Christmas sprinkling its pixie dust upon them. How could she be sure things would be different once they left this magical setting? Chandra wasn't sure if she should trust it, but it felt right. Sitting here with Derek, holding his hands, the snow falling, the Christmas tree, all of it—it all felt so *right*.

She was willing to take a chance.

Not trusting her voice, Chandra could only nod.

Relief flooded Derek's face. He brought her hands up to his lips and held them there for a long time before saying, "Thank you."

Chapter Six

"I'm sure this wasn't the Christmas Eve dinner you had in mind," Derek said.

"Not really"—Chandra smiled across the table—"but the lasagna was good. I rather we save the turkey and all the trimmings for dinner with the kids tomorrow." She pushed away from the table. "Let me get started on these dishes."

"I'll help," Derek said, rising as well.

"You don't have to. I can do it."

"You always pick up after meals. There's nothing wrong with me helping out a bit," Derek pointed out. "I'm going to help out more when we get back home, too."

Chandra shoulders drooped and she took a breath. "Derek, I've never regretted being a stay-at-home wife and mother and all the work that comes with it. And what happened to us not talking about this anymore this weekend?"

"I know we agreed not to talk about it, but you have me thinking about all I've taken for granted." He looked into her eyes, hoping his apology shone through. "I hate that you've felt neglected all these years, Chandra, when I never intended to make you feel that way."

"Just remember that you're not the only one to blame here," she told him. "As much as I may think you should be, you're not a mind reader, Derek. I should have spoken up a long time ago," Chandra reminded him. "Now I want to enjoy the rest of our Christmas Eve."

He deposited the glasses on the counter next to the sink, and shrugged a shoulder. "Since you don't want help with the dishes, let me at least put the leftovers away."

"Fine, knock yourself out." Chandra laughed.

Derek packed the last of the leftovers from their Christmas Eve dinner in the refrigerator and carried the dirty dishes to Chandra, who stood at the sink full of sudsy water. Derek deposited the two plates in the water, then moved behind her and slid his arms around her waist. He hesitated only a moment before placing a kiss behind her ear.

"Do you mind if I do this?" he asked, holding his breath as he awaited her answer. After what felt like a full minute, Chandra shook her head.

"No, I don't mind," she said with a soft voice.

"Good," Derek let out in a rushed breath. "Because it would have killed me to let go." He trailed light kisses down her neck and snuggled closer, pressing himself more firmly against her. "I miss this, Chandra."

"I do, too," she admitted.

Derek inhaled a lungful of the light, powdery scent that lingered on her skin. "When did my hugging you become such a rare thing?" he murmured against the column of her throat, relishing her sweet, unique essence.

Chandra delicately hunched a shoulder. "I can't pinpoint it. We just stopped."

"That was very stupid of us."

He felt the giggle ripple through her body. "I agree," Chandra laughed.

Derek nestled more snuggly against her. God, she felt good. He trailed his hands from her waist upward, closing his palms over her breasts. Chandra moaned, her hands falling still in the sudsy water. She lulled her head to the side, granting him access to her elegant neck.

Derek took full advantage, nibbling at her skin with

gentle bites. Her nipples grew taut beneath his palms, and his groin tightened. Derek could think of nothing but pulling her shirt over her head and peeling away her bra. He wanted to feel the evidence of her arousal against his bare skin.

Using his tongue, Derek traced a path from her ear to her jaw, moving one hand up and dipping it into her shirt. He delved his hand down to the valley between her breasts.

Chandra stiffened.

"What?" Derek rasped, stifling his disappointment. He raised his head from where he'd cradled it in the curve of her neck.

"Look outside the window," she said.

Derek's eyes followed where she pointed. It looked as if it were closer to midnight than early evening. "Does the snow seem to be falling twice as hard to you?" he asked, unwrapping his arms from her waist.

"At least," Chandra answered.

Derek headed to the front door, Chandra following a few steps behind. He flipped on the outside light, which illuminated the snow swirling chaotically just beyond the door. It moved swiftly, the strong wind whipping up the snow that had already fallen to the ground, and whirling it in a small, twisterlike frenzy.

"This has to be more than your run-of-the-mill snow-storm," Chandra said, ducking under his arm to take a peek. "This is serious."

"I think this is what they consider a blizzard," Derek said. "Let's see if we can find something on the Weather Channel." He shut off the outside light and the entire house went dark.

"What happened?" Chandra cried.

"I shut off the porch light," Derek said. He flipped the switch up and down a few times, but nothing happened.

"Maybe it's a breaker," Chandra said. "The fuse box is inside the broom closet next to the kitchen. I saw it when I was looking for cleaning supplies," Chandra admitted.

They went back into the house, the glow from the fireplace the only source of light for the entire downstairs.

"Stay here," Derek said, motioning for her to stand at the entryway to the kitchen. He waited a few moments for his eyesight to adjust, then cautiously made his way to the broom closet. Derek turned on his cell phone and used the meager light provided by the screen to illuminate the electrical panel. "None of the breakers have tripped off," he said.

He walked back to Chandra. "It must be a blackout. We can try calling the sheriff's office. Maybe they can tell us what's going on. The number is on the refrigerator, right?"

"Yeah," Chandra answered.

Derek found the refrigerator by memory, and used the cell phone light to locate the sheriff office's number. He called and had his prediction confirmed. Power was out to the entire mountain. And, although the operator at the sheriff's office claimed this was still just a really bad snowstorm, she had to admit that she hadn't seen it this bad in quite a few years.

"Well?" Chandra asked, walking up to him just as he was disconnecting from the operator.

"We just have to wait out the storm," Derek answered. He turned her in the direction of the living room and put his hands on her shoulders, giving her a gentle squeeze. "It's a good thing we've got that extra firewood, since we just lost the central heating, too."

"Lord, I hadn't even thought about that," Chandra said. "We may just have to burn our Christmas tree."

"At least it'll go for a good cause." Derek chuckled.

"Unless we can find some candles somewhere, that fireplace is all the light we're going to get."

Chandra stopped short. "There's a flashlight in the top drawer of the nightstand in the room I slept in."

"I'll go up and get it," he said.

Chandra caught his arm. "You're not leaving me down here by myself," she said. "No, we can go together."

Derek's head fell back with a crack of laughter.

"Don't you dare make fun of me, Derek."

"I'm sorry," he said. "I forgot about how you get in the dark sometimes."

"Only in unfamiliar places," she argued.

Chandra's fear of the dark had been a source of joking for Derek for the entire twenty years of their marriage. Chandra had come to accept his teasing a long time ago. He missed teasing her.

"Lead the way," Derek said, motioning for her to go ahead of him. They traveled gingerly up the stairs with only the light from the cell phone to guide them. "I'm going to need to shut the phone off once we get up the stairs," Derek said. "I don't want to run out the battery."

"Mine is still on the charger downstairs," Chandra said. "Though having it there is pretty useless now." She snorted.

They arrived at the top of the stairs, and headed in the direction of the second bedroom. Derek turned off his cell phone and the entire area was awash in darkness. Chandra gripped his hand even harder. He gave her a light squeeze, but didn't comment.

Chandra felt her way through the bedroom. "I'm relying on tactile memory," she called. She found her way to the bed, and then to the nightstand next to it. Derek heard her open the drawer and rustle around in it.

"Ow," she muttered.

"You alright?" he asked, stepping a few feet into the room.

"I'm fine," Chandra said. "Just stuck my hand on something."

"Be careful, baby," he said. "You need my cell phone?"

"No, I think . . . thank God," Chandra breathed, then a tiny stream of light shot forth from where she stood. She motioned it toward the doorway. "And the good Lord said, 'Let there be light.' Now what?"

"Keep warm," Derek answered, following the beam to her. He captured her by the hand. "Why don't we head back downstairs? We should stick as close to the fire as we can."

"I was just thinking, it's probably a good thing the kids couldn't get here. With no light, or television, or Internet, they would go crazy."

"And drive us crazy in the process," Derek agreed.

Now, he was happy for the kids' absence for an entirely different reason. Being here in the dark with Chandra created a heightened sense of awareness. Everything about her seemed larger than life—her scent, the softness of her skin, the remembered taste of her lips against his.

Derek's fist clenched with the need to touch her. It had been months since he'd last been intimate with his wife, but if he had anything to say about it, their drought was about to come to an end.

He guided Chandra down the stairs and to the great room. She plopped down on the sofa with a huge sigh.

"Never mind the kids, I don't know what *I'm* going to do without electricity," she said.

"I'm sure we can find ways to entertain ourselves."

"What, making hand puppets on the wall with the flashlight?" Chandra laughed.

"We can come up with something better than that,"

Derek said, tossing one of the throw pillows to the other end of the sofa and taking the seat right next to Chandra.

Chandra settled against the cushions. "What time is it? Just after eight, isn't it?"

Derek quickly checked the time on his cell phone. "Eight seventeen."

She sighed again. "It's going to be a long night."

He was counting on it.

Chapter Seven

Resting her elbow on the arm of the sofa, one hand cradling her chin, the other wrapped around the stem of a wineglass, Chandra sipped the 1996 Merlot. With a lazy smile edging her lips, she admired the view provided by Derek's khaki pants that stretched taut over his rear end as he knelt on one knee next to the fireplace and pushed in a couple more logs. After all these years, the man still had a butt worthy of the pages of a magazine.

"How are we doing on firewood?" Chandra asked, swirling the wine around in her glass.

"We've still got a good bit," he answered. He stood and dusted his hands on the sides of his pants. The soft glow from the fire cast a gentle glimmer to his features. The effect was hypnotic. "As long as the temperature outside doesn't drop anymore than it has already, that is."

"How likely is that?" Chandra laughed.

He put his hands on his hips, and with a grin crinkling the corners of his eyes, answered, "About as likely as all this snow melting in the next hour."

Chandra raised her glass to eye level. "Well, at least I've got this delicious wine to keep me warm," she said, taking another sip.

He grabbed the candle from the mantel, and walked over to the sofa, placing the candle in the center of the square coffee table and returning to the spot beside her. When they'd arrived back downstairs from their flashlight expedition, Derek had gone in search of candles, finding two stout pillars with fresh, unblemished wicks. Chandra figured they were for decoration only, but desperate times called for desperate candle burning.

Derek retrieved his wineglass and took a sip. "I almost didn't bring the wine," he said. "I packed the bottle at the last minute. I wasn't sure if I'd need it for fortitude."

Chandra threw her head back with a laugh. "That was probably a good idea. I'd much rather we enjoy it this way, though."

"I'll toast to that," Derek said, stretching his glass to her.

Chandra touched her glass to his with a soft clink. She looked at him over the rim of her glass as she brought the wine back to her lips and took another healthy sip. She wasn't sure if it was the effect of the alcohol, or the extra logs Derek had added to the fire, but she was suddenly much warmer than she had been just a few minutes ago. She shifted on the sofa, bringing her legs up and tucking them under her.

Derek scooted closer. He stretched his arm over the back of the sofa and ran a finger under the collar of her shirt. Chandra's eyes closed and she let out a soft moan. It felt so good to be touched, to have his hands upon her skin. He used to touch her like this all the time, light insignificant little strokes that now held so much more meaning after going so long without them.

Chandra lolled her neck to the side to give him better access. It was all she could do not to purr in satisfaction. He applied light pressure, and this time Chandra did purr. His fingers were like magic.

"I have an idea," Derek said. He placed his wineglass on the coffee table and stood.

Chandra peered up at him. "What's that?"

He plucked the wineglass from her fingers, placed it next to his, and, capturing both of her hands, pulled her up from the sofa. Her body was a scant inch from his, and the heat radiating from him was nearly as addictive as the wine.

"I think we should dance," Derek said.

"You do?"

"Sure," he said, applying soft kisses to the tops of each hand as he pulled her to the open space before the fireplace.

"One problem," Chandra said. "No electricity means no CD player."

"We can't let that stop us," Derek smiled.

He enclosed her waist in his palms and began to hum. Chandra brought her hands up and wrapped them around his neck. She rested her head against Derek's chest, and together they swayed from side to side as he sung Nat King Cole's version of "The Christmas Song" in his deep tenor. Goose bumps traveled along her skin as his intoxicating voice brought new life to her favorite holiday song.

His hands traveled up her back, then down and over her backside. He pulled her against his body, which hardened with arousal against her stomach. Chandra brought her fingers up and trailed them over his clean-shaven head. She lifted her face and kissed along his neck.

For a moment, Derek stopped singing. He took a deep breath, and then resumed the song.

Chandra allowed herself to succumb to the magical spell that had been hovering in the air. Its enthralling effect had been creeping over them both since the lights went out. Derek pulled her even closer, and Chandra melted in his arms. It had been so very long since she'd felt the skin-tingling effect of his chiseled chest against her. Her body ached for him.

"You feel so good, Derek," she murmured.

Chandra felt his body shudder. "I can't even describe how you feel right now." He put his hand under her chin and lifted her face. "I just know it's been too long since I felt this way."

He lowered his head. Chandra lifted her face to meet his mouth as it landed lightly upon her lips. He moved with ease, his tongue gently prying her lips apart. Chandra moaned, accepting Derek's tender, yet insistent, prodding. They continued to sway, though the crackle of the logs in the fire was the only music left in the room.

Derek lifted his head. "Chandra?" he softly whispered.

"Yes?"

"If I asked you to make love to me right now, how would you answer?"

Chandra's breath caught in her throat, sensual hunger holding her captive.

"Derek," she started.

"We're still married," he reasoned, shutting down her protest. "And we both want it."

Yes, she wanted him. Chandra could no more deny it than she could her own name. And there was no mistaking Derek's desire; it was pressed firmly against her stomach, sending sparks of anticipation shooting through her. Chandra debated the wisdom of surrendering to her desires. Months ago, she'd accepted the fact that nights of making love to her husband were a thing of the past. If she did so tonight, how would it change things between them?

Despite the questions floating back and forth through her mind, Chandra could not deny one simple truth. She wanted him. God, did she want him.

"Yes," Chandra finally answered.

Derek stared into her eyes. His own were naked with need. He ran his hand through her hair and pulled her to him, bringing her mouth in contact with his again. Her body answered with a shiver. Chandra groaned, parting her mouth and accepting his tongue.

Derek grabbed the hem of her shirt and pulled it over her head, then did the same with his own. He threw them to the side. He hooked his thumbs in the waistband of her lounging pants and pulled them down her smooth, shapely legs, leaving Chandra in her matching bra and panties.

For a long moment, he just stared at her. His breathing slowed as his eyes glazed over with longing so raw it wrenched a moan out of her. Chandra's entire body blushed with heated desire at his frank perusal.

"You have always been the most beautiful woman in the world," Derek said. He shucked his pants and dropped them next to hers, then he kicked both pairs to the side.

"One second," he breathed against her lips. Chandra followed him with her eyes as he went over to the sofa and grabbed the soft throw that lay across the back of it. He situated it over the hand-tufted rug, and taking her by the hand, guided her down on the makeshift bed in front of the fire.

Derek settled on top of her, his lips meeting hers in a gentle, yet mind-drugging kiss. Chandra pulled his tongue between her lips and sucked, his taste as sweet as ever in her mouth. It was paradise, being back in her husband's arms, feeling his weight upon her.

He slipped his hands behind her back and went for her bra strap. "Damn," Derek muttered as he fumbled with the tiny hook. He tried, but still couldn't unclasp it.

He rolled her over. Chandra leveled herself above him, reached behind her and released the single clasp on her bra. It fell away from her chest and down her arms. Chandra flicked the bra on top of the pile of clothes that had accumulated a few feet away.

"Oh, baby," Derek said with a husky whisper. He drew his hands up her stomach, then closed them over her breasts.

Chandra covered his hands and squeezed, throwing her head back and releasing a moan from deep within her throat. Good Lord, his hands felt good on her skin. They had smoothed a bit over the years, but there was still a hint of roughness to the palms that tantalized her sensitive nipples as they rotated in slow, sure circles.

Derek slipped his hands free and moved them to her waist. He lifted her and settled her onto his erect form. Chandra gasped, her head back, her eyes shut tight. With supreme strength of will, she held herself still, giving her body a minute to adjust to the width of him. Her body stretched in delicious remembrance, yielding to Derek's arousal with a familiar ease.

With the assistance of Derek's hands upon her hips, she rose and fell upon him, moving with a cadence that matched Derek's labored breaths. Her hands still on her breasts, Chandra clutched her nipples, pinching and squeezing.

"Oh, God," Derek groaned. Chandra looked down to find his eyes on her breasts. "Don't stop doing that," he pleaded.

She continued to fondle her breasts, Derek's heated gaze stoking the flames of her own desire.

Their lovemaking became feverish. Pleasure, fiery and intense, flowed throughout her entire body. Derek gripped her butt and began to pump with wild, frenzied strokes. Chandra threw her head back and cried out, the pleasure coursing through her veins unlike anything she'd ever experienced. She fell onto Derek's chest, rising and falling with each breath he took.

Derek rolled her over, and with his hands still gripping

her backside, lunged into her. With insistent strokes, he pumped in and out, harder, faster, driving her out of her mind.

Chandra exploded in another orgasm, this one so powerful it shot from every nerve ending in her entire body.

With one final lunge, Derek groaned between clenched teeth and collapsed on top of her, his breaths coming in heavy pants.

"Oh, my God," they both said at the same time.

Derek looked down at her, and Chandra couldn't contain her laughter. She was giddy with the pleasure still flowing throughout her body. He eased himself out of her, rolled onto his back and pulled her on top of his chest. He rubbed his hand up and down her sweat-soaked back.

Chandra sighed into his chest, too exhausted to even lift her head. "Well," she said. "I guess finding something to entertain ourselves wasn't so hard to do after all."

Derek's chest rumbled with his laughter. "I knew we could come up with something if we just put in a little effort."

Chapter Eight

Derek wasn't sure how much time had passed. It seemed as if he and Chandra had been lying on the rug wrapped in each other's arms for hours. She'd fallen asleep, woken after a half hour, and allowed him to make love to her yet again.

She was like a drug to his brain. Derek couldn't get enough. Even now, just thinking about all they'd done, and feeling Chandra's warm, soft skin against him, caused his body to harden. He ran his hand from the top of her head to the base of her spine. Chandra shivered beneath his touch.

"Are you cold?" he asked.

"I'm okay," she said, snuggling closer to him.

Derek tucked the blanket he'd pulled from the sofa more securely underneath her and pressed a kiss to her bare shoulder.

She let out a satisfied sigh.

"Actually," Chandra said, "I need to go to the bathroom." She unfurled herself from the confines of the blanket.

"Take the blanket." Derek stretched it out to her, but she shook her head.

"It'll just trip me up."

Naked, she headed for the downstairs bathroom, just to the right of the great room.

God, that woman had a body on her, Derek thought as

he watched her scamper away. The embers that remained in the fireplace made her skin shimmer. Derek stared up at the logs that crisscrossed overhead, and let the smile that had been on the edges of his mouth have life.

How had he gone so long without making love to his wife? They had always been hot for each other, from the very minute their eyes met over his busted fender when she'd backed her car into his all those years ago. In the twenty years they'd been married, Derek had never tired of her body. She'd fit him perfectly in every way. She still did.

He heard Chandra's bare feet padding toward him on the hardwood floor. She ran up to him and quickly dropped to the floor, wrapping herself in the warmth of the blanket.

"I guess I need to put a couple more logs in the fireplace," Derek said.

"No." She tugged on his arm. "Just hold me. That'll warm me up."

"Sounds good to me," Derek said, folding her into his arms and clasping her middle against his increasingly aroused body. He wanted her again in a bad, *bad* way.

One elbow on the floor, Chandra rested her chin in her upturned palm and traced his goatee with the index finger of her other hand.

"It's just after ten o'clock," she said.

"We're in Mountain Standard Time, so we gained an hour," Derek pointed out.

Her hand traveled down his chin, to his throat, then to his chest. "Hmm," Chandra purred. "What do you think we should do with that hour?" she asked, her hand skimming down his stomach in a march to the part of his body that was straining for her.

She closed her palm around him, and Derek gasped.

"Uh . . . I can think of a few things," he said.

A deliciously wicked grin curved the edge of her lips. "Why don't you show me?"

After one of the most pleasurable hours of his life, Derek rolled off his wife, gasping for air. He was spent; completely, wonderfully spent. His muscles felt as if they would need at least a week's recuperation before he could resume normal activity.

"We should probably get dressed," Chandra murmured from where she lay next to him.

"I don't know." Derek yawned, tucking her head in the cradle of his arm. "I could easily stay like this for another forty-eight hours."

"Oh, that's something Anika and D. J. would love to see when they walk through the door," Chandra laughed.

"Point made," Derek said. Despite his utter exhaustion, he disentangled her from his hold and stretched his arms above his head. "I can run up and get you something more comfortable to wear."

"Would you?" Chandra looked up at him, her eyes full of gratitude. With that vulnerable look on her face, he would jump off a bridge if she asked him to.

He pushed himself up from the floor. "I'll be right back," he said, snatching the flashlight from the coffee table.

"My UT Arlington T-shirt is in my carry-on bag," Chandra called as he headed up the stairs.

Derek went first to the master bedroom and grabbed a pair of pajama pants from the drawer where he'd packed them last night. He'd left half of the top drawer for Chandra's clothes. As soon as the power was restored, she would move her things in here with him. Derek would insist.

He pulled on the pajama bottoms, even though he would have been just fine remaining snuggled up to Chandra in the buff. He used the flashlight to guide him to the second bedroom and found Chandra's carry-on bag next to her bed. He pulled out her UT Arlington T-shirt and a pair of underwear. Derek had a mind to stuff the underwear back into the bag, but she would just send him back up to get it. He drew the line at bringing her a bra.

He unzipped the front compartment of the bag in search of socks, but all she had in there were a few paperback novels and a couple pieces of mail. The return address on one of the envelopes caused Derek to pause.

Palmer and Associates, Attorneys at Law.

He took it out of the bag and pulled the papers from the envelope. He shone the flashlight on them, thumbed through a couple, then stopped cold.

Listed in a neat table was nearly everything he and Chandra owned: the house in Dallas, the condo in Florida, both cars, each location of Stovall's Body and Detailing Shops—including the two that had yet to officially open— artwork, and collectibles they had amassed over the past twenty years.

Derek's hand shook as his brain registered what lay before him. He flipped back to the first page and read over the letter from attorney Anya J. Palmer. It spelled out, in no uncertain terms, everything Chandra would be entitled to if she and Derek were to divorce.

Divorce?

What happened to just separating? When had the talk turned to divorce? Chandra hadn't mentioned anything about making this separation—something that had yet to happen—permanent.

But apparently, she'd been thinking about it. Hell, she'd already sought out an attorney.

A sharp ache pierced his chest. Just a few minutes ago, Derek had been thinking of how they would end this foolish talk of separation. But she'd had bigger plans in mind. All this time, she'd been preparing for a divorce.

Derek's hand fisted around the papers, the sound like a crackling fire in the darkened room.

Pitching her T-shirt and underwear on the bed, Derek stalked out of the room and pounded down the stairs. The fire had dwindled to a low burning bed of embers, but Derek dismissed it. He sure as hell didn't need the flames to keep him warm right now.

He shone the flashlight on Chandra's face and tossed the envelope on the blanket next to her.

"You want to explain that?" he motioned with his head.

She sat up, holding the blanket to her chest. "What is this? What happened to my clothes? And stop shining that light in my eyes." She shielded her eyes with her hand.

"I found that envelope in your bag," Derek said, leaving the flashlight right where he had it. He wanted to see her face while she tried to explain this. "So, have you and your attorney figured out how to take me for all I'm worth?"

Chandra groaned. "Derek, it's not what it looks like," she said, propping her elbow on her raised knee and cradling her head in her upturned palm.

"Really?" he sarcastically quirked a brow. "Because it looks to me like you've been planning for a hell of a lot more than just a separation, Chandra. How long did it take you and your attorney to compile that list of every damn thing I own?"

"*You* own?" She shoved herself up from the floor, wrapped the blanket around her. "How about what *we* own? Twenty years of working alongside you as your wife, and you still see it as *yours*."

"Don't start that stuff again," Derek warned. "You've been planning this a lot longer than three weeks. And it's not just a separation. This is the start of a damn divorce, Chandra!"

She put her hand up. "Derek, please don't do this right now."

"What in the hell do you expect, Chandra! I can't believe you. After everything I've given you."

"You have not just *given*, damn you!" She flung the papers at him. "You did not do all of this on your own! It was not just you!"

She brushed past him and ran for the stairs.

Chapter Nine

Chandra stumbled through the darkness until she found her way to the bathroom that connected the second and third bedrooms. She shut the door and braced her back against it, sliding to the floor just as the tears began to cascade down her cheeks.

Had she honestly believed Derek had undergone this miraculous transformation over the course of an afternoon?

After everything they'd gone through today, after all that had come out through their discussion, he still didn't appreciate a single contribution she'd made to their marriage.

Chandra had known this before she left Dallas, yet she'd foolishly allowed the magic of their surroundings to influence her thinking. Like an idiot, she'd fallen under Derek's spell, and look where it had landed her: sitting in the dark, naked, with only her tears to keep her company.

Chandra angrily wiped her cheeks and pushed herself up from the floor. She felt around until she found the sink. She fumbled over the knobs, turning on the hot water that only ran lukewarm. She splashed water on her face and braced her hands on the sides of the sink, letting the droplets fall along with the few remaining tears she would allow herself to shed.

Chandra took a deep, steadying breath, her decision made.

She turned, and screamed.

Derek stood in the doorway. In the window behind him, moonlight broke through the falling snow, which Chandra noticed was not coming down as heavily as it had been earlier in the day.

"I'm sorry," he said.

"I don't want to hear it," Chandra whispered. She stooped and retrieved the blanket. She held it up to her breasts and tried to walk past him, but he caught her elbow. Chandra tried to jerk it away, but he only squeezed tighter.

"Chandra, please," he pleaded. "Please just hear me out."

"No, Derek. I don't care what you have to say."

"I was caught off guard," he tried to explain. "Look at it from my perspective."

"Why should I? You refuse to see it from mine. After everything we talked about today, you still think of everything we own as yours. I just have no part in it, right, Derek?"

"That's not true. If you would just—" She jerked her arm from him. "Chandra."

The lights flickered, then came on, and the first thing Chandra noticed was the anguish on Derek's face. He stood before her, his brow creased, his eyes filled with regret.

Chandra spotted her T-shirt and underwear atop the bedspread and snatched them up. She dropped the blanket and quickly drew the T-shirt over her head, then stepped into her underwear. Derek remained where he was, his expression awash in contrition.

"Chandra." Her name was a whispered plea on his lips. "Please hear me out."

As much as she wanted to fight it, Chandra could not steel herself against his tormented appeal. She wrapped her arms around her waist and briefly shut her eyes before opening them and looking into his eyes. They were filled with such agony Chandra's heart constricted in empathy.

"It was a knee-jerk reaction," he started. "I saw those words, and just how coldly they were laid out by the attorney. It . . . I don't know. It just struck me that you'd put more thought into leaving me than I'd first imagined."

She spoke slowly. "I only went to the attorney to figure out what my options were. It was a preliminary visit, and it meant nothing. The attorney ran away with it. I was as surprised as you were when those papers arrived in the mail." She pressed a hand to her throat; the lump of despair lodged there was thick enough to choke her. "Derek, right now—a divorce is so far off my radar, it doesn't bear mentioning, especially after everything that has happened between us today."

"Baby, I'm sorry for not listening—really listening to you. I guess old habits are hard to break." He took a few steps, closing the distance between them. He took her chin in his hand and raised her face to meet his. "You know everything I have belongs to you. All of it, my heart included."

Chandra melted at the genuine sorrow that washed over his face. She loved this man so much she ached with it. How did they drift so far apart?

"I'm sorry," Derek said, the words drenched in hurt.

"How . . ." Chandra hiccuped. She swallowed back her tears and tried again. "How are we going to get past this?" she asked him, because she truly didn't know where they were going to go from here. The one thing Chandra did know was that she still loved her husband with every part of her soul. She did not want to lose him.

"I don't know," Derek answered. "But we have to. Chandra, I can't live my life without you. You have to know that."

"I can't either," she said with a small sob.

"It's going to take more than an evening in each other's arms to fix whatever it is that's happened to us, but we have to fix it," he said. "There's no other option I can live with."

He reached for her, and Chandra could not make herself turn away. She fell into his arms and buried her face against his chest.

"God, I'm sorry, baby," Derek breathed against her hair. "I'm so sorry."

"I am, too," she said. Chandra raised her head and looked into his sorrowful eyes. They were brimming with remorse. "Promise me we'll work to get through this," she said. "When we get back to Dallas, promise me we'll do whatever it takes to get back to being the husband and wife we used to be."

Derek brought her hand up and brushed his lips across her fingers. "I promise."

Chandra inhaled a deep breath and burrowed her head against his chest.

Tranquil minutes of holding each other passed before Derek whispered against her temple, "Can I give you your gift now? I know we still have a few minutes before Christmas gets here, but I don't want you to go another minute without it."

"What is it?" Chandra asked, wiping a wayward tear from her cheek.

"Give me a minute." He placed a kiss on her forehead and left the room. Moments later he returned, carrying two small boxes.

Handing her a long, thin, rectangular box, he said, "Open this one first."

Chandra's hands shook slightly as she lifted the top. Inside was a simple gold chain with a heart-shaped locket. There was a small purple gemstone in the center of it.

Chandra lifted it from the bed of brushed velvet that lined the box and opened the locket.

Her breath caught in her throat. Inside the locket was her favorite picture of Anika and D. J. from when they were kids.

"Oh, Derek," she said, her heart melting.

He gestured at the locket in her hand. "The stone is your grandmother's," he said softly.

"What?" Chandra gasped.

Derek placed the other box he'd brought with him in the center of his palm and lifted the top. Tears formed in Chandra's eyes as she instantly recognized the grapevine pattern carved into the ring band.

"I found your grandmother's ring a few months ago," Derek continued. "Since the stone was always falling out, I decided to put your grandmother's amethyst in the locket and replace it with a diamond."

"Why didn't you tell me you found the ring?" Chandra whispered, staring at the ring in awe. It was as exquisite as always, but the beautifully cut diamond made it even lovelier.

"I wanted it to be a surprise," Derek said. "You always talked about how romantic you thought it was that your grandfather proposed to your grandmother on Christmas morning."

Derek slowly lowered himself to one knee. Tears started streaming in earnest down Chandra's cheeks as he captured her left hand and slid the ring onto her ring finger where it butted up against the simple gold wedding band Derek had placed on her finger twenty years ago.

He captured both of her hands in his and placed a kiss upon the crest of her fingers. "Chandra, I love you," he said, staring up at her with all the love in the world in his eyes. "Forgive me. Please make this Christmas the best ever by promising to stay my wife for the rest of my days on this Earth."

She nodded her head and choked out a sob. "I promise," she said.

Derek stood and grabbed her, lifting her in his arms and carrying her to the bed. He placed her gently on the soft covers and followed her down. "I love you," he said, his face an inch above her.

"I love you, too, Derek," she said, meeting his lips in a magical kiss that ushered in the Christmas morning.

Epilogue

The next morning, Chandra woke ensconced in Derek's embrace. The joy she felt at being back in his arms again eased every ache in her heart. He was everything she'd ever wanted; how had she thought she could survive without him?

"Are you awake?" came a husky voice.

Chandra started. She hadn't realized he was up. "I am," Chandra answered, snuggling closer to him. He draped a heavy arm around her middle and tugged her closer against his strong chest.

Her cell phone began to chime. Chandra groaned. "Oh, I don't want to answer it," she said.

"I'll get it," Derek said. He unfolded himself from the bedcovers and walked over to the bureau where she'd sat her phone last night. "It's Anika," Derek said, flipping the phone open. "Hey, baby." A smile broke out over his face. "Give me a minute," he laughed.

"What?" Chandra sat up in the bed.

"Your son and daughter are waiting outside."

Chandra bounded out of the bed and wrapped herself in Derek's robe. They raced down the stairs and Chandra jerked open the front door.

"Mom!" Anika shrieked. She ran into the house and into Chandra's outstretched arms.

"Baby!" Chandra wrapped her daughter in a hug.

"You're finally here. Derek Jr., get in here," she said, holding her arm out.

"Merry Christmas, Mama," her son said, the smile on his face so much like his father's.

With Derek and D. J. carrying the bags, they all piled into the great room.

"Is that supposed to be a Christmas tree?" Anika asked, pointing to their makeshift tree still propped in the corner.

"It took great pains to get that tree here," Chandra said.

Derek came up behind her. He kissed the top of her head. "But it was worth it," he said.

She looked up at him, took the hand he'd placed on her shoulder and kissed the back of it.

"Yes, it was."

Can You Believe?

by Stefanie Worth

Written with thanks for the blessing of my kids—
who believe at Christmas time and beyond.

Chapter One

Fallon Terry would've bet her whole week's overtime pay that she'd never get her husband Naymond to Crystal Mountain. But, if she'd done that, she'd be broke—considering that he surprised her with a getaway to the Northern Michigan ski resort for their first anniversary. She teetered between anticipation and anxiety, wondering what other surprises awaited two flights and a few hours into her future.

With her weekend wish list pared down to the simple things—an uneventful trip, unforgettable first anniversary, and a tad of leftover holiday "magic" to reconnect her heart with her husband and erase the stress of their last three months apart—Fallon speed dialed Naymond from her cell phone for reassurance.

"Ready for me, lover boy?" She whispered her greeting to avoid the ears of the woman in front of her on the moving walkway.

"You know I can't wait to see you, babe." Naymond's voice melted through the mouthpiece and drizzled into her ear.

"That's not what I asked." Or rather, not what she meant. Beneath the sugarcoated seduction, her heart begged to hear that her husband wanted this weekend because he missed *her*—not just the loving.

"This'll be just what we needed. Watch and see." He spoke faster now. Fallon could hear his footsteps on tile.

They kept pace with his breathing as he raced through the faraway terminal that led to tonight.

Naymond's haste forced him to speak in short, cryptic phrases that made his answer sound a bit patronizing, as if he was patting her head from afar saying, *Quit tripping, Fallon.*

"You're right, hon." Time off from their nine-to-fives, which were more like twenty-four-sevens, was the least their first anniversary deserved. "Thanks for all this. See you there."

"Not soon enough." He sent a kiss through the receiver that calmed her nerves and piqued her libido. "Later."

They ended the call with Fallon feeling less anxious and more eager to see her husband. *Can't wait to tangle my fingers in that untamed 'fro of his.* She smiled at the thought of how he'd bite the corner of his pouty lower lip when she did that, or how he'd glare at her when she threatened to shave off the fashionable hint of five o'clock shadow he wore across his cleft chin and block jaw.

She imagined that any future babies she bore would inherit a blend of Naymond's maple syrup complexion and her French vanilla tone and wind up with creamy peanut butter–colored skin. She hoped they lucked up on his hooded brown eyes, too.

You'll be staring into that sultry face before sunset, Fallon reminded herself. No, she really couldn't wait.

She'd never traveled on Christmas Day, but the trip was cheaper this way. Lugging her carry-on luggage behind her, she focused on the hum of its wheels to quiet her racing mind and transition her thoughts from a long day of massaging wounded joints and muscles at the Physical Therapy Rehab Center to the notion of getting a rub-down of her own from Naymond.

Most travelers had already reached their destinations

and loved ones, leaving Fallon with a few Friday night stragglers who, like her, anxiously awaited the remnants of Yuletide hugs that awaited them across the miles.

Must be close to five o'clock, she surmised by the setting sun outside the concourse windows. That left her a few minutes to spare, maybe tick off a couple of to-do's before boarding. She swerved into the nearest sundry shop.

Since Christmas would be pretty much over—and the getaway used up most of the money they had saved—they'd decided to celebrate Kwanzaa, replacing materialism with quality time and focusing on each other. She strolled the angled aisles, searching for something significant. The cultural celebration called for meaningful gifts—books, things of that sort—but Naymond was a singer, not a reader. He was too spontaneous and imaginative (and she, too practical and thrifty) for any of the ordinary souvenirs shelved in this overpriced shop.

"Not quite what you had in mind?"

Fallon turned toward the voice, coming from the somewhat familiar face of a stout woman with gray wisps around her hairline and faint parentheses in her cheeks that betrayed her youthful tone and sparkling eyes.

Early fifties with one facelift, Fallon guessed. She shook her head at the friendly stranger and responded, "All the good stuff must be gone."

The quip hung in her throat. She couldn't help but compare the comment to the state of her marriage. They were so broke, she was so tired, and Naymond had been so far away for so long, that deep inside she wondered if all the good stuff was gone there, too.

"You'll be all right, Miss Terry."

"Mrs." Fallon instinctively corrected her title. "Do I know you?"

"No, but everybody knows your husband." She paused

long enough to unnerve Fallon further. "I recognize you from that video they did of him on the show. The one with him back home selling houses and you tending your flowers."

"Oh, so you're a *Chart Toppers* fan." Too old to be a groupie, Fallon hoped the woman was crazy. Reality shows brought out the best and worst in folks, so she imagined that even a jazzy old woman could get caught up. "Don't believe everything you see. Nobody's selling houses in Michigan these days and my sister planted that garden," she joked.

"Doesn't matter. We watch that show every week and I've got plenty of reasons to put my vote on your husband." The woman shrugged as her eyes took on a distant cast. "Don't you wonder why? Or want to know what's waiting for you on the other side of this trip?"

That would be LA and the final taping of the show when we find out who wins. Then we either go home or start a brand-new life—which will probably, unfortunately, include weird people like you.

But Fallon decided to humor the woman. "If I could see into the future, what would I do with today?"

Funny the conversation had turned to fortune telling of sorts, considering that she was on her way to Crystal Mountain. Fallon surveyed the stranger with renewed interest. Her mind fumbled for a name to fit her familiar face. An older version of a family friend? A grade school teacher maybe?

The woman's gaze returned to the present and met Fallon's brooding expression with an ear-to-ear grin she suddenly knew from late-night TV. "Trixie DuCayne?"

The celebrity nodded her approval of the recognition.

She had achieved stardom as the 1960s lead singer of Motown's Diamondaires and 1990s host of the *Psychic*

Dimensions show. Suspicion-tinged excitement prickled Fallon's skin as Miss DuCayne reached into her purse and withdrew an object she kept hidden within her fist.

"Hindsight never did me any good," she whispered. Grasping Fallon's hand, she spread her fingers to reveal a small snow globe and pressed it into her palm. "So, how about a peek at tomorrow?"

"Too bad that's impossible." Still, intrigued, Fallon shook the globe. Glitter flakes settled around a miniature jet plane suspended over a snowcapped mountain range. Were those tiny skiers on the ground? She must be selling these to promote her sideline. "It's cute, but still not quite what I'm after. I wanted a book—"

"There's more than one way to tell a story. Books, sure, but television, movies, songs, even . . ." She placed her hand over the snow globe in Fallon's and shook them both. "See what I mean?"

With a second look, the jet seemed to have progressed on its journey, hovering over a building that resembled the one on the ski resort brochure. A small sign in the landscape read "Holiday Inn 2008."

I must've missed that the first time, she thought, though her feeling of being pranked morphed into an uneasy sense of manipulation. Fallon didn't have the patience or time to be toyed with.

"Thanks anyway." She managed politeness despite her annoyance. Trixie DuCayne might be eccentric, but she was, after all, a fan. "My husband will love this gift."

"*Glimpse*." This time Miss DuCayne did the correcting. "I said it was a *peek*—and it's for *both* of you."

Ending their chat with a wink and a quick swivel, she sashayed toward a uniformed man waiting just outside the doorway. A passerby stopped Miss DuCayne for an autograph, which the pseudopsychic superstar songstress obliged—pausing to raise a pair of crossed fingers at Fallon in a gesture of good luck.

Fallon nodded in return, shaking the snow globe at her in a show of appreciation. She took one last look at the gift—glimpse—and was startled to see the snow falling on a new scene: a mirror image of herself standing in front of a Swiss-style chalet labeled "Crystal Mountain."

"How does it do that?" she wondered aloud, mesmerized. Shrugging off the illusion, she jammed the snow globe in the corner of her oversized tote and turned her attention to getting on the plane and seeing her husband.

Still without a purchase, Fallon wheeled toward the counter, searching the racks for a copy of *her* favorite reading material. Entertainment news would be a perfect distraction during the forty-five-minute flight to Chicago. There she'd hook up with Naymond so they could fly together to Crystal Mountain.

Finding the tabloid she sought, Fallon plucked a copy of the *Star Gazer* celebrity "newspaper" from a rack beside the cash register, dropped two dollar bills on the counter and hurried toward the departure gate as the airport's public address system announced that her flight was now boarding.

Shifting her purchases, purse and her carry-on bag to one hand so that she could display her driver's license and boarding pass with the other, Fallon heaved a sigh of relief as she wormed her way through the narrow tube that deposited passengers into the belly of the commuter plane. In this era of super-sized jets, small aircraft like this one made her nervous.

She staked out a window seat on the nearly full flight and settled in to clear her thoughts. Closing her eyes and mind against the outside world and the nearby shuffle and chatter of passengers, she uttered a quick prayer for a safe trip and readied herself for the short flight.

Flurries wafted past her view. Fallon smiled at the sight. She hated the cold, but loved the way snow blanketed everything in its path, painting the scenery fresh and new. Picturesque gave way to practical in the urban landscape. Every inch of pavement she could see had been dutifully cleared from the plane's ground route.

The plows had heaped piles of blackened snow along the runway's edges. Most of the snowfall she watched hit the salted pavement and vanished. Luckier flakes tipped the plowed snow mounds bordering her view, creating a mini-panorama of the scene she'd soon share with her husband. She was so desperate to lay eyes on Naymond that she hoped he'd made the *Star Gazer*'s gossip column this week—in a good way.

Though she knew its stories were all—or at least mostly—bunk, she also believed there must be truth to the stories that showed up again and again. Her mother used to say "where there's smoke there's fire" and that stuck with Fallon—even when applied to gossip. Still, she wondered if the *Star Gazer* had been following contestants on the *Chart Toppers* reality show.

While seeing him only via TV for the last twelve weeks was little consolation and a newspaper photo offered even less, the pseudo sightings provided at least something to soothe the emptiness his lengthy absence had created.

Fallon knew how hard he'd worked for this break and, at first, she'd been more than willing to carry the financial load of their marriage as he pursued his once-in-a-lifetime opportunity. But, when she was honest with herself, she looked forward to the new normalcy they would have when the show ended next week. Hopefully, he'd win, start making some money, and she could stop working overtime.

Meanwhile, she needed to relax so her stress didn't show when she finally saw him.

Fallon fished the newspaper from her gift-store bag. The way she figured it, by the time she finished reading the latest copy her tension would be replaced by mindless up-to-the-minute gossip, they'd be back on the ground and Naymond would be waiting for her.

She lowered the tray table on the back of the seat in front of her, unfolded the paper and laid it flat on the snack-sized surface. Page one featured full-figured bodies that the headline proclaimed FAT!

"These women are just fine." She mumbled loud enough for the broad man squeezed into the seat beside her to hear. "Those other girls are just too skinny. Don't you think?"

Her neighbor chuckled. "Gotta have something to hold onto," he said, agreeing with Fallon.

Photos of pregnant starlets littered pages two and three, hyped as today's Hollywood baby boom. Who knew photos of buying diaper bags or simply exposing a round tummy would be considered engaging news? She shook her head and flipped through the pages until her eyes landed on the center spread.

SOUR NOTES KNOCK CHART TOPPERS TO FIVE, the two-page headline screamed. Fallon eagerly scanned the performance shots and behind-the-scenes pictures for Naymond's sparkling amber eyes and full-lipped smile.

She found it all right: in an arms-around-each-other, eyes-closed kiss with the reality show's rising star: backup singer, Eva Barrow. Tuesday night viewers had already made her the face of the year and, according to the caption

below their photo, ON-STAGE CHEMISTRY BUBBLES BACK-
STAGE FOR EVA AND NAYMOND.

Naymond hated that Fallon loved the gossip rags.

He never dreamed when he auditioned for the *Chart
Toppers* reality show last year that he'd make it to one of the
five finalist slots. Winning would earn him a record deal
and guaranteed creative freedom on an upcoming album.
But being a contestant also turned him into tabloid fodder,
a side effect as unpleasant as the nausea, headaches and upset stomach so many miracle drugs came with these days.
The cure for his career aches was about to make his marriage very sick.

He sat at the edge of the double-width vinyl-covered
bench bordering the baggage claim area, trying to figure
out how to explain the photo of him and Eva before Fallon arrived to meet him. It wasn't fake, but it looked bad,
and he was going to have a hard time making his wife believe the kiss etched in ink wasn't what it seemed. Even
the three-hour flight from California to Chicago hadn't
given him enough time to come up with a way to make
her believe.

The timing definitely sucked. In less than an hour,
they'd be together. He didn't want the strain of tabloid
talk to show in the way he looked at her or in his voice or
demeanor. She'd know something was wrong.

Naymond owed his wife for basically supporting him the
whole year they'd been married. With Detroit's wrecked
economy and a housing market in crisis, his real estate
commissions didn't even cover the cost of their mounting
cell phone calls. And part-time work as an *aspiring* singer-
songwriter didn't pay any bills.

I'm gone too much and contributing too little, he thought.
Now this.

With any luck, she hadn't seen the tell-all magazines yet. And by the time he finished handling his anniversary business over the weekend, she wouldn't want to doubt a word he said. All this would be cleared up by Monday—if he could just keep it away from her until then.

He turned his energy to writing, attempting to pen a tune he'd premiere on the *Chart Toppers* finale, which taped on Tuesday.

"Are you a teacher?" The perky smiling woman beside him craned above her turtleneck sweater to peer at his tablet.

Choosing not to respond, Naymond shook his head no, and shifted his work slightly out of her sight, placing his left hand atop the text to display his wedding band. While some women considered a ring the covert signal for "I'm available," he hoped this one would leave him alone. Right now, he didn't even want to look like he *might* be flirting.

"Are you in school or something?" Undeterred by his silent dismissal, the stranger continued her interrogation.

She's nosy, but probably just trying to make conversation, Naymond told himself. He came up with a polite, noncommittal answer and kept working. "Guess I'm enrolled in the school of life. That's about it."

"You really are modest. I thought maybe that was just an act for TV." The friendly stranger smiled like she knew him. "You *are* Naymond Terry, right? From *Chart Toppers*?"

Naymond did a quick gut check. He'd been holed up in LA so long—where everybody's a Who's Who—that he forgot he might be considered a Somebody in the low-key Midwest. Trying to avoid the appearance of wrongdoing while feeling utterly flattered (and a little bigheaded) was hard to do. He smiled back.

The fan leaned in to whisper as Naymond's grin widened.

A camera flashed.

The woman rose, winked and melted into a throng of passersby, adding "foolish" to his list of feelings.

"Dangit! She set me up," Naymond muttered.

Wanting to hide, he shoved the tablet into his laptop case and slipped the carrying strap onto his shoulder. He examined the crowd gathering at the baggage carousel, looking for other potential traps amid the grins and hellos. Naymond watched the carousel spin for a moment as passengers emptied it suitcase by suitcase.

It seemed like his life had suddenly become the same kind of conveyor belt: loaded with love and opportunity just days ago, but rapidly losing its focus as people kept carrying away bits and pieces of him.

Where was *this* snapshot going to land? And what would it say? He could just imagine.

Is this what I have to look forward to once I win Chart Toppers? *And Fallon . . .* He grabbed his two suitcases from the carousel and readied himself to face his wife. Naymond rubbed his hand over his head. *My dream's been a nightmare lately. Makes a brother think maybe selling real estate will work and that me and Fallon's life isn't so bad after all.*

What he craved was a quick fix—the reassuring sound of the way she said his name, the way he made her giggle, the way his heart hung on after they said good-bye—just enough to get him from this madness to her arms. Naymond called Fallon, planning to hear the same happy anticipation her voice carried an hour before.

Instead, unanswered ringing ushered Naymond to her voice mail. "Leave a message, I'll catch you later," left him more than unsatisfied. Either Fallon was still on the landing strip or she was ignoring his call because she knew about Eva.

The automated phone attendant followed Fallon's

instructions with details of its own. Naymond mustered an upbeat, but conciliatory spiel he hoped would help ease him into his wife's good graces.

"Time to start the rest of our lives." He blurted his spin on the truth and rose to go meet her. His words kept time with his brisk footfalls as he hurried through the terminal toward tonight. "Love you."

Within minutes he'd be eye-to-eye with his wife for the first time in three months.

Still trusting that maybe she hadn't seen the article yet, he set out for their departure gate with half a mind to buy out every newsstand in the concourse. Just in case.

Chapter Two

The short flight from Detroit to Chicago was barely long enough for Fallon to read that crap about Naymond, forget trying to process the accusation.

Sure, she only half-believed most of the stuff she read in the *Star Gazer*, but seeing her husband hugged up with somebody else was definitely a slap in the face. Nothing fake about that feeling. The baggage carousel began to circle in front of her, spitting out luggage, baby seats, guitars and boxes.

Her jumbled mind whirled with the baggage—passengers picking up their items and another woman trying to claim her man. Fallon couldn't call her what she wanted to, but neither could she blame one person for an act it took two people to perform. The photo's kiss was burned into her vision like the shadow left by the sun if you stared directly at it.

And it hurt just as much.

She watched her oversized pastel Fendi bag roll by once, twice, again and again, until it was the only suitcase left on the carousel and all the other travelers had left her alone with her dismay.

Her cell phone rang. Naymond's ring tone.

Fallon didn't answer, but grabbed her luggage, extended the handle and pretended she was still happy with her husband. Cheerful couples tripped by, hand-in-hand or arm-in-arm, up the escalator, through security, across the strolling walkway. They seemed to be everywhere.

Did her devastation and loneliness show to them? Would Naymond know the moment he saw her that something was wrong? He had that knack for picking up her emotions, no matter how she tried to hide them. He had to know she'd find out. What did he plan to say?

Hands full and too wound up to stop for a cup of designer tea, she glanced at the overhead signs and turned down the concourse toward gate A10. Naymond stood on the other side of the wall, eyes searching the crowd for her.

"Hey, you," she stammered and came to a stop. Surprise grew to shock when she noticed the bundle of *Star Gazer* newspapers tucked beneath his arm. *I know he didn't think he could hide that from me.* "Is that your 'glad to see you' gift? How thoughtful."

"Nothing but trash." Naymond dropped the stack onto a nearby chair and extended his arms for a hug.

Fallon hesitated. Oh, how she missed being held by him! But she couldn't. Yet. The jealousy was too fresh. Instead, she shifted her Pullman and continued wheeling toward the gate without waiting for Naymond. His luggage wheels whistled as his footsteps pattered behind her.

"Hold up, babe," he called.

She all but skidded into the waiting area surrounding gate A10, opting to take a seat in an empty row near the window. Naymond rolled his bag beside her and leaned on the extended handle.

He *looked* sorry.

"I saw it." She tried to hiss, but the sound came out syrupy and sentimental, teary instead of ticked off.

"I figured. But I hoped—"

"That you could hide it from me."

"More like buy some time, that's all." Naymond sat on the edge of the chair beside Fallon and stared into her eyes.

Mad as she was, her heart wanted to brush the whole thing under the rug. Instead, her gut stood guard. "The fact that you didn't tell me when it happened must mean there's something to that 'chemistry.' Otherwise—"

"I didn't lie." His gaze didn't waver. "If I say 'it's not what you think,' you'll think I'm treating you like you're stupid." At last he looked away, out the window behind them. "It's gotta be some kind of publicity stunt. Fallon, girl, you know I would never—"

"Kind of hard to believe that right now, so don't say it." She held her fingers against his lips. Soft, full, slightly moist. Ready. She pulled her hand away, leaving a trail of second thoughts. "Say it is a stunt, why would you agree to something like that? How am I *supposed* to feel?"

"Like you know me better than that." He looked away once more. "At least that's what I hoped after it happened."

"*It?*"

"The kiss." Naymond leaned forward and dropped his head into his palms. "Okay. We're backstage, right? Everybody geeked because, hey, we made the cut. People hugging and rubbing, getting real friendly—especially Eva. But she's always all over the cat with the most votes."

"Like 'I better hang with him'—" She began.

"—'he can take me places.'" he finished. "So you only get Eva's attention if she thinks you're in. And for a minute, the light was shining on me." Naymond lowered his gaze with mock humility. "You heard the judges. They said real good things about me this week."

True. And Fallon practically burst with pride after every comment and score. "I remember. 'Real music. A whole new sound. The next level of NeoSoul.'"

"Right." A broad smile crossed his face, pleased— Fallon could tell—that she'd memorized the praise. "So she grabs me. Slobs me with this kiss. I push her off. Everybody laughs and starts teasing her about me being taken. Next thing I know, she's bringing me the *Star Gazer* with that picture."

Slightly relieved, Fallon asked, "What's her deal?"

"Camera hungry? Who knows." He tapped Fallon on the nose with his forefinger. "Me, I got a girl. My wife. Whether the cameras are rolling or not. You are the only one, I swear."

Still, thought Fallon, *that was one heck of a grab, to wrap him up like that in a second or two. Girlfriend either had skills or a very willing victim.*

She looked into his eyes for telltale signs of a lie. No twitching, sweating or stammering. And he didn't avoid her visual interrogation.

The control freak part of her wanted to be right, even now. The rest of her relaxed into a smile and a hug of her own. No way would she let Eva's arms be the last ones holding her husband.

In a welcome and overdue public display of affection, Naymond buried his head in Fallon's neck and placed a soft kiss beneath her earlobe.

"I'm sorry to put you through this," he whispered. He pulled away and grasped her shoulders. "I love you too much to hurt you, Fallon. Things are about to change for us, babe. We gotta be stronger than the bull that's about to come our way."

"It's done. In the past." She hoped.

"Now boarding for Crystal Mountain." The gate announcement interrupted their moment.

"Time for the best weekend we ever had." Naymond stood, tossing his carry-on bag onto one shoulder and lifting Fallon's Pullman. He pulled his own suitcase in the other hand.

Both their cell phones rang.

"Should we?" she asked him, ready to cut off the rest of the world and submerge herself in seventy-two hours of anniversary Naymondness.

"Last call till Monday. Deal?" He dropped one bag and answered his call.

Fallon glanced at her caller ID first, saw her sister's number, and flipped open the phone. "Hey, what's up? We're boarding."

"Your two-timing husband, that's what's up. Girl, he is all over the *Hollywood Hot Sheet* tonight. Have you seen these pictures?" She paused for half a second to take a breath and start again before Fallon could interrupt. "How dare he do this after the way you supported him all this time."

"Mimi. Everything's fine, really. Let me call you later, okay? Bye." Fallon hung up without waiting for an answer.

Pictures, her sister said. Plural. A single ambushed hug that happened to be caught by a lucky paparazzi was one thing. More than one . . .

Maybe playing it cool would have been easier if Naymond didn't look so shell-shocked from his own call.

"Who was that?" he asked.

"Mimi." She folded her arms and nodded at Naymond's cell. "That?"

"My brother."

Heaven help us. Fallon groaned. "And?"

He shrugged. "From the look on your face, Trevor's probably talking about the same thing as your sister."

"Now it's all over the TV." She resisted the urge to scream at him only because she didn't want to embarrass herself more than she already was. "Sounds like Eva stole more than one kiss."

"Calm down, babe. This is getting all out of proportion. I told you how Eva was all over me." Naymond reached for her.

She snatched her hand away. "Sure you didn't forget something? Were you doing your own share of hugging and rubbing?"

"Final boarding call." The flight attendant addressed Fallon and Naymond, the only passengers left to board the small plane.

With any luck we won't have to sit together. Fallon fumed. It didn't matter that she was running with gossip, judging on hearsay. She was angry, yes, but far more disappointed that her husband didn't have much to say for himself.

Naymond peered beyond the plane's wings, onto the kind of sky a kindergartner might draw. Handlike sunrays poked through cotton candy–shaped clouds, finger-painted salmon stripes ran along the horizon's straight blue edge. The illusion convinced him the world must be square.

Why not?

If anyone had told him this morning he'd be accused of infidelity on grocery stands across the country, he wouldn't have believed that either. Now he knew anything was possible; even a flat world in which Fallon had lost faith in him.

A demoralizing mix of fury and hopelessness wrestled inside him, sprinkled with a salting of self-pity and naïveté. He finally got to sit beside Fallon on the plane, but only because he told the man next to her that it was their anniversary trip and asked if they could *please* exchange seats.

Despite his hard-fought physical nearness, they remained distanced by seat belts, a metal armrest, the over-sized tote Fallon insisted on calling a purse, and a palpable current of anger, fear and pride that swirled beneath their silence. He'd bet that the emotional temperature inside the plane matched the chilly wintry countryside they descended into.

His wife avoided the issue by pretending to be asleep. Her mask allowed Naymond to recoup one of the pleasures he'd missed most during their separation: stolen moments of adoration like this when he could bask in her beauty.

With the high cheekbones, wide-set eyes and lush lips a top model would fiend for, Fallon bore the look but carried none of the diva-tude similar faces might tout. She preferred blue jeans and flat boots over killer heels and clingy clothes any day of the week. It made sense to Naymond that a woman with his wife's complex personality probably needed the respite a classic appearance offered.

She sat dancer erect beside him, sandwiched between his window seat and the sympathetic stranger now on the end, head flumped against the backrest. Strands of chestnut-brown hair splayed to each side of her face, glued to the seat by static and restlessness.

Faint worry lines rippled across her forehead. They deepened into sunken crinkles at irregular intervals, as if painful thoughts snagged between her brows, knotting, then untangling when the threat of hurt passed.

He yearned to make it all better, to erase the strain of her twelve-hour day spent kneading away the strains of her athletic clients and rehab patients. Fallon's touch did wonders for them. Naymond wished he could do the same for her.

From the corner of his eye, he saw something tumble from her bag and roll between their seats. He reached for the object, careful to touch her thigh as he retrieved a small snow globe. He held it up to the plane window and watched the artful sun rays fill its liquid with light, then gave it a shake.

Flakes soft as powdered sugar melted into a snowscape surrounding a Swiss-style chalet and a miniature woman that resembled his wife. He ran his fingers along the glass scene, longing to switch the toy he touched with the woman he loved.

Moments later, the plane thudded onto the ground. Passengers wobbled and righted themselves. Naymond tipped conveniently into Fallon. She grabbed his hand—instinctively, he was certain—but he held it tight nonetheless.

The plane wound through the tarmac's looping runway. Every turn revealed a picturesque scene Naymond thought existed only on professionally staged postcards—or in expertly crafted snow globes. Even the pilot's announcement of "Welcome to Crystal Mountain" didn't shake his awe.

Ordinarily, his wife would be chattering away as they prepared to exit. Her continued silence prompted him into nervous conversation. If he couldn't inspire her to talk, maybe landing amid happy childhood memories would. "It's just as beautiful as you said it was."

"More so, I'd say. A lot of change."

He sensed Fallon warming and turned to see her staring past him into the wonderland enveloping them. First anniversary. First time together in months. No way some video vixen wannabe was going to ruin his weekend or his marriage. A hint of his wife's smile boosted his determination to get things right—quick. He hoped the place wasn't *too* different.

"So does it still meet your expectations?" Overhead, stay

buckled/no-smoking signs went dark, signaling passengers that it was time to gather their belongings and get off the plane. Naymond needed a few more minutes to sway her, feeling in his gut that if their feet touched ground in their current state, she'd be lost to him for the weekend and beyond. He ventured another icebreaker. "I knew it would be nice, but it even outdoes my imagination."

"It's always had that fairy-tale quality." Fallon paused to shift her tote and began unfastening her seat belt. "You know how you'll see something and remember how you liked it as a kid—like snow cones or candy corn—and you buy it because you're feeling nostalgic?"

"Um-hm. That would be eggnog and fruitcake for me."

"Well, nobody likes fruitcake except you," Fallon teased. "Anyway, let's say it's hot outside and so you get a cherry cone with extra juice and it tastes . . . all wrong."

"Right. Too sweet usually, or it has a funny aftertaste. Makes you wonder why you used to beg for it."

"Exactly." Fallon stood and stretched. "Well, being here isn't like that at all. Every memory from here is a good memory. Playing in the snow, hanging decorations, sipping hot chocolate and piling logs in the fireplace. Mom let me and Mimi stay up late and count stars when the sky was clear. I used to think Crystal Mountain was magic back then."

"So you're saying it still is?" Naymond tried to bring Fallon's flashback to the present. "Or not?"

"There *is* that holiday tingle in the air." Her tiny smile returned. "The one that makes you believe reindeer will be flying overhead any second now."

Too late to ask Santa, Naymond wished for whatever help he could get.

He scanned the snowcapped mountains surrounding the small airport once more, searching for a sign. "Did you have to be sleeping for the charm to work? My mom always said if you're awake when Santa comes, he won't leave you any toys."

"We didn't have to be asleep." She squeezed into the aisle, reached into the overhead luggage bin, and tugged on her suitcase. Her tone twisted into sarcasm. "We just had to *behave*."

I'm obviously on the naughty list, Naymond thought. He gritted his teeth and counted to ten to pull himself above Fallon's dig while making his way to her side. "Considering we opted out of his visit and decided to do Kwanzaa, then sleep, wake, good or bad doesn't matter. It's about us being together. *Umoja*."

"Unity." Fallon translated the Swahili term for Kwanzaa's first day, the one they'd celebrate tomorrow. "Right."

With a final yank, her suitcase tumbled out of the bin above and onto their heads. They both staggered under the assault. Tangling in each other's legs, they stumbled backward and plunked onto the empty seat across the aisle.

"Ouch!" Naymond winced as his butt hit the armrest, but his main concern was steadying Fallon, who was still tilted toward the floor. He wrapped his arm around her waist and pulled her into his lap.

Her face skewered into an embarrassed frown, she rubbed the top of her head as if to erase the incident.

Naymond grabbed her hand mid-jerk, leaned her backward, and kissed the wounded spot. His own head throbbed, but he ignored the pulsing pain and asked Fallon about her injury.

"Smacking you might have been easier, but you know I like drama." She grinned, then erupted into weary laughter.

"Well, if you were trying to knock some sense into me, all you did was put more stars in my eyes." He looked into his wife's eyes, struggling to express how much he loved her—now and always.

She stared at him as if she was trying to remember his face. Naymond hoped her heart was taste-testing their memories, looking for that familiar flavor they used to share. He prayed the moments ahead would not turn out to be based on bittersweet nostalgia. No syrupy snow cones, please.

"You'll believe in me again, Fallon. I promise," he whispered into her ear. He hugged her again before lifting her hips from his thighs and rising to leave, determined to make his words come true.

When she reached for the fallen suitcase, Naymond pushed her hand gently aside. "I got this." He retrieved the rest of their bags and urged her ahead down the empty aisle with a joke of his own. "Who knows. After that collision, we might not ever see right again."

Chapter Three

Fallon deplaned ahead of Naymond, her head a little foggy from the suitcase injury. No walkway from plane to inside gate, this small jet required they clamber down a steep flight of steps to ground transportation. She did so, feeling her way down the steel stairs, her vision obscured by self-induced stars, swirling snow, and misty steam rising from an invisible chasm beneath her feet.

For a moment, Fallon felt like the miniature woman locked inside the gift snow globe from Trixie DuCayne. She couldn't see a thing for the snow.

"You there?" she called to Naymond through the surreality, willing to set aside her anger until they reached solid ground and familiar sights.

"Right behind you, babe."

The snow fog cleared amid a flurry of flashing lights, a crowd shouting her husband's name, and a gaggle of young girls clawing at each other to get a glimpse of him. He stepped beside her, trying to shield her from the crowd with his body and their luggage, to no avail. The throng swallowed them up.

Now this is not the cherry snow cone—or magic getaway—I remember, Fallon thought. Panicking came to mind.

If they'd traveled by train, she'd say they must have missed their stop. Or, if by car, that they'd lost their way and ended up in an off-the-map town where the residents confused them with some long lost local royalty. But, while she was sure the pilot said Crystal Mountain, she had no idea where they really were.

The group pressed harder, pinning them against the plane's stairway. Panic took hold. Fallon pushed back.

"Do you know what's going on?" Naymond shouted through the din. Without waiting for an answer, he reached through the fans, grabbed her wrist, and pulled her past the first photographer, only to be ambushed by two others. "Let's get out of here."

Holding his hand, Fallon ducked and scurried behind her husband as they began to plow through the grasping strangers. She looked up at the sound of her name—not Naymond's voice—to see a hulking man wearing a full-length leather duster waving them forward. His shoulder muscles bulged through the fitted outerwear and gave him a superhero appearance. He certainly seemed like one at the moment.

"Honey, there." She tugged Naymond's hand to turn his attention to the man who beckoned.

Following his lead, they soon stood beside a black luxury sedan, door open, awaiting their arrival.

"You went all out, didn't you?" she murmured, sliding onto the warm leather seat and pulling Naymond into the car beside her.

"On whose tab?" He shook his head. "I haven't won yet, remember?"

"Always the funny man." The superhero laughed before he planted himself beside Naymond and slammed the door. "Maybe traveling was easier before you crowned yourself King of *Chart Toppers*, but it's too late to turn back now."

It was silent as Fallon absorbed the statement.

"We must've hit our heads harder than we thought," Fallon whispered to Naymond.

"No doubt," he whispered back. "This is one heck of a hallucination."

Or glimpse.

Impulsively, Fallon reached into her tote to retrieve the snow globe. Same scene, new caption. The mini resort sign now read, "Holiday Inn *2009*," next year instead of now.

Inside the car, the air oozed tranquility in total contrast to the din outside. Kenny G's saxophone ebbed from surround-sound speakers into a wordless smooth jazz version of a John Legend song. She looked up from the globe to see the superhero stranger staring at her with hooded eyes and a half snarl.

"Sorry, I didn't get your name," she asked. He looked at her with a hint of distrust that made Fallon feel intimidated asking him to identify himself. But maybe he would help her figure out if this was part of Trixie's glimpse—and if so, of what.

"My bad, ma'am. You all weren't together when I started." Superhero threw his gaze in Naymond's direction and followed it with a quick smirk, as if they shared a secret. "Jeff. New bodyguard."

Jeff the Superhero Bodyguard seemed to assume she knew his predecessor.

"Didn't know I had an old one," Naymond whispered to Fallon, echoing her shocked sentiments. Then his eyes widened with a sudden ah-ha. "You set all this up with the *Chart Toppers* people, didn't you? They're trying to prank me, right?"

"Naymond, honey, I couldn't even imagine this hoopla, Less know how to pull it off."

But, what if Trixie's glimpse remark was a bunch of hogwash and somebody—Eva maybe—concocted this charade to show me up? Is she trying to tighten her grip on Naymond by impressing him with the star treatment?

But the limo, the bodyguard . . . it was almost as if this was *real*. Fallon closed her eyes, slumped against the backseat and laid her head on Naymond's shoulder, thinking that maybe when she opened her eyes they'd be in a cab, watching the meter miles chip away at their precious spending allowance. Jeff, of course, wouldn't exist. Maybe the Eva-kiss wouldn't either.

"Okay, let's pretend you didn't arrange for the attention and maybe they're mistaking me for some other Naymond Terry who's famous. If this is what you meant by the holiday magic here, I'll take it." Naymond laughed, raised his voice and prodded Jeff the Superhero Bodyguard. "So where's the camera, man? You're not going to keep this up all night, are you? I've got plans for my wife that we don't want on video."

Fallon lifted her head to shush her husband with a mock scowl. He leaned down and kissed her heavily. She pulled away as his tongue entered her mouth, placing two fingers against his lips and shaking her head gently. The scene reminded Fallon of making out in the backseat as a teenager while her boyfriend's best friend and his girl sat mute up front.

Jeff feigned indifference, as if he'd politely ignored worse.

"Can you do us a favor, please?" Fallon asked him. "How can I get a copy of the latest *Star Gazer* newspaper around here?" As excited as she was to be here, she hadn't forgotten the still lingering issue of her husband posed similarly with another woman—now on sale for the whole world to see.

Jeff shook his head and gave Naymond another Boys Club glance.

Naymond furrowed his brow and rolled his eyes. "I can't believe you," he mumbled, scooting away from Fallon.

"Likewise," she hissed.

Jeff cleared his throat in an awkward attempt to silence their rumbling. "For reasons you can probably understand, that's not a paper they carry at the Inn. But, I'll see that you get a copy, Mrs. Terry."

They rode in silence through the middle of nowhere until they reached The Holiday Inn, which looked exactly like the photos in the brochure they used to book the trip and the scene in the snow globe.

Jeff exited ahead of the couple, scanning the grounds (for trouble, Fallon assumed) and opened Fallon's door. Naymond scooted along behind and exited beside her. Unwilling to break the silence as she absorbed the atmosphere, she walked a small arc around her husband and began strolling the wide bricked walkway toward the entry.

A doorman readied the door for their entrance. She heard Naymond's footsteps quicken behind her, then pass to her right. He spun quickly in front of her, stopping her determined path, scooped her into his arms newlywed style and followed Jeff's lead through the lobby and into a mahogany-laden elevator. He placed her feet gently on the floor, but held tightly to her hand.

She found herself reeling not from the elevator's rise, but from Naymond's obvious attempt at making up. He made it hard to stay mad, but she tried her best.

The elevator arrow dinged as they reached the top floor. The doors opened as Jeff escorted them across the hall and around the corner to a STAFF ONLY elevator. He shoved a small key into an unmarked slot and held it until the elevator car arrived. The unlit floor selection panel displayed only six buttons, each marked in a sequence beginning with PH. Jeff pressed PH3 and they began their final ascent.

"At last." Fallon exhaled loudly. Her feet hurt. Her

mind raced. A hot bath and short nap seemed the perfect remedy.

Jeff exited first, entering the suite's private foyer and scouting the perimeter before signaling "all clear" to Naymond and Fallon with a nod and a wave.

Their "this must be a dream" sequence reached a new level of impossibility when they entered the room—clearly the *wrong* room. Even with two decades of renovation and redecorating, Fallon's girlhood memory couldn't conjure the palatial accoutrements the suite contained.

The living room alone was larger than the entire first floor of the Detroit bungalow she and Naymond lived in. A full-size overstuffed sofa occupied one wall, flanked by two leather armchairs, all grouped around a large carved coffee table. Holding center court on the wall across from the sofa was a flat-screen TV that Fallon estimated to be at least sixty inches wide. An electric fireplace burned brightly below it.

A spacious dining area boasted a stately dark wood table set for company and lined with six chairs. A bar dressed with four tall, dark wood bar stools separated the eating space from the kitchen. All Fallon could see of the cooking area was a gorgeous set of cabinets. That was enough.

"Coffee has been prepared for you, Mr. Terry, and hot water for your tea, Mrs. Terry," Jeff noted as he scouted the room's perimeter before circling back to the entrance where Fallon and Naymond stood awestruck. "And I'll get that newspaper to you, Mrs. Terry. Let me know what else you need."

"Yes, I believe there's been an error." Dollar signs clicked through Fallon's head as she surveyed the sturdy wood and exotic fabrics peppering the room.

"Oh—" Jeff pursed his lips and steeled his gaze as if bracing for a verbal slap.

"No, everything's great." Naymond interrupted, trying to shoo the bodyguard toward the door. "We'll call if we need you. Thanks."

To Fallon's dismay, Jeff ignored the hint, grabbing the remote from atop an end table, flicking on the television and plopping onto the nearest armchair.

Naymond and Fallon turned to look at each other.

"You mind, Jeff?" asked Naymond. "It's our anniversary trip . . . Please?"

"My bad. I forgot." Jeff rose and strolled toward the door. "I'll be out here if you need me."

Naymond closed the door behind him. "Fallon, this is some crazy stuff. Think we're being set up?"

"Yes and no." It could be the *Chart Toppers* people playing a trick on Naymond, sure, or it could be that Trixie had more psychic power than her laughable TV show let on. Fallon could see celebrity written all over their circumstances.

This Inn was not the Crystal Mountain resort her parents' Jim Dandy Ski Club vacationed at when she was a child. Nor did their *MTV Cribs* suite fit within the paycheck-to-paycheck life she lived with Naymond. This beck-and-call, wait-on-you-hand-and-foot excursion fell far outside the realm of their wildest dreams.

What she needed was a glimpse at a real date before she told Naymond anything.

A Holiday Inn amenities menu scrolled across the television, offering touch-tone options for laundry and messenger services, concierge assistance, room service, free movies and wireless Internet access. Photos of smiling patrons and diligent staff morphed across the listing, ending with a flurry of snowflakes that landed to form the words, "Welcome to Wonderland. Your Dreams, Our Magic."

* * *

Naymond watched the Inn's marketing slogan fade from the TV screen. They obviously took their advertising seriously. Magic was the only word to describe seeing everything he'd ever wanted appear before his eyes when they stepped off the plane.

Would Fallon do this for him? Were Eva or those *Chart Toppers* producers up to something else to make him look bad, like saying he'd stiffed the hotel on this bill? He should've let Fallon finish her sentence when Jeff asked if they needed anything. This was a mistake they couldn't afford.

He watched his wife walk around the room touching and admiring the finishes and room accents she craved for their home. "One day, babe." Though he wished it could be today. "But you were right. This whole setup is wrong. There's no way we can afford this."

She looked tired and rightly so. A full shift, two flights, the *Star Gazer* nonsense. And her long day would now be longer because they'd have to backtrack and get to the right room.

"I just don't understand the mix-up. Not just the room, but a limousine and bodyguard, too. For us? This must be a joke—like I need more trouble." Naymond craned his neck to search for a restroom in the house-size suite. "Let's take a few minutes to stretch, then go downstairs and find our real room."

He tossed the remote onto the couch. The television channel changed. *Hollywood Hot Sheet*'s opening music cascaded from the screen.

On tonight's show, we'll be talking to Chart Toppers *winner, producer Naymond Terry, whose first CD,* All I Want, *went platinum this week.*

Naymond sat in disbelief as his publicity headshot faded into the background video of him and Fallon entering the Inn a short while ago.

"Did you see that, babe?" He stood and spun toward the kitchen.

Fallon had migrated into the living room area, staring at the screen, hands on hips, jaw dropped, eyes wide.

"Looks like we *can* afford our fun." He shook his head and laughed. "What'd we do? Fly through a time warp?"

A "Merry Christmas 2009" graphic served as backdrop to the story following Naymond's, giving Fallon the proof she needed to believe that the possible time warp her husband snickered about was probably the glimpse Trixie promised.

Fallon loved a good surprise, but not this. Her whole life disappeared when she got off that plane. The world she knew had been swallowed up by her husband's vision of life after *Chart Toppers*.

She didn't like it.

Not the bodyguard on twenty-four-hour duty, those groping groupies, or the cameras in her face. Sure, she supported Naymond's audition for the show. But, once he made it and then kept winning, she realized her man was mushrooming into a household fantasy for millions of desperate, conniving women all across the country. Week after week, they dialed Naymond's "number" to bring him back so they could lust over him the next Tuesday.

Between the pressure of becoming sole breadwinner, managing the household, and supporting her husband's bid for stardom, Fallon had started to wish for the end. If only he'd realize that, like this room, the spotlight was just a dream.

She was ready for Naymond to lose and come home.

Eventually the mortgage market would rebound, houses would start selling once more, and he'd be bringing in his fair share of income as a realtor to help cover household expenses. They'd assume the life *she* pictured: stable jobs, happy home, cute kids. No groupies.

Stupid holiday magic.

She strolled across the room to click off the television. Naymond balked (he was in the middle of watching a program), but she needed to be able to sound rational when she laid this glimpse story on him.

"So did you wish on a star during the flight or what?" She thought maybe a mystical conversation starter would make the discussion easier.

"All I've wanted for three months is to lay my eyes and hands on you."

"Well, hon, we got that, but I think we got a little more."

"Talking about the celebrity treatment?"

She nodded. "But I don't think it has anything to do with your *Chart Toppers* people. I met Trixie DuCayne at the airport in Detroit."

"The singer with the psychic show?" He raised his eyebrows and scoffed.

"She gave me a gift. Hold on." The snow globe with its 2009 sign and morphing scenery would make her sound sane. Fallon crossed the room and rummaged through her tote tossed on the couch until she found the snow globe. She shook it to demonstrate her point. "This. First it had an airplane. Then it had the Inn inside with a 2008 sign. Now it says 2009."

"Yeah. I saw that during the flight when it fell out of your purse." Naymond took the globe and gave it his own shake. "But it had a girl inside. I swear it looked exactly like you in front of this hotel."

"When I thanked her for the gift, she called it a *glimpse*."

Fallon paused, pursed her lips and crossed her arms. "You think she hexed us or something?"

"A hex would be bad," Naymond offered. "A glimpse of what?"

"I didn't know until we got here." Fallon took the globe back. "It's a little freaky—the scene inside the globe keeps changing. But everything it shows is one step ahead of where we are. And you saw the date on that entertainment show."

"Even though that seemed real enough, you're telling me this is supposed to be a glimpse of our life—when, next year?" He laughed and reached for the TV remote, flicking the television back on. "Sure, why not? But, I'm supposed to be the one with the crazy imagination."

Fallon knew she was pushing her luck asking her husband to believe something she wasn't sure of. "Okay, so what if all your fame does turn out to be a prank by your show's producers? Groupies included."

"There you go." He scooted away from her. "Is this your way of bringing up the *Star Gazer* mess again? I told you it's not true."

"Hmph. If you ask me, your weak explanation is about as hard to believe as this." She threw the snow globe onto the couch and walked away. "I'd be very interested in knowing how you're going to act when I'm not around."

"You gotta stop reading that stuff, Fallon. What? Tabloids are all lies unless they're about me? Thanks." Naymond leaned forward and drummed his fingers on the coffee table. "How are *you* going to act once I make it? You gotta be a lot stronger than this if we're going to be together."

"What do you mean 'if'? Listen to you talking about splitting up already!"

"That is not what I said." He growled beneath the

words, then took a deep breath to regroup. "Us being to-gether means you trusting me. I'm about to give you everything you ever wanted."

Fallon plopped back onto the couch beside Naymond. "From the glimpse I've gotten so far, I'm not sure *your* dream is *our* route to happiness."

"Think about all the magazine pages you've torn out. The samples you collect. All that *House TV* you watch." Naymond waved his hand to show off the room. "You're talking money, money, money every time I call. Now it looks to me like you can have anything you want—and you're still complaining. What do you want me to do? Fail?"

"No," she lied. "Well, not exactly. I just don't need us to be *too* famous."

"Oh, I see. You'll be cool if I'm just a *little bit* successful, then? So I shouldn't work so hard to provide for my wife and the family she wants. Is that what you're trying to say?"

His eyes narrowed and his nostrils flared. Fallon real-ized she'd ticked off her husband.

"You know I'm with those professional athletes all day." She tried to erase the sting sharing her insecurities caused. "I hear about their escapades—who does who and all that nonsense. I know what you're up against."

"Yeah, sure, if I was a *single*, multimillion-dollar-a-year, endorsement-happy athlete on a championship team. But I'm married. To you. And I love you more than anything. I have never done anything to betray you—and I wouldn't. How could you even think . . . ?"

"You're a man."

"I'm *your* man."

"But women like Eva—"

"Got nothing on you." Hurt hooded his eyes, washing Fallon in a flood of guilt.

"I'm—"

Pounding on the door interrupted her apology.

"Naymond! It's Tana. Open up."

"Just what I'm talking about." Fallon rolled her eyes and folded her arms across her chest, glad she didn't finish her sentence after all. "Get it. Probably some groupie. I'm going to take a bath and lie down for awhile."

"Yeah, whatever. But I'll tell you what, whether this is magic or a mistake, I'm about to enjoy this ride. You do what you gotta do." Naymond rose to answer the door, shouting, "Just a minute. I'll be right there."

Chapter Four

"I know it's Christmas and all, but that's no reason not to answer your phone." An average-height woman wearing cat-eyed glasses, a short blonde afro and a very tall attitude barged through the door, leaving Naymond standing tongue-tied and confused in a cloud of her Oriental cologne. "I told you we need to review your schedule for the weekend. We have to get an early start in the morning and—"

"Tomorrow's our anniversary." Even though Fallon had really gotten on his nerves this evening, he knew she was overworked and underloved lately and that the tabloid article added one more issue to her stack of insecurities. He had making up to do. "We've already booked the entire weekend. Together. Alone. Who are you to undo our plans?"

"You in the market for a new manager? I can go home and spend the rest of the holidays with my family instead of you." She poked a forefinger into Naymond's chest and planted her other hand on her hip. "Just 'cause you suddenly decide to pretend you have an anniversary—what? I'm supposed to throw out all our work?"

Her all-business-no-bedside-manner demeanor offended Naymond. Nobody talked to him like that. But just in case she was part of this whole celebrity gag *Chart Toppers* might be playing on him and Fallon, he didn't want to show up on TV acting like a jerk. He took the cool route.

"Obviously, you just don't know. December twenty-sixth. As in tomorrow. Me and Fallon." He paused his low-key tirade to wonder what this Tana—his manager?—had waiting for him. "What's so important that you want me to mess up my wife's weekend?"

Tana peered over her glasses and laughed. "You're kidding, right? Because *you* approved the 8 A.M. interview for National Black Radio, the noon photo shoot with *Rolling Stone*, and dinner with the R&B Awards staff about producing the opening segment for June's show." She leaned back and looked up at Naymond with a direct, accusatory glare. "Tell me that's what you meant by *we're booked*."

Wow.

Naymond weighed his options: A whole day handling his music business *or* endless hours of Fallon's pouting accusations and his useless explanations?

"You know I meant to say *Fallon's* booked. Sit down. Relax." The invitation was more for himself than his manager. He ushered her to a chair at the dining room table and plunked himself into a seat beside her. "Maybe she can go get her hair done after breakfast and I know she has some last-minute shopping to wrap up before she joins us for dinner. How's that sound?"

"Dinner's fine. She knows the drill. I'll arrange for the extra reservation." Tana whipped out her rhinestone-studded BlackBerry and began inputting words into the PDA with her thumbs. "But since when does she *go* to the salon? I'll call tonight and have her spa coordinator up here around ten o'clock, after her workout. Speaking of which, where's the treadmill I asked for? It's supposed to be against that far wall." Tana's thumbs took to pecking once more.

He played along with Tana's demands, afraid that saying "no" would end the excitement as mysteriously as it appeared. What if the *Chart Toppers* producers really had turned a critical life moment into a final judging test?

His "manager" said he won. It worked for him.

He'd have to deal with the fact that bailing out of the planned His-n-Her massage, facial and pedicure session in favor of face time with his new followers would kill their weekend. Naymond could even picture her icy silence during dinner—if she bothered to show up. But he wasn't willing to risk missing out on what might be real. Naymond mentally postponed making up with Fallon until Sunday.

"She's pretty tired, Tana. Not sure she'll feel like running that early. We'll let her sleep in." Which meant he had a whole lot of work to do tonight to compensate for disappointing her tomorrow. He nodded toward Tana's PDA. "That takes care of Saturday. What's up for Sunday?"

"Since tomorrow's pretty tight, you get a reprieve Sunday. Keep dinner open, though. I may have some people I want you to meet. Let's say six o'clock, tentatively." She tapped the PDA. "Monday we fly out to LA so you can perform on the final show of the 2009 *Chart Toppers* season and close out your reign. Time to crown your successor!"

"It's already been a year since I won?" Now that part he didn't like—missing his whole first year of being famous. An in-flight time warp sounded more and more like the answer he wanted to where they were.

Since the funny stuff started as soon as they stepped off the plane, would they get that time back when they flew home? Or would his best memories be lost forever in this "glimpse"?

"Can't I get another week to wallow in the glory?"

"What's up ahead is way better than what you're leaving behind." Tana laughed. "That's why I can't believe you brought *her* with you—why it looks like you're taking her back. Now especially, when Naymond Terry can pull any woman he wants. Of course, you pick the one that comes with the drama." She shook her head and threw her hands into the air. "What's with that?"

Obviously, his twelve months of magical celebrity hadn't boosted Fallon's confidence in his ability to be the man she needed. Did he fail on his promise to her after all?

"Lay off my wife. Somebody's gotta keep it real around here." He had to defend her, though she seemed to have a bad reputation where he was concerned.

"That's the problem, Naymond. All she ever did was bring you down. Where is she, anyway?" Tana whispered the question and peered toward the doorway that separated the front suite from the bedroom. "You let your wife annoy certain people who could have opened doors and taken you places."

Why the past tense? What happened to him and Fallon during the months they missed in this imaginary time warp? Or were the producers trying to split them up on national TV?

"Tell me what she supposedly did again? And to what people? Be specific."

Tana furrowed her brows at Naymond. "Your Regional Promotions director, for one, won't even take her calls."

"Why would she be calling him anyway?"

"Good question." Tana rolled her eyes. "After him, pick anybody on your staff and they'll name their pet peeve with Mrs. Terry. So, if your bookings slow down once you reunite, don't blame me."

The comment hurt Naymond. To get back together, there had to be a breakup. Fallon was all good. His dream caused most of their grief. First it was financial and, as of today, emotional. How did his wife become the bad guy?

He didn't like this future scenario at all and wouldn't play along if the show's producers were wrecking his family in the name of ratings.

"Enough about Fallon. What else do you and I have to take care of tonight?"

Tana looked over her glasses again. "That's it for me and you. I'm about to leave, though, because it sounds like you've got some explaining to do around here." She tapped the PDA once more, stood, stretched and turned toward the door. "I'll arrange a wake-up call for six A.M. I'll have the car downstairs at seven. Be ready—on time, okay?"

"No problem."

Oh, but it was.

Naymond walked his manager to the door and wondered if every special occasion had become just as impersonal. If so, Fallon must be miserable.

With or without magic, they'd never make it like this.

A commercial jingle caught his ear. He turned to find himself on-screen hawking a diamond-studded designer watch. No words—just him, his pricey timepiece, and a studio full of musicians playing a jazzed up version of his winning *Chart Toppers* tune. The ad faded to black with the watch hands saluting midnight.

Time.

Naymond felt theirs slipping away. In order to change Fallon's attitude toward the life he wanted, he'd have to persuade her that his dream was worth following.

Let me get started.

He picked up the phone to call room service and ordered lobster and petit filet mignon to be delivered in two hours. The second call was to the concierge with a request for ten dozen red rose petals, a bottle of Cristal on ice, and candles.

* * *

A little miffed, but more jealous, Fallon slid deeper into the tub, feeling its whirlpool currents whipping her cares away. Magic or mistake, whatever happened here brought Naymond's dreams to life. In that same flash of fate, all her material lusts had been satiated.

Was that so bad?

"I've been dreaming of a full-length black fur that swings just so." The kind her ball-playing clients draped their wives in during winter games. She slathered an armful of bubbles across her body to mimic the wrap-around warmth she no longer had to envy. "And maybe I don't need to worry about that Eva Barrow wench in 2009 either."

Without Eva in their way, celebrating Kwanzaa's Unity and Self-Determination days tomorrow and Sunday would be a whole lot easier. Someone probably did set up Naymond for that fake photo in the first place. Her mind hesitated, but her heart wanted to believe her husband was innocent, like he said.

Besides, Eva wasn't the only problem between her and her husband. There used to be the matter of his wannabe career overshadowing their very real bills. Or the stars in his eyes keeping him away from her for months at a time. And the overtime she worked week after week to hold their fragile life together.

Their tough times made her overlook good things—how Naymond taught her to play pool, watered the garden because she seldom remembered the chore, and called her every single night to say "I love you."

Now, the longer she soaked, the sillier being mad at him became. "We needed a miracle to make a happy first anniversary and it looks like we got one."

As much as the snow globe appeared to be the culprit, the thought that Trixie DuCayne held some power over their lives was eerily unnerving. Despite the evidence, Fallon preferred to pretend Naymond's automatic celebrity status was a *Chart Toppers* joke that would air on the reality show finale next week. That meant he was going to win. Who else could afford to go to these lengths?

"It doesn't matter how we got this break. What's important is now. My husband told the truth. I overreacted to gossip. I get a chance to see that our new life is just what I've been dreaming of, too. Time for me to apologize to my man."

"Naymond, hon," she shouted from the tub, "can you come here a minute?"

Humming preceded his entrance. No words needed. Fallon knew the song, "Splash," a tune she helped him write for the *Chart Toppers* audition based on a poem she started shortly after they met. Naymond brought their mutual feelings to life by adding his own musical arrangement and production expertise.

He sang, *Got me thinking of rinsing off these old ways . . . Putting on your new love, cool and calm . . . Diving in your well . . . Making waves of my own . . .*

"Knock, knock." He spoke the greeting.

"Who's there?" she answered with a singsong, schoolgirl lilt to her voice.

"Wondering if you'd like to go skinny-dipping?"

"What kind of girl do you think I am?"

"Just the one I've been looking for." A shirtless Naymond pushed through the door and, with an open bottle of champagne in one hand and rose petals in the other, began scattering a trail of flower bits behind him as he crossed the room toward Fallon. He climbed the three wide steps to the raised whirlpool and knelt beside the tub, sprinkling a final handful of petals across her bath's fading bubbles. "Need a refresher?"

"I was about ready to get out." Fallon's legs quivered against the whirring jets beneath the water. She watched Naymond's eyes leave her own and caught the smile that creased his mouth at the sight of her trembling bubbles. "It's getting chilly."

"Better let the official temperature tester handle this." Naked by the time the last syllable left his lips, he slid into the water beside her. He took a sip of the champagne and offered the bottle to her. "Remember when we used to play like this in the morning?"

"Been a long time." Truly, she'd forgotten how incredibly sexy liquid love could be. Fallon took a sip and set the bottle beside the tub. Then, finding the soap, she sat upright and began to lather Naymond's back.

"Two years together, twelve months of marriage—amazing how fast we start taking these pleasures for granted." Naymond slipped the soap from Fallon's hand and washed his chest, abs and arms.

"I had to be at work so early . . ." She thought back to those first months together. Baths like this happened regularly. Taking the soap once more, she worked her hands full of bubbles and rubbed them up and down Naymond's legs, around his feet and back up between his thighs.

"Then I tried out for the show . . ." He splashed clear water over his body.

"Who knew we'd have to go months without seeing each other?" More statement than question, she wondered aloud as she splashed his back.

"Eighty-one days this time." Naymond reminded her of the count, though she knew it by heart, too. "No wonder you're cold."

"Not anymore," she murmured, sizzling beneath the water.

Naymond stood and stepped out of the tub. He removed

a body-sized towel from the warming rack behind Fallon's head and wrapped it around his waist. Then he reached for her hand and helped her from the whirlpool bath, wrapped her in a matching towel and led her along the rose-strewn path into the bedroom.

There, the room glowed with the light of a dozen candles. Their half-spent wicks cast trembling shadows along the wall and ceiling, swaying in time to Fallon's tentative footsteps.

Petals covered the floor and the bed, their thick rose aroma mingling with the fragrant vanilla and sweat pea scent of the room's candles.

"Welcome to Che Na-mone," he said in a faux French accent. "Tonight I bring your dreams to life."

What more could she ask? Fallon released his hand and unwrapped the towel.

Teasingly near, he stood inches from her body, pursed his lips and began to blow her skin dry. Behind the ears, down her neck, across her shoulders, his warm breath chilled and teased.

He didn't touch. She wished he would.

Wordless whispers hung in the soft breezes he swept across her nakedness. Between her breasts, around her navel, down to one hip, slowly over to the other.

Unable to stand another second steeped in his heat, yet separated from his skin, she reached to touch his cheek.

He threw his head backward, smiled, knelt and blew a long, hot kiss into the space between her thighs.

Fallon's knees buckled, tumbling her into his waiting arms. Naymond's want washed over her passion-scorched body in a purifying wave, laying her mind empty and breathless like sand beneath the tide.

He carried her to the bed and laid her gently in the center. "Turn over."

Fallon obeyed, closing her eyes and falling face-first into the pillow. She felt him kneel astride her, sitting gently atop the backs of her thighs. His hands caressed her shoulders. Softly he began to massage the muscles in her arms, first one side, then the other.

She felt a trickle of liquid at the base of her neck that dribbled down her spine to her hips. She smelled the oil—lavender and musk. Her body responded to its warmth by writhing beneath him.

He placed his hands along her hips. "Be still," he commanded and began to rub, knead, mold her skin, pressing away what remnants of worry remained in her mind by moving the oil across her back and buttocks, down her thighs, knees and calves, to her heels. He covered every inch of skin within his reach with warmth.

Toying with her senses, he flexed each ankle, traced his fingers along the soles of her feet, between each toe, and then began to work his way back up her body. Sitting between her thighs, he lifted the right leg, then the left, kneading each calf while massaging oil onto the front side of her body.

Moving the oil between her legs, his hands lingered, moving upward with deliberate precision, freeing the muscles, teasing to elicit her response, only to shush her to silence each time.

She didn't know which of them enjoyed the game more. She arched her back.

"Be still, Fallon." He pretended to be serious as he rolled her over.

"I can't." Her whine was genuine. *How can he hold out so long?* she wondered, trembling, quivering in her effort to restrain her desire.

He leaned over, kissed her neck, nibbled her earlobes.

She could feel him, firm between their bodies. She wanted to move, didn't want to wait any longer and tried to lift her hips against him.

"You're being bad," he said.

"Feels so good," she moaned.

He licked her shoulders, raised her arms above her head, and slid his hands along her body, squeezing the nipples, crisscrossing her belly and waving his hand above the space between her legs.

"I want you now," she gasped.

"Just gotta have it your way, huh?" He teased. "Then again, that is what I said you'd get, isn't it? Tell me what you want then."

She lifted her hips to invite him inside.

He scooted backward, instead gliding his hand from her navel to the steaming space he airbrushed moments before, dipped his fingers into her warmth and kissed her belly.

"Stop!" she moaned.

"Don't want it after all?"

"Quit playing with me, Naymond. It's been too long to waste time on games, baby."

"Oh, you're saying get down to business?" He placed his hands on her hips and slid atop her, pausing, then plunging. "I missed you."

"Me, too." For once, she did not need him to defer his climax to wait for hers.

The whirlwind of emotions pummeling her all day swirled amid her passion, spinning her physical desire into the emotional cyclone that made for the best orgasms. Anticipation, anger, want, uncertainty, desire, confusion, elation whirled inside her belly.

She dug her nails into his back. Whether he tensed

with pain or pleasure she couldn't tell and didn't care. She squeezed the muscles deep inside her body until he pulsed in rhythm with the circular motion of her hips. Fallon thought she would dissolve with satisfaction as he came and collapsed, finally empty, atop her.

He wrapped her in his arms and held her close, breathing heavily into the space between her neck and shoulder. She knotted her legs around his hips and they rolled as one onto their sides.

"Tonight was beautiful, Naymond." She smiled, a bit ashamed about feeling so complete. "Everything I hoped for."

"I try, you know." He kissed her lightly and laughed.

"I can't believe you did all this for me."

"C'mon, Fallon. I feel like I owe you the world. Everything you've done for me. You've always believed in me. I would not be where we are without you."

A twinge of guilt burrowed beneath her contentment, separating her from his adoration. Sure, she supported him. But, her belief in Naymond had lately been laced with doubt. She worried that the shimmer of Hollywood would distract her husband and lure him from her and toss him into the arms of others who might be more gorgeous, more glamorous, more connected than his wife, the physical therapist.

Her insecurities followed her right up until this afternoon. He knew that, yet he was still grateful.

"Even here, with all this, Fallon. I can see through the gloss and glimmer, that you're the one who keeps me grounded. Thank you for giving me us."

"All I wanted was a simple anniversary weekend away, and you give me Wonderland."

"Not me, really. I had no idea when you talked about the good things that always happened here, that we'd be in line for a little holiday magic ourselves. So, we got more than we bargained for coming here. Is that bad?"

"No. I guess not. It is like a glimpse into the life we'll have when you win." Fallon tried to speculate and apologize in one swoop. "I've been so scared that the show would take you away from me, but I see now that by having the things we worked for, it just brings us closer. Thank you for putting up with me."

He gave a bright smile. "Woman, please. I'm not about to let you get away."

"And to think. This is just the start of our anniversary celebration. What other surprises are waiting for us?" Unburdened by telling Naymond what she'd harbored for so long, Fallon grinned and relaxed. "I know you wanted to make tomorrow all about me, but this is *our* weekend. So, now it's my turn. Tell me what you want, and I'll make it happen. Where should I begin? Or maybe we could just lay here until Monday morning and do absolutely nothing but make love and get room service. What do you say?"

Naymond's fingers, slowly tracing lacy loops along her chest, around her breasts, suddenly stopped. He withdrew his hand.

"What?" Fallon asked. An alarm went off in her gut. She stared at him, watching him close his eyes, and listening to him sigh. "What, Naymond?"

"I'm still not sure what's going on—with the people around me, our room, the service we're getting. You call it magic, I still think it's a joke or some mix-up. Whatever's happening also has me booked all day tomorrow."

"What do you mean, 'booked'?"

"From sunup to sunset."

"Well, call your producer and tell him you already have plans. It's our anniversary!"

"Yeah, but say it's just part of this game. What if they already know I'm going to win next week?"

Anger grew in Fallon's chest. "I see your priorities—"

"Us. Nothing's changed except that now we might be getting everything we want—for real." He returned the intensity of her gaze. "Yes. Tomorrow I have an interview, a photo shoot, and an awards show meeting. I'm sorry, Fallon, but it'll be worth it in the end."

She couldn't believe he was ditching their getaway for some reality show joke. "You're saying this is it for *our* weekend?"

"Not necessarily." He stumbled over his explanation. "Well, at least until tomorrow night. Maybe we can start again on Sunday."

Naymond went from heroic to pathetic in ten lousy seconds.

Fallon wriggled out of his embrace and rolled away from him. "Candlelight, roses, that Cristal dip, not to mention the massage. I thought you were giving me a preview—"

"Who says it's not?"

"How can it be?" She sat upright. "Come sunrise, you're out of here, while I—what?"

"Well, you seemed so tired after the flight. I thought you might want to sleep in."

"With *you*, yes."

"Or if you want to get started early, Tana said she could get you some exercise equipment here first thing."

"Oh, that's a blast."

"Why are you acting like you ever miss a workout?"

"I had other kinds of cardio in mind." She'd left Detroit hoping her husband missed more than her body—knowing good and well she would've taken him up on a midair romp if he dared her. Yet a Mile High quickie couldn't compare with what he concocted tonight. Still, it wasn't that. "I really didn't want to share you this weekend, Naymond. The whole point of taking a trip for our first anniversary was to get away from everybody. But, no. We're surrounded by a bunch of strangers who followed us here to ruin our anniversary!"

"Fallon, let me find out what's happening. We'll have our time. I promise."

"You're not doing so good keeping the first one—about making me believe in you. Remember that? What, three hours ago? Maybe you should reconsider—"

"Admit it." Naymond leaned against her back and whispered into her ear. "The weekend turned out different than you expected. But not one thing has been bad about it. Am I right?"

"Unless you're on a totally different trip right now, how could you possibly think that, Naymond Terry?"

Chapter Five

Morning after in the "Fabulous Life of Naymond Terry," greeted Fallon with the leftover scent of rose petals and vanilla candles. Satin, gold and marble accents throughout their suite at the Inn confirmed that yesterday's surreal time warp was indeed her glimpse at their future reality.

Except for last night's lovemaking, she wasn't sure she liked what she'd seen so far. Her husband's space beside her lay empty—an ominous start to their first anniversary and this first day of Kwanzaa named "Unity." Some unity. She sat alone with her future and her conflicted feelings about what awaited her.

"Make the most of it," she told herself, tossing aside a mound of tousled linen and stepping out of bed. "What choice do you have?"

She wished her internal timer was set to something besides eight A.M., that she could have slept until noon to shorten the time between now and when she'd see Naymond again. Angry as she remained, he was Fallon's only certainty in their new famous world. Her marriage and a consistent workout schedule were the two things she clung to when life grew overwhelming. Now seemed like the perfect time for her iPod favorites and a cardio circuit.

She stretched, washed up and dressed to work out—all without leaving the bedroom suite. Not until she walked into the living room area did she wonder if managers, bodyguards or other hangers-on lurked in the shadows. She double-checked the room for strangers and found only a state-of-the-art elliptical machine and continental breakfast—complete with Cristal mimosas, smoked salmon and cheese grits—awaiting her in the dining room.

Fallon put her hands on her hips and marveled at the machine before her. Envied it, actually. She'd only seen these things at a really good gym. There were buttons to create your own level of intensity, highs and lows to challenge your heartbeat. There were sensors to take your pulse every few seconds, tell you how many miles you'd traveled, and how many calories you were burning. It was ideal.

Turning on her iPod, Fallon started the machine and picked a preprogrammed workout that promised to churn up 750 calories over the next forty-five minutes and climbed aboard to the sound of Wyclef Jean and his ode to the traps of making money.

Her mind wandered with the melody to a place of physical perfection she always seemed five pounds within reaching, a state of emotional satisfaction—which, until last night, she equated with financial freedom.

The pulsing LED display before her wound down the seconds as she cycled her legs in time to its diminishing numbers and her escalating thoughts. Around and around she pulsed until the clock told her she'd finished, reached her goal, done enough for today. She shut off the iPod.

The machine cooled her down automatically, taking her through a systematic circuit to lower her heart rate and return her to the empty day she started with.

The room phone rang, setting a cacophony of several cordless handsets in motion throughout the suite. She didn't know where a single one of them was. When she finally located a phone, behind the buffet table, the ringing had stopped. She missed the call, but the hunt did lead her to a Post-it note from her husband, attached to the table beside the phone.

> Didn't want to wake you. I know we're not supposed to sleep on anger, so I hope you woke up happier than you were when you fell asleep last night. Maybe you're not up for another massage, but I still sprang for the spa. They'll be there to treat you at 10. I'll pick you up for dinner at 7. Miss you till then.–N

"Ah, you think you know me so well." She unstuck his attempted apology and placed it on the counter, picked up the phone and asked for the spa. "I'd like to cancel my session for today. Thanks."

Feeling quite pleased with herself, she hung up the phone and surveyed the excess of her surroundings. If the glimpse held true, chances were good that there would be plenty of other pampering opportunities in the days ahead.

For now, Fallon wanted more information about her and Naymond's life between Christmas Day 2008—when they'd left yesterday—and their two-hour leap to Christmas Day 2009 last night—yesterday. It appeared he won *Chart Toppers*, so was it really all they dreamed? Did they move? Did she still work? Was Eva a fluke or the first of many like her?

Naymond obviously had one kind of day planned. She had another, filled with questions. Fallon decided to spend her hours of "me" time finding answers.

"You want to know what's surprised me most since my win, huh?" Naymond paused to digest the interviewer's question. He had no idea how he should answer.

His eyes darted around the radio studio, looking for

clues: a copy of his CD, a photo of the deejay and one of his *Chart Toppers* colleagues, a magazine cover—something with a headline that hinted at what he'd been doing all this time. Nothing surfaced.

He'd been so excited about the day ahead, that until Tana started prepping him for the interview, it never occurred to him that he didn't have answers to potential questions about how he'd spent the last year or what he planned to do in the days and weeks ahead.

Desire Whitten, the interviewing deejay beside him, leaned closer, brows raised, grin pending, as if she expected a profound response.

"I'm probably most surprised at how fast the year passed—almost like I was competing one week and sitting here the next." Though he blew off Fallon's Trixie DuCayne encounter as whimsy last night, everything around him now proved her tale true. The new reality made his answer authentic. "I feel like I haven't even started my journey. I'm still curious to see where the future leads and anxious to get there."

"So who's been most instrumental in getting you on this path? Fans . . . friends . . . family?"

"Everybody plays an important part." Naymond nodded for emphasis as if the radio listeners could see him. "People who know you only by the two dimensions they see on the television screen every week, and people who know all of the things you wish they didn't—because they're the real people in your life. They keep you straight, keep you true to yourself. Like my wife."

"So you're telling us there's nothing to those rumors that started when you were on the show about you and Eva Barrow."

I'd hoped we'd left that behind. "Absolutely not. Without question, tabloid 'reports,' unfounded rumors, and the people who run with those stories have definitely been the hardest part of my newfound celebrity."

Tana gave Naymond the thumbs-up sign from the corner. He smiled as Desire fumbled through her notes for a new line of questioning.

"So does that motivate you or bring you down?"

"That fake stuff doesn't get to me." He shrugged. "You take that negativity, mix it up with some perseverance and some faith and you spin out some song lyrics like the ones in my new hit, 'Keeping it Real.'

"When your life reads better than a television script,
It's time to step back and get away from it.
Free your mind and try to find
The magic you need when reality won't let you be."

"So sometimes you even gotta escape your dream?"

"Exactly."

"That's tough." She checked her notes and the clock on the wall. "So as of next week, you're no longer the reigning king of *Chart Toppers*. Where's your dream taking you then?"

Naymond's eyes gravitated toward Tana, looking for assurance that he was giving the right response. They reviewed this in the car, but everything was new. All he could think of was—

"Looking forward to getting back into the studio, laying the groundwork for the next album. I'm ready to take my sound to the next audiosphere, if you will, with some new partnerships. I've got my eye on a couple of collaborations I'd like to make happen."

"Anything you can tell us? Like a Chris Brown or Mary J. Blige project maybe?"

"Good ideas, but everything's under wraps for now." He laughed at her attempt to get him to spill news he didn't even know about. "Stay tuned."

"Well, thank you for joining us, Naymond." She turned toward the microphone, but kept her gaze on her interviewee. "I'm Desire Whitten. You've been listening to National Black Radio."

She pressed one of a multitude of square buttons on the soundboard in front of her. A car dealership commercial filled the airwaves Naymond had just vacated.

He removed his headphones, stood and stretched. The quick thirty-minute stint went better than he thought it would when he first plopped into the chair.

Maybe the '09 Naymond was used to early mornings, but the old version still preferred getting up after traffic died down, once the second pot of coffee was brewing, and all the syndicated morning radio teams had cleared the airwaves for the middy deejays.

"Want to hang around for awhile? Help me host the rest of my program?" Desire spoke with a syrupy tone that Naymond recognized as more than an invitation to share her studio.

Judging by her demeanor, he suspected her Eva Barrow question was a ploy to feel out whether he was the philandering or faithful type. He took pleasure in disappointing his host.

"Sorry, but I've got a full day and Fallon waiting for me at the end of it." He smiled—a little too broadly—to help emphasize his point.

"Speaking of which, I was distinctly instructed to not ask anything about your wife on-air." Desire tilted her head toward Tana and raised her eyebrows. "But now, off-air and off-the-record, how are you two doing these days?"

"Great. Really. She's still the best thing that ever happened to me."

"Well, good luck to you both." Desire extended her

hand for a shake. "Belated Merry Christmas. Stay safe in the New Year."

"You, too. And Happy Kwanzaa."

She takes rejection well, he thought. *Even though she gave my ego a good stroke.*

Naymond knew one thing about himself that he was determined to keep unchanged: He was not a liar and he would never betray his wife.

"It's our anniversary," hummed Fallon.

Showered and stuffed from the continental buffet, with all the fruit, pastries and exotic tea she could swallow, she sat at the desk, watching Denzel Washington in *The Preacher's Wife* on the flat-panel TV across the room and logging into Naymond's laptop.

When the singsong tones played that let her know the computer was ready for her pursuit, she typed EVA BARROW NAYMOND TERRY into the search engine and hit the ENTER key. More than five thousand results appeared on her screen, scattered among dozens of pages. She tried to avoid jumping to conclusions, not wanting to assume that every story she scrolled through was one she didn't want to read.

While staying positive was tough in the face of all the Eva Barrow mentions that flooded the pages Fallon scrolled through, harder yet was adjusting to the December 2009 dates. Days, weeks and months she hadn't experienced yet were already recorded for posterity. Anything the search revealed about Eva was already a done deal.

Since this trip is a glimpse of our future, does this mean we'll be able to undo any damage I discover?

In and out of the limelight, the focus on Eva and Naymond didn't keep to any pattern she could decipher.

The articles were nearly all identical: Allegations of

trysts based on fuzzy photos of a woman Fallon couldn't identify supposedly on vacation with Naymond.

Frustrated, she typed in EVA BARROW only and still pulled up yet more articles tying her husband to Eva. The same grainy beach photos appeared on the Eva-only pages.

Seemed like everyone jumped on the story when they left—Christmas Day '08—abandoned it temporarily for hotter topics, and returned to the familiar fodder of the musician and his prodigy in September '09.

"Try looking for *us*."

Again, hits seemed heaviest the week of Naymond's 2008 win (this time "last year"), leveling off in the month or two that followed, only to spike again in the weeks before time jetted them here to 2009. She found a few photos of herself arm-in-arm with her husband at several miscellaneous parties and outings.

"Well, I haven't been hiding in the closet the entire time, that's good to know."

Fallon tried to piece together their relationship based on the faulty news reports and discovered that they reveled in the fact that Naymond played all his own instruments. They compared his voice to everyone from Sam Cooke to Anthony Hamilton, and his production skills to a young Diddy and Jay-Z, but in R&B instead of hip-hop.

She thought of her current resentment over Naymond's potential fame and wondered if she gave him a hard time when his dream came true. Once more, she turned to the search engine, now looking only for mentions about herself.

A slew of articles picked up her story in early September 2009, just over three months ago, when she apparently joined her husband at a movie festival in Hawaii. As he conducted a promotional tour across several of the islands, she went sightseeing with a group of celebrity wives also along for the trip and stumbled across her husband having lunch with an unnamed model at a high-profile eatery.

According to online tabloid speculation, the embarrassment of catching her husband (while a group of strangers watched), the ongoing rumors about Eva Barrow, and the stress of being the media's latest "It" couple proved too much for the newlyweds.

Fallon left Naymond and filed for divorce.

"Ohmygosh, ohmygosh, ohmygosh!" She leaned over the keyboard and stared at the words on the screen. They swam before her eyes, ebbing in and out of focus. "By December 2009, we're not together."

According to the article now full-screen before her—which described their personal tragedy in graphic detail—her husband was involved in the latest in a long line of Eva-like entrapments. Naymond denied doing anything to jeopardize his marriage, saying that he was merely taking time to counsel an aspiring songwriter.

Apparently, Fallon thought otherwise.

News reports said she left Hawaii that night and moved out a week later, refusing to talk to the media since. Naymond carried on with his contractual obligations as the *Chart Toppers* winner—touring, interviewing, making guest appearances on late-night television, and writing music. Not a single other compromising photo appeared after they separated, but articles dated yesterday—December 25, 2009—had begun to appear about their arrival at the Inn together.

She pushed away from the desk and stood, unsure what was spinning faster, her mind or the room around her.

A breakup would explain the scant number of articles about her and Naymond in recent months and Jeff's wary scrutiny of her in the limousine. Apparently, the superhero bodyguard didn't expect her to join Naymond on this trip.

The time jump was now far less of an issue than what took place in the fast-forwarded year. Yes, within a few hours, she'd skipped a year of her life, but three of those months were spent without her husband. That's a long time to leave a man like Naymond alone.

Has another woman taken my place? Would I even want to know?

Sure things were shaky between her and Naymond, but—hopefully—nothing some concentrated quality time couldn't cure. Even with the interruption of Eva, she never doubted they'd work things out.

But that was yesterday, Christmas Day 2008.

Today, one year and one day later, they were separated by anger, misunderstanding, and the threat of divorce, and joined only by a fluke of fate: a two-dollar snow globe. Fallon thought of the mini version of herself, standing in front of the Inn *alone*.

She shut the laptop with a new perspective on Naymond's schedule and heightened appreciation for today's anniversary. Discovering answers about their new life she never would have dreamed stirred a new set of questions only one person could address.

Chapter Six

If anybody had a handle on her life, it would be her best friend and confidante, the older sister she told everything to, and the woman who wasn't afraid to tell Fallon exactly what she needed to hear. She needed Mimi to verify what the Internet stories proclaimed.

Fallon forced calm into her voice. Few things fooled her sister, especially fake "everything's great" calls. "Hey, girl. What's up?"

"I was wondering when you'd call." Mimi laughed. "Why do I have to find out from the *Hollywood Hot Sheet* that you sneaked off with your almost ex?"

"I don't think creeping counts if you do it with your husband. This trip isn't what you think."

"Oh, I get it. You just happened to bump into him at the airport and decided to share a limo when you found out you were both staying at the Inn. Right?"

Fallon debated telling her sister about Trixie DuCayne's globe and glimpse. "I couldn't convince you if I tried."

Mimi did indeed seem to be living in 2009 like everyone else around them, which was enough to convince Fallon that the last eighteen hours weren't a joke. If someone was trying to prank Naymond, her sister would've ruined the secret immediately after she heard it.

That question aside, Fallon got to the point of her call. "Remind me why I filed for divorce."

"Personally, to me, you let Fallon's unlucky past block the Terrys' promising future."

Fallon expected to hear a reason involving Eva, not her own insecurities. Mimi made her defensive. "With the string of strikeouts I had, can you blame me?"

"Nothing is ever entirely the other person's fault, no matter how *wonderful* you were." She exaggerated the wonderful as if to remind Fallon that sometimes she wasn't.

"Remember the physicist who made enough money to support ten kids?"

"Book smart. Love dumb." Mimi offered her assessment of the former beau.

"Then I had the community activist with the huge heart and incredible aspirations," Fallon continued her roll call.

"Great for the kids, bad for you." Mimi surmised his shortcomings as well.

Fallon rattled off another suitor. "The sports agent."

"Fine as the day is long. But, all defense, no offense. Had you checking in 24-7."

"So what was I supposed to think when I ran across a singer who sells real estate?" Fallon argued.

"That maybe he deserved as much of a chance as all those other knuckleheads." Mimi paused just long enough to launch into her lesson. "See, this time you hit the ball so far out of the park, you didn't even see the grand slam. Everybody's shouting, 'Run, Fallon!' and you're standing at the plate, afraid to claim your victory."

"Then why didn't you stop me from leaving him?"

Mimi hmphed. "Please, girl. You know how you are. Get an idea stuck in your head and—no matter what—there's no talking to you."

"It was important, I would've listened."

"The issue was Naymond and infidelity. You refused."

"I gave up without proof, or second chances, anything?"

"He said he didn't know how to prove his innocence when all you wanted to see was guilt."

Fallon gave a heavy sigh.

"When did all this start?"

"Hard to say because you didn't say anything to anybody and no one suspected a thing. But I'd say I started to notice something strange about a year ago. Last Christmas."

That would be right about now. Fallon calculated the distance between her real time today and their future disaster.

"Naymond's good people," Mimi continued, "but you let the marriage go and I didn't want to interfere." Mimi paused, long enough to let Fallon's heart sink and resurface. "So, I shouldn't tell you that, yes, he called, every now and again, just to see if you were okay or if you needed anything since he could finally afford to give it to you."

Fallon hesitated to ask the question that would probably do her the most good, but finally blurted it out. "What does he think about me now?"

"Well, at first it was usually couched in, 'I'll get over it,' but he always wonders how you couldn't trust him, wonders what he did to make you not believe that he'd never, ever betray you. Then after a while he was simply insulted that you thought he would even want somebody like Eva Barrow."

"T-true . . ." she stammered. Knowing that she was about to lose him, Fallon realized how much she wanted Naymond back. "What do I do now, Mimi?"

"If you're still carrying those doubts, I'd say leave it alone. You'll only make yourself miserable trying to be with him but not believing in him. Have you talked about it?"

"Not a word. I guess being here is fate's way of saying the breakup doesn't have to happen."

Mimi continued her flippant commentary, but softened her tone. "Girl, look. Maybe it would help to remember that before this all-of-a-sudden reunion, you and Naymond *were* on the verge of divorce for a lot of different reasons. Don't lose sight of that reality as you fall in love all over again today."

"Tomorrow, more likely," Fallon muttered, hesitating as she anticipated Mimi's response. "Naymond's not here . . . right now. Tana has him booked all day."

"How convenient on your anniversary. Don't you sit there moping and let him ruin your getaway. You're supposed to be getting pampered this weekend. Have you even been to the spa yet or are you sitting around waiting on him?"

"I cancelled the session. It was supposed to be a His and Hers appointment, so I didn't want to go alone. What do you think I should do, Mimi?"

"Figure out what you're trying to go back to by being with Naymond, that's what."

What if it's not up to me? Fallon worried. *What if when Naymond and I get off the plane in LA, we go right back to where I started at five o'clock yesterday afternoon? Then next week he wins. Eight months from now, I'm fed up and leave.*

"What if it's not my choice anymore?" she whispered.

"Sounds like you need to talk to your husband—while he's still yours."

"What kind of game are you running on my sister, Naymond Terry? Seducing her in front of the cameras and then dumping her on today of all days?"

The fury in Mimi's voice roared through the cell phone receiver and singed Naymond's better judgment.

He walked from the broadcast building into the cold outdoors, holding up his index finger at Tana, whose scowl indicated he didn't have time to be talking on the phone.

Mouthing "One minute," he used his free hand to shoo Tana into the limo that would take them to his *Rolling Stone* cover shoot. Handling Fallon's sister required full concentration, even for lighter topics. He could already tell that this would take all the cool and creativity he could muster.

Admittedly, he'd abandoned his wife today; he was still so caught up in his new reality that he didn't want to part with the fringe benefits, even if it meant Fallon had to take a temporary backseat to his limelight. Naymond's sister-in-law—one of those people willing to call out anybody at any time for any perceived wrongdoing—obviously recognized his selfishness for what it was.

"Look, Mimi, she was so tired, I thought she'd appreciate the rest." Why'd he lie? It really wasn't his sister-in-law's business how they spent their anniversary. "Anyway, is it that hard for you to go a day without bugging my wife?"

"Oh, so she *is* your wife again. No wonder Fallon called *me*, thank you, questioning her reasons for the divorce."

Divorce?

"Who said anything . . ." First Tana, then the deejay, now Mimi. He shuddered—from the cold *and* his shock. "What's with everybody and us breaking up?"

"Can you say Eva Barrow?"

The seriousness in Mimi's tone made Naymond pause. "You're about as bad as Fallon with these rumors. Everything that Eva woman tells the papers is a lie and you know it."

"You are quite the actor, aren't you? Now let me guess,

you're pretending nothing happened between you two, even after the split. Right?"

"Nobody's pretending, Mimi. I'm here to try and make up for the rough couple of months me and Fallon have had. This has nothing to do with anybody else. I swear."

"Well, you've got some way of showing it," Mimi scoffed. "Even your wife's confused about your intentions—seeing as how you're not even around on your anniversary."

He ignored his sister-in-law's sarcasm and stomped his feet to warm his toes. "I understand she's upset about me working today."

"Is this how it's always going to be with you— Naymond first? Fallon needs you, too."

"I know how to take care of my wife." Naymond tried not to shout. "This nonsense you're talking—I don't have time for it right now."

He snapped the phone shut and noticed his hands were shaking. He was sure it wasn't just because they were freezing.

This place, this time—2009, missing a year, the divorce—it was all real. That crazy singer at the airport must've given Fallon more than a lousy snow globe to make all this happen in order to tear him and his wife apart. Even *Chart Toppers* couldn't pull this kind of joke.

He had to talk to Fallon before things got even more complicated than they'd become in the last few hours. He flipped open his cell phone to dial her cell, pacing until she picked up.

"Happy Anniversary, sweetheart." His breath warmed the air, condensing in the cold around him, creating a puff of steam. He hoped his voice thawed his wife's mood the same way.

"Today is nothing like I planned."

He heard the sadness beneath her words, pictured her eyes looking downward, the corners of her lush mouth set in a pout, her free hand twirling her hair. He switched his phone to the warmer hand and ditched the other into a pocket for warmth.

With no good way to spring this news, he pounced. "Did you know we're not together by December '09?"

"It's all over the Internet. I couldn't believe it until Mimi told me it was true."

"If we don't fight for us, they win, Fallon." Naymond exhaled quietly, determined to be patient. Fallon seemed so negative, almost determined to believe what the future supposedly held instead of what they knew to be true. "Let's make our life what we want it to be. Not what these people here claim it is."

"You mean what *you* want it to be." Fallon huffed. "A record deal and a divorce would work out great for you."

"Now you know better." He maintained his cool—easy, considering the frigid temperature—determined not to let this news or her mood ruin what had been an incredible day so far. "What good is fame if I can't share it with you? Look, you said this weekend is a glimpse, true? That means it's just a *sample* of what we're going to face when I make it big." Her silence that followed challenged Naymond's ego to take a stand. "Tonight, we have a chance to have a great time, celebrate our anniversary—and a little unity, right?—and rub elbows with people we only see on TV. The limo will be waiting downstairs at seven."

"Yeah, well, I'm tired. I'll take a nap and let you know if I'm coming when I wake up."

"I'm not sure what Tana has in mind with these

award-show guys, but it sounds like an important meeting and I really need you there." Naymond backed off his bravado since it didn't seem to be working. "You don't have to dress up, but you can run down to one of those boutiques at the Inn and pick up something special if you want."

"Maybe."

He thought he heard her change her mind. "I love you, Fallon."

"Mmm. Me, too."

If she was trying to convince him, the attempt failed.

"I don't know what Mimi said, but it's just me and you, Fallon. Always." The last thing he needed was to have his wife thinking he was making excuses to be away from her—especially for some other woman.

Naymond kicked at the snow like a small child muzzling a tantrum and began walking toward the much delayed limo. Listening to Fallon's silence, he wondered what she was thinking, if she could have faith. No way did he consider the leap into the future his fault, but he felt obligated to get them back to better times.

He just had no idea how.

"Can you forgive me?" Fallon asked.

"What did you do?"

Quick speech at a slightly raised pitch hinted at her husband's thinly veiled panic. Not wanting him to think she had more bad news, Fallon hurried on with her apology.

She spoke slowly, nearly wincing with each syllable. "According to my sister, the divorce is *my* fault."

"Funny. She told me just the opposite."

Fallon's instinct was to fume, even if she'd never known Mimi to toy with people's emotions. Then she calmed, understanding what her sister had done.

"Sounds like we're both to blame." The admission brought a small measure of relief. "I can't figure out whether I should be thankful for this so-called glimpse, or pitch that doggone snow globe out the window."

"I'm with you there." He spoke in his head-shaking voice. "How long have we been separated?"

"About the same amount of time you've really been in LA. Three months. And the divorce is supposed to be final next week." With unity the theme of the day, Fallon figured she'd give him her view of what happened. "It seems Eva—and my insecurities—got in the way. She was a convenient excuse to exercise my doubts."

"And that's why you're asking me for forgiveness?"

"Sorry." She was. Yet she was also angry about the pictures she'd seen and the new things she discovered about their relationship. Fallon found herself caught between her heart's desire to keep Naymond and her gut's instinct to protect herself.

"I know I don't want to lose you, Naymond," she explained. "I'm apologizing for doubting my husband and asking him to help restore my trust, before it's too late."

"Can I start by saying 'sorry' for planting that doubt in you? When we came here, I said I'd make you believe again—and I will, Fallon."

"Until we arrived, I didn't know how important my faith in you would become."

"This is where a crystal ball would come in real handy," Naymond joked.

"I think we got that and more, don't you?" Fallon laughed along with her husband. "Snow globe, Crystal Mountain, a glimpse of our messed up future."

"No, it's not," Naymond interrupted her litany. "Now that we know, we fight for us. Deal?"

"Can we kiss on that?"

"Seven o'clock?" he asked.

"I'll be there." She agreed to his second request for dinner, anxious to seal the agreement and start securing their union, but, worried whether a day and a half would be enough to fix their issues.

Chapter Seven

Naymond hung up and checked his watch.

"Yes, we're behind schedule," Tana quipped. "Blame yourself. What's up with you today?"

First of all, he didn't know what the heck he was doing in front of all these lights, cameras, and strangers. Second, even if he did, the "trained" lion manager they brought in for the photo shoot kept him too nervous to feel much like *Chart Toppers*' NeoSoul King. Finding any kind of groove seemed impossible in this unfamiliar place under unexpected circumstances and amid growing uncertainty about his marriage. The strain obviously showed.

"Just not myself today. Maybe tired from traveling." Naymond shrugged.

"No, you're not the Naymond I know. That Naymond loves attention. A day like today? That's heaven to him. You? You look miserable."

"The time away from Fallon is taking its toll, Tana." True in his real present and this imaginary future, he spent too many days apart from his wife. "And this is our anniversary, you know. Least I could do is be around for once."

"What? You all really are back together then?"

Okay, how to answer that one? He hadn't pictured himself without Fallon since the day they met. It hurt to discover that his success brought so much pain. Absorbed with his analysis, he didn't answer Tana.

She flicked her wrist at him. "Boy, you've got it bad. I haven't seen you this distracted since the split." She rolled her eyes and scrunched her brows. "You cost me a lot of money canceling gigs with your moping around. We're not about to go through that again, are we?"

Naymond didn't know. When he left this place, would it be without his Fallon? Or were they headed home to greet his escalating career and their deteriorating marriage? Was fame at fault for their problems? Should he be trying to get her back or make her stay?

Tana interrupted his personal interrogation. "That's on you, but if you ask me—"

"No," he interrupted. "I didn't mean to." He didn't realize he was talking aloud and hated that Tana, of all people, overheard. She acted like she couldn't stand Fallon anyway and was probably glad to see them divorce.

Though Tana might not see the beauty of their arrangement, Naymond had always appreciated Fallon's hands-on approach to his career. The way she offered insight on riffs, suggestions on lyrics, hung out at the studio while he worked on his demo. Today, Tana gave him the distinct impression that nonmusic people—"civilians" as she called them—belonged only in record stores and the balcony seats at award shows.

"Oh, I get it!" Naymond groaned.

"Okay, now you're talking to yourself out loud a little too much." Tana raised her eyebrows and placed a palm on Naymond's forehead as if to check for a fever. He no longer cared that she eavesdropped on his confusion.

His epiphany came as a flash. "This is the *only* way I would spend an anniversary away from my wife—is if we weren't together anyway." Now the day filled with back-to-back appointments made sense. He wouldn't want time to think about the woman he missed. With a wide smile, he looked at Tana. "Maybe I've been taking her for granted and this twist in time is how we find our way back to where we need to be."

"You're about to back out of dinner, aren't you?"

He started to answer with an automatic, "Yep," but stopped short to consider the possibility that he might *not* reconcile with Fallon, that their new state of being was the path they were meant to tread.

Tana shook her head and shouted at the photographer, "It's a wrap!"

Photo shoot ended by her authority, he thanked her with a sigh.

If I turn down dinner, they'll find some other singer to step into my segment during the awards show, I'll earn a reputation for backing out of commitments, and the domino effect will kill my brand-new career.

He focused his eyes on Tana's jawline, rigid with forced patience, as if she wanted to understand Naymond's dilemma, but didn't care for the inconvenience of accommodating his choice. *If we're meant to reconcile, that means Fallon will understand how crucial this is to me.*

"Hold up, Tana. Keep the dinner reservations." Tana rolled her eyes, yet he could see relief in the relaxed eyebrows and tentative grin.

Besides, Fallon will be beside me. He tried to rationalize his career-over-cuddling choice. He hoped.

She tried forcing herself to rest, but sleep only teased Fallon. She lay on the overstuffed sofa wondering how they wound up here: Not just a year ahead, but estranged and unhappy in the midst of all they ever wanted.

"Lord, please don't tell me I'm about to become one of those wives who's never satisfied with anything her man does." But, that's exactly how she felt; like she pushed him to the finish line with one hand while sticking out the opposite foot to trip him as he crossed the yellow tape. "Maybe I turned into one of those women who taunts and tests until her man breaks."

Again, she closed her eyes against the ideas assaulting her. Behind her lids, an image emerged like a Polaroid snapshot, revealing a bitter, disgruntled, jealous woman—unfulfilled, unwanted and alone.

Like the tiny woman in the snow globe?

Fallon flashed back to the *Star Gazer* story—her husband in the arms and on the lips of Eva Barrow. Thanks to this jump through time, knowing she left him over that tramp validated her fears, no matter how irrational Naymond tried to make them seem.

"I've gotta get out of here." Regretting her initial, impulsive cancellation, she picked up the phone and called the concierge. "I'd like to reschedule my appointment at the spa."

Taking advantage of her celebrity-by-association status to indulge herself felt empowering, especially since she knew the Inn's staff would do whatever was necessary to keep her husband happy—even if it meant fitting her into an overbooked spa schedule with no notice. Attitude made Kimora Lee Simmons fabulously famous; maybe it would work for her, too.

"How soon would you like us to fit you in, Mrs. Terry?" The concierge asked.

"Immediately." Not wanting to come off as totally high maintenance, she softened the request. "If possible."

"We'll be happy to see what we can do for you, Mrs. Terry. Would you prefer an in-room service or will you be joining us in the salon?"

"I'll venture out, thanks. There's some shopping I need to take care of before dinner."

"Anything we can assist you with?"

"The boutique. Can someone tell me what handbags they have available? I'd like a black clutch. And I'm looking for a tunic-style sweater, velvet pants and matching boots in a size nine. Medium."

"Certainly, ma'am. I'll call to arrange a showing." He paused as if to jot a note. "Do you want the items brought to the salon or would you prefer to see them in your suite once you've finished your service?"

"Let me see them while I'm at the spa in case the choices affect my hairstyle or makeup." She'd seen Kimora do this a hundred times and tried to recall the type of answers and commands she gave on her television show.

"You'll hear from me shortly, then, Mrs. Terry."

"Thank you. I really appreciate it." She did—mostly because she pulled off her I'm-a-star charade—and made a mental note to send him a gift certificate for his efforts before the end of the weekend.

Post-workout clean, but self-conscious about her attempt to act famous, Fallon jogged into the bathroom to check herself once more.

The phone rang; concierge, she hoped. She grabbed the bathroom extension and swallowed her jitters, pretending to be calm.

"Yes."

"Concierge, Mrs. Terry. Jerrilyn at the spa is now awaiting your arrival."

Waiting for me! Fallon stifled a giggle. "Certainly. I'll be down shortly. Thank you." She hung up the phone and clenched the edge of the bathroom's marble counter.

"Wow. Is there a back elevator? Should I put on sunglasses? A wig? How do I hide as I stroll through the lobby? Or do I just pretend I'm nobody and go on about my business?" She stood and stared at her bare face, feeling as socially naked as her undressed skin.

Far from the familiarity of exercising clients back to good health, figuring out ways to stretch her overtime pay to cover their growing bills, and entertaining regularly timed calls from her husband and sister, she didn't know how to perform as a celebrity wife.

"I'll take the bold approach," she decided. Donning a makeshift diva persona, she sifted her fingers through her hair, and lifted her chin. She left the bathroom in search of her backless gym shoes and no-name purse, put them both on and strolled with confidence toward the in-suite elevator.

She pressed the button to summon her "ride" to the new outside world awaiting her. Once inside the elevator, she heaved a sigh of relief. The unlit floor choices on the panel included SPA.

All this worry for nothing. No need to see a soul between here and my afternoon of pampering.

She traveled downward in a vacuum void of time, people, and clarity until the rear doors opened to reveal a white room littered with robed women in turban–toweled hair and freshly pedicured toes draped in terry and straw flip-flops. Smiling attendants adorned each client.

As she stepped into the room, one such friendly face approached; the woman possessed a flawless olive complexion, commercial perfect brunette waves and a restrained runway strut. "Shall we start with your usual, Mrs. Terry?" she asked with a tinge of a Georgia drawl.

And what, pray tell, is that? Fallon assumed this to be Jerrilyn, but wondered what she was about to undergo. She'd always liked her skin and treated it simply. No dermabrasion or peels or harsh cleansers and she wore little makeup. Had living in the limelight changed the require-ments of her longtime routine?

"Of course . . . Jerrilyn."

"So formal today. Bad mood?"

"Sorry. Tired, that's all."

"No problem. I expect to be back to Jerri before you leave here. Guaranteed."

The promise elicited a smile from Fallon. It was nice to be doted on.

Jerri led her to a private area at the back of the spa. "Your robe has been warmed, your masseuse is waiting. Change and come on out when you're ready." The atten-dant waved a hand to usher Fallon into a circular space filled with the scent of vanilla—her favorite—and closed the door behind her as she left.

Fallon surveyed the room: a small vanity, stuffed recliner, sunshine through a high window, mirrors everywhere. She began to undress, acutely aware of exposing body parts that only Naymond and her physicians ever saw.

"Don't think I caught this episode," she murmured. "Is this no undies beneath the gown like the gynecologist's office? Or panties no bra like the internist? Or swimming pool cover-up over all underwear?"

Erring on the side of prudence, she discarded the bra and opted to leave on her panties, cinched the robe around her waist, and crossed the room to peer out the door.

"I understand you're in a hurry. You're not acting like it!" Jerri chided her with a broad smile and a reproving gaze. "Here she is."

She handed Fallon off to a tall, slender man. Blond, blue-eyed, square-jawed. Gorgeous. Was looking like a beauty or bodybuilding contestant mandatory for work-ing here? A smile escaped her lips, dragging her reluc-tance along behind it.

"How much time *do* you have for us, today, Mrs. Terry?"

Fallon searched the room for a clock, found none, and tried to recall when she'd hung up from Naymond. "What is it, two?"

"Thirty," Jerri answered.

"Four hours then." Fallon gave herself an extra half an hour before Naymond said he'd pick her up—just in case the appointment ran late.

"Wow. Plenty, for a change. Let's go with a hot stone treatment, hour and a half. Then send her over for hair and nails. Thanks." Jerri disappeared and the blond Adonis took over.

"Sounds good." Fallon worked her voice into an expectant instead of surprised tone.

She tried to remember the last time she had her hair done. Probably for Naymond's *Chart Toppers* audition and maybe once more after that for his first trip to LA and the taping of the show's premiere.

Since then, she did the old school perm-in-a-box thing, stashing a good pair of beauty supply scissors in the medicine cabinet to keep stray hairs and split ends in check, and two cabinets full of heat protecting, detangling, shine layering products to make her *look* like she went to the salon every week.

This was so much easier.

She reveled in the pleasure she'd soon get from leaning her head back over the shampoo bowl and feeling someone else's fingers on her scalp.

I may get that nap after all, she thought, disrobing and laying herself atop the massage table.

Hands landed on her shoulders, moving outward toward her arms, back, then down the muscles alongside her spine. She knew the drill, performing similar techniques for her physical therapy patients, though their treatments generally consisted of more aggressive deep tissue and sports massage. It was all work to her and, she assumed, a perfunctory drill for her patients.

Seldom on the receiving end of laying hands, little did she know that the sprinkling of water, dabbling of oil and therapeutic movement of palms on her skin by a stranger could be a near orgasmic experience. Though the treatment wasn't quite on par with Naymond's performance the night before, today's massage rivaled his skill in terms of pure spirit uplift.

She scarcely noticed the minutes passing by. When the first stone was placed at the base of her spine, just above her panties, Fallon gave in to sleep.

Jerri awakened her after what felt like an eternity, feeling far from the room she'd entered, and forgetting for a moment exactly where she was.

"Hey, that's a first," Jerri laughed. "Where'd you drift off to?"

"Home, I think." Fallon replied with a yawn, noting how disoriented, yet refreshed, she felt.

"Since you brought it up, do you mind if I ask? How are things going? I hear—"

"Great. Just like nothing ever went wrong." Unsure how well she knew her attendant, Fallon refused further details.

"Behold the power of 'sorry,'" Jerri remarked, eyebrows raised.

True, Fallon had apologized—and she meant it. Though as the hours passed, her heart reverted to feeling more wronged and less at fault. She strolled silently behind Jerri to the beat of sidebar banter from three women gathered in the pedicure chairs.

Her attendant deposited her in the care of a hairstylist who already had an array of perm, pomades, and hair color waiting for Fallon. The neighboring women gabbed throughout her shampoo and conditioning, blow dry and trim.

As the stylist spun Fallon toward the mirror with her back to the trio, they seemed to peak with chatter, providing her with lively and nonstop entertainment while she sat staring into space and half-listening. Their flat Midwestern voices floated and wove among each other until it sounded like one woman talking incessantly to herself.

"Girl, you see Dalinda in the paper yesterday?"

"Looks like she finally trapped herself in her own web."

"Who are you all talking about?"

"Dalinda—oh, excuse me—what's she call herself these days?"

"Eva Barrow, honey."

"You mean, *Evil* Barrow—"

"No, Eva *Borrow*. As in take your man."

"I can't believe she ain't changed in all these years. Same as in high school."

"Most likely to steal your husband."

"So who caught her?"

"The girl she hired to help fake those photos with that boy from the singing show last year."

"Oh, yeah, I remember him."

"He had a pretty wife, too, didn't he?"

"Hear they split up."

"Not over some nonsense like this girl, really? Nobody believes that mess those papers print. Half those pictures don't even look real."

"I think they were kind of young, though. Maybe they didn't know how to handle it any better."

"Evil, I tell you."

"Well, the story said the assistant turned on her when she caught Eva with *her* man."

"Um. That'll teach 'em all a lesson."

"Glad she took that mess to the other side of the country. One less problem we have to worry with around here."

"Amen to that."

Problem for Fallon was, Eva's trouble did strike home. *My home.* She seethed inside—at Miss Evil Borrow for setting the snare, at Naymond for falling into it, at herself for forcing her husband to handle it alone instead of standing by his side. *I hope those women don't recognize me.*

"Scoot up and lean back, hon." The hairstylist tapped Fallon out of her slumped position and into the present.

The rejuvenation left over from her massage teetered beneath the weight of the bad decision that lurked between her and Naymond. She stared into the mirror, wishing the stylist could cover her guilt and naïveté much like she'd washed sunshine highlights into her chestnut-brown hair.

The women's conversation wandered back into Fallon's range. "Ever wonder how many other couples she tricked into splitting up?"

"Like I spend time following that woman's comings and goings."

"You have. Ever since she took your prom date you been waiting for something bad to happen to her."

"And honey, you need to let that go."

"But, in the beginning, didn't you ever wish you could get back at her?" Fallon interjected.

A moment of silence was followed by a hesitant response. "No. I just wished I could've done something to keep him."

"Probably right about that one. 'Cause you sure haven't had a bit of luck with men since."

"Why, sugar? You got man troubles?" The anonymous voice echoed the tone her mom might use.

"No. Not anymore," Fallon answered. "I'm sorry, but I just couldn't help piping in."

"Don't worry about it. We're not talking about anything real anyway."

They laughed and moved on to a discussion of New Year's dinner menus and last-minute shopping deals. Fallon was glad they were finished with Eva. The coincidental conversation let her know that she could let Eva go as well. She focused on the night ahead.

The stylist gave Fallon a cut that hung just below her chin in the front, tapered upward toward the ear, and ended in dramatic short layers across the back of her head. Highlights around her face uncovered a level of sexiness she hadn't seen on herself in years, making her feel like she'd been depriving poor Naymond of all she had to offer.

During the styling, the Inn's boutique staff treated her to a mini show of suggested fashions, precisely what she'd requested and a few more choices that, according to the owners, were items she'd like based on previous purchases.

She went with red boots instead of another black pair, and a tan suede hook-up consisting of a knee-length button front coat and paisley printed skinny pants, and a boxy red Kate Spade bag to match her footwear. *Now this will win my husband back.*

The celebrity indulgences, exotic spa and personal shoppers, reminded Fallon once more of where she was. That the life she was currently experiencing might not be hers to live—yet.

Chapter Eight

Fallon wandered into the lobby to wait for the limousine. Oversized, ultradark sunglasses and fur coat to match, she avoided the spectators awaiting her husband's reentry to the Inn. Not sure how she felt about being so obviously cast aside, she smiled when waved at (which most of them did). A few of them spoke; she nodded hello. But, nearly all of them inched closer as the moments passed, suspecting her husband the star might show up any second.

That people thought they were getting back together was a plus. The Inn staff, management, entertainment reporters and other miscellaneous onlookers seemed to think the couple had worked things out. That meant she could ogle and fondle her husband in public if she wanted to and enjoy some semblance of an anniversary.

She wanted to tempt fate by walking through the door alone to see what would happen, but her heart pounded and her belly gurgled and churned at the idea, afraid deep inside that if she stepped out alone, she'd find no Naymond—just her former life on the other side of the door and he'd be lost to her forever.

Her purse vibrated, jiggling, then stopping to let her know a text message awaited. She reached inside her new handbag to check the cell phone's display. WHERE ARE YOU? JEFF'S BEEN LOOKING FOR YOU. WE'RE HERE. DRIVER'S COMING IN TO GET YOU.—N

Before she'd flipped the phone shut and dropped it

back into her clutch, a long black luxury sedan pulled up to the lobby doors, beckoning beneath the overhead valet lights. She hesitated for a moment, not sure whether she should bolt through the growing crowd surrounding her, or if she should wait for the driver to enter, wrap his arms around her and lead her through the throng to safety.

"Where's *my* bodyguard?" she asked, envying her husband's shepherding crew.

Tall enough to glance over most of the crowd, she finally saw the familiar face of Jeff, the Superhero Bodyguard. Before she could raise her hand to signal him, he'd cleared a path to her merely by his oversized presence, without speaking a word. He grabbed her arm and led her to the waiting car.

He opened the rear door of the chauffeured sedan and ushered her inside. She scooted across the black buttery leather and landed beside her husband. The razor-sharp crease in his jeans had softened over the course of his day. The collar of his shirt lay open, slightly crumpled.

Head laid back upon the seat, Naymond turned to face her and muscled a small smile for her entry. His eyes spoke louder, carrying the light of eager recognition she craved.

"You're so tired," she whispered, smoothing his eyebrows with her thumbs as Jeff slammed the door and disappeared. "Did you accomplish everything you set out to do today?"

"What I intended to do at seven this morning and what I think needs to be done now have nothing to do with each other. How about your day? You look incredible, by the way."

"Thanks, sweetie. I like this cut she gave me." She blushed and brushed her hair from her cheek with one hand. "It's all really weird. I still feel like I did yesterday when we left, but nothing's the same, is it?"

"We are." He sat upright.

"But only to us." Fallon shook her head in disagreement. "So now that we're here, what do we do?"

"I haven't figured that out."

"Would it make the most sense to hope that when we wake up day after tomorrow and leave for LA, that time will put us back where we belong? What if nothing changes when we leave—that we're really split up?"

"Then we put things right ourselves. If we're living in separate places, we move back in together."

"I have to admit, Naymond, even though I was upset yesterday, knowing we might lose each other gives me a different point of view. I don't know much about what the future holds, but I definitely want our marriage to work."

"What about *my* new reality? Can I send you back to physical therapy—working seventy hours a week, putting in your own perms, doing your own pedicures—when I can make your life so much more comfortable? Should I give it all up to keep you?"

Fallon knew that Naymond liked their new reality. "So, what if this does turn out to be some prank by your show's producers?"

"Whether it's Trixie's trick or a *Chart Toppers* treat, it's going to be hard getting back to 'normal.'" Naymond emphasized his point by forming quotation marks with his fingers. "Last night, everything was perfect. I mean, sure, our date books are a little off, but it doesn't feel like we've been apart."

"Right. Not like *that*." Fallon understood Naymond's haphazard explanation perfectly.

"It's been too long since I've seen, touched, made love to you—"

"But I don't hate you or not want you around."

"Exactly. Me, too. If Tana hadn't questioned me about 'taking you back'—"

"And if I hadn't gone on the Internet—"

They spoke their conclusion in unity. "—we never would have known we broke up."

"Naymond, if we're past the bad times and this is what's on the other side . . ." She waved her hands at the opulence surrounding them. "Do you remember what you were thinking when you stepped off the plane yesterday?"

"Exactly." Naymond turned to look into her eyes. "My goal for this whole weekend was to make you believe in me again. What about you?" He tapped her on the forehead. "What were you hiding up here?"

"Truth is, Naymond, I'm just as petrified of blowing this relationship as I am of seeing all our dreams come true. I love you, I don't want to lose you, and I don't want to be wrong again."

"Look, babe. If or when I win *Chart Toppers*, there's going to be so much pressure on us. Not just people like Eva, but more time apart with me on the road, the whole celebrity trip. How many famous couples even make it? Are we up for the fight we're about to face?"

Maybe that's what this glimpse was all about, she thought. *Preparation for the fight of our lives.*

"If we weren't before, I'd say we are now." Fallon was ready for her second chance.

The backseat intercom buzzed as the sedan slowed to a stop. "Mr. and Mrs. Terry, we've arrived."

"Let's start over with dinner," he said. "We'll just be Naymond and Fallon, together to stay, no questions allowed."

They missed their reservations. Perhaps the twenty-car valet line and bumper-to-bumper street parking would have forewarned them—if they'd been paying attention to anything besides each other during the entire ride.

Tana arrived before them and Naymond and Fallon found her at the head of a long line of patient patrons waiting their turn in the cold. She barked Naymond's name to the security personnel to no avail and soon resorted to complaining spoiled-celebrity-style about how "We never," and "How dare they?" and finally, "Where's Chuck?" in an attempt to prove Tana knew the owner well enough to call him by nickname.

"Okay, now this kind of nonsense I can do without," Fallon whispered to Naymond.

"Absolutely." He nodded in agreement and grabbed Tana's arm, pulling her away from the battle she was attempting to launch. "This isn't necessary."

"The hell it isn't. We have reservations. I don't care if we are late. You are Naymond Terry. We're here with the executives from VIP Records and it's your anniversary. They're going to seat us now. Not in forty-five minutes."

Fallon leaned toward Naymond and murmured into his neck. "We could hang out in the back of the car until our table's ready."

He turned to whisper into her hair. "You mean maybe find something to pass the time?"

"Come on." Fallon tugged his hand and giggled.

"Yeah, Tana. We'll wait. Hit me on my cell when our table's up."

They ran back to the car, still stuck in valet gridlock, and clambered into the backseat, crawling over each other like teenagers at the drive-in.

"Did you lock the doors?"

"Heck, I don't know." They laughed at their inexperience with the protocol and gadgets accompanying their exclusive ride. "Should I ask the driver?"

"Unless you want company." Fallon peered through the darkened windows into the crowd surrounding the car. "Anybody could just drop in on us."

"You work on dropping that sexy getup you got on and I'll take care of our privacy," Naymond growled.

No cool, calm, extended foreplay this time. Naymond lunged for Fallon as soon as she slid her pants down. He pinned her to the seat with a piercing kiss as he unfastened his jeans and slid inside her. "Happy Anniversary."

"And Happy Kwanzaa." She clenched her teeth and raised her hips. "Here's to *our* unity."

"Um-hm. This togetherness works for me."

It worked for her, too. Quick and incredible, their crazed pounding probably rocked the car, but who cared?

They laughed. Fallon hugged Naymond close, her legs wrapped around his, their gazes locked on each other. She remembered the first time they made love, how he left her breathless and made her believe in forever—just like now.

"We started out so good," she murmured.

"And now we're even better." Naymond writhed atop her playfully, then lifted himself to sit and redress. His cell phone began to belt out his *Chart Toppers* song entry. "Hungry, too."

"That Tana is always right on time, isn't she?"

"From what I saw today and comments people around us were making, I'd say she has a knack for getting things done."

"Then let's go make this awards show opening act happen so we can go back to the suite and get down to some real business."

Chapter Nine

Humming her own rendition of "Let it Snow," Fallon held her breath as she steadied a tall, thin candle atop its narrow crystal holder. On each side waited one matching candleholder. She placed a green tapered candle in one and a red taper in the other.

Since they were away from home and all things familiar, Fallon had used what she could get to make up a cultural love renewal ceremony combining elements of Kwanzaa, Christmas and first anniversary traditions.

The black candle used to represent Unity in Kwanzaa ceremonies made a perfect centerpiece. Her plan was to have Naymond hold the red candle to represent creativity while she held the green taper representing faith. Together they would light the Unity candle, just the way they did in their wedding.

After this "glimpse," the best gift they could give each other was a future together.

Fallon continued to hum as she admired the handiwork most Kwanzaa purists would scold. She might not have Naymond's best-selling voice, but she shared his love for mood-making music and his penchant for perfection. The song in her heart and her decorative display would meet both of their expectations.

Maybe next year I'll be decorating to the sound of his first Christmas CD. The warm thought gave her a sense of optimism about their tomorrow that she'd been afraid to confront all morning.

Unable to rest most of the night—despite Naymond's best attempts to rock her to sleep—she watched snowflakes stream past the undraped balcony window against the cloud-heavy sky. She thought of how she could watch the fat, fluffy flakes drift for hours without a clue as to whether they were sticking or melting, piling up or disappearing.

She related the scenario to her life. The way she and Naymond drifted in their day-to-day lives, floating past each other without ever stopping to see whether their actions might be amassing into problems.

Is there a disaster recovery agency for love gone awry? She smiled at the throngs of imaginary workers in hard hats and goggles, armed with roses and sex toys, dedicated to rescuing couples from themselves.

The love rescue notion wove so well with the events of Fallon and Naymond's trip that the idea creeped her out. She closed her eyes against the swirling storm outside and decided to arise early, alone, intent on making their remaining "magic" hours memorable.

They had agreed not to do a present exchange for Kwanzaa and Christmas this year since their money was tight. But, she qualified for a cell phone upgrade on her two-year plan and used the discount to buy Naymond a music/PDA/mapping phone. He'd need one to keep his life in order once he won *Chart Toppers* in two days. And she was looking forward to attending her first Hollywood awards show as a result of his success.

Last night's dinner, dominated by Tana's deft negotiating skills, landed Naymond just shy of where he hoped to fall: as the *intermission* opening act of the Urban Entertainment Awards Show. They opted for a bigger name to start the show, but Fallon figured half the television audience would miss the beginning anyway. Midshow was probably better.

With premier placement among his industry peers, a substantial payment (that in their 2008 world would allow them to live debt free for three years), and the promise of top-notch production and promotion, the group settled into discussions of the best paparazzi escapes, who'd missed the most flights, how to avoid snow on a ski trip, and New Year's Eve plans. A round of Cristal and triple chocolate dessert closed out the evening and sent everyone their separate ways.

Naymond's singing drew her back into the present.

"*What are you doing New Year's Eve?*" He sang an old bluesy holiday tune that used to be her mother's favorite. Smiling as he took a ballroom dancing glide toward her, he scooped Fallon in his arms and twirled her around the coffee table. "How's Santa's favorite helper this morning?"

She leaned into his silent, sexy sway. "Better now."

"Something wrong?"

"I wish I knew for real. That's all."

"Stop it. We're taking this minute-by-minute today, you hear? I can see your mind's already revved up." He leaned back to look into her eyes, then glanced over her shoulder. "Unless I had more champagne than I thought, *that* was not here last night."

"Thought I'd surprise you," she said. "I asked for three things before we came: a trip with *no* surprises, an anniversary we wouldn't forget, and a little magic to help us find our way back to each other. This is my way of saying thanks for making my wishes come true."

"Except for the surprise part, right?" He pulled her close once more. "Still, it's great. I wouldn't trade these crazy two days if it means you'll always be mine."

Fate had given them so much to think about over the last day and a half. About all she could do was make a symbolic gesture to preserve the life they now wanted so badly.

Snow outside the window fell faster, with bigger flakes that blended into one another, creating a sheet effect, like linen flailing on a clothesline in the wake of a storm. She turned and snuggled closer to Naymond for warmth.

"What's on your schedule for today?" Fallon asked.

"I told you last night, Tana gave me permission to take the day off," he answered with a kiss.

"Things change so fast around here, I wasn't sure if that was still true." Fallon laughed. "So how shall we spend our hours?"

"We can stay in all day. Or we could sneak out, go skiing or out to eat, maybe hang out in town and do some sightseeing."

"Might be fun to pretend we're famous while we're here. Just in case this magic doesn't stick once we leave."

Fallon thought of melting snowflakes, how they dissolved from carefully formed icicles and snowmen to nothingness with the slightest touch of warmth. And how she and Naymond's dream weekend might go from reality back to fantasy once they left the Inn for Los Angeles tomorrow. Fallon hoped that wherever they landed outside the Inn's doors, they'd remember the lessons learned and the love they rekindled here at Crystal Mountain. She wanted to believe that they would either take the events of the weekend back into their past to avoid the mistakes of selfishness and mistrust that tore them apart, or use the wisdom they'd gained to secure their future together and overcome the challenges they'd face as a happy celebrity couple.

"Sure. Let's do some shopping. Pick up some souvenirs for our parents, Mimi, your brother."

"That'll work. I don't know if I've holiday shopped for my crew yet, either. Tana mentioned something about me getting a list together. I don't even know what they would want."

"I know what you mean. It's weird having strangers *know* you." Fallon faked a shudder. "When I went to the spa yesterday, this woman named Jerri knew what services I usually requested—like my nail color preferences, how I used to wear my hair, even the amount of tension I expect from my Swedish massage."

"That is a little creepy." He kissed her on the nose, spun her around and swatted her butt. "I'll call room service and get breakfast. Okay with you?"

"Sounds good." She frowned. "Naymond, we've been so focused on our new reality since we got here, I don't have a clue what's happened in the rest of the world over the last year. Do you?" She gauged from his expression that he hadn't thought about the bigger picture either.

"Why don't you turn on the TV and check on society while I order?"

She flicked on the television to the beeping of an emergency broadcasting alert. Winter storm warning news crawled along the bottom of the screen as the on-air anchor discussed the best ways to return Christmas gifts.

"You see this?" Fallon asked Naymond as his phone rang. He answered the call as she continued to read the information and tried to decipher the diced-up map depicting their area.

"Right now?" Naymond practically shouted into the phone.

She heard the heat in his tone and suspected Tana's voice was on the other end of the line riling him up. Leaning into his ear, Fallon whispered, "Is she trying to make you work today?"

He shook his head and mouthed, "We're leaving. Now."

Fallon turned back toward the TV and reread the news flash. In four to six hours, an incoming storm would begin blanketing the entire viewing area with ten to fifteen inches of snow. They'd be stuck here for days. Naymond would miss the final taping of *Chart Toppers*. None of this dream would have a chance of coming true.

"Okay. I'll start packing." Snow was sneaking up on them. Likewise, Fallon feared that if they didn't get out now, the problems they glimpsed would start piling up, too.

Chapter Ten

Despite the smattering of fans scattered throughout the lobby, Jeff commanded his post just as if a crowd of thousands threatened the safety of his boss. The bodyguard exuded the alertness of a lion protecting his pride. He escorted them briskly through the lobby and to the entrance to wait as the airport limo pulled up to the doors.

"Let me get your bags."

"Thanks," they murmured in unison.

Fallon watched him tote their load back and forth. Her pulse quickened as the mound of luggage became smaller and smaller.

So were they headed to the taping of Naymond's winning night on *Chart Toppers* or his one-year anniversary guest appearance on the show? Fallon wished for the guest slot.

Naymond reached for her hand and gripped it so tight Fallon thought she could feel the blood coursing through his veins. She squeezed his fingers in return and looked up into the wonder and worry in his eyes. "Tell me you love me." His gaze pierced her, draining any last ounces of doubt she held in reserve.

"You know I do, Naymond, more than anything." And she did. She always had. She always would.

"Same here." He pointed a finger at his heart. "I love you, Fallon."

Fallon didn't want to go and tugged at his hand to pull

his body next to hers. The heat between them grew, their blood pulsed in unison. "Tell me *you* believe."

Solemnly he said, "I believe everything's going to be alright." He kissed her, lightly at first, then deeper, giving her time to taste all the reasons she loved him. "If we get separated, meet me in LA."

"Sir, it's time to go." Jeff beckoned.

"Ready?" Naymond hesitated, then lunged forward, pulling her hand.

Fallon's coat caught on the door as he ran. The tug was just enough to jerk their hands apart as her husband crossed the threshold.

Chapter Eleven

"This man has proven to be a fan favorite, here on the show and in your homes." The *Chart Toppers* announcer paused to add drama to his introduction. "Ladies and gentlemen, it's time to bring this week's final contestant to the stage. Give it up for Naymond Terry!"

Since they stepped off the plane in LA, nobody recognized her husband. There was not one adoring fan, side-long glance, or autograph request that surfaced when they arrived in the concourse, or as they stood curbside awaiting a cab and trying to figure out how they were going to pay for an unexpected extra night's stay.

She wanted to cry.

Yes, she remembered the weekend. Every shimmering detail mocked her now. She didn't even have on the same nail polish she'd left the Inn with or that hot new haircut. Fate dumped them smack-dab in the center of their former less-than-comfortable lives where Naymond now faced the performance of his life and Fallon had an unbalanced checkbook to look forward to back home.

She slumped into the auditorium seat with a sniffle, then coughed to mask the sound of her crying.

Naymond began to sing. A midtempo ballad unfamiliar to Fallon's ears broke through her introspection and regret. Its soulful melody and poignant lyrics floated through the crowd, silencing the audience's chatter and inspiring most of those seated to sway in time. The tune rose above the crowd and caught Fallon's ears.

Her husband was serenading her on national television.

"This song is not what he rehearsed," she whispered to the stranger beside her.

In long-distance conversations weeks ago, Naymond and Fallon decided to showcase an upbeat R&B song he wrote that featured him doing a syncopated rap just before the bridge. The idea was meant to remind the judges—and the voting television audience—that Naymond's talent embodied everything *Chart Toppers* said it was looking to expose: songwriting, vocals, production skills, and style. She knew he had all that and more. They just had to develop a routine that let viewers see his range of talents.

The love song he was belting out tonight fell short of the mark.

With words that were achingly personal and the song's haunting quality, Naymond's performance became a one-man-to-one-woman show.

No matter where we land in space and time, now is forever with you. As long as you're the one who's by my side, I'll stay here in love's wonderland with you. He sang it as if he could see her, feel her beside him.

Fallon stared up at the stage as the song ended and women in the audience jumped to their feet. She stood and craned her neck above the crowd, trying to catch her husband's attention.

And to think that two days ago in a place so far away, she dared to want his dream cut short. How could she expect just a little bit of fame for Naymond? Without question, the show's producers made him the closing act because he was obviously the contestant pegged to win.

He deserved the *Chart Toppers* star. Her selfish insecurity was embarrassing.

Wild clapping and whistling died down as people in the audience and at home waited for the judges' reactions.

"Not what we expected," came the first comment. "A song like this belongs in Week Two at best."

The next judge was kinder but no less surprised. "It says here"—he looked down at a sheet in front of him—"that you'd be playing keyboards. The acoustic guitar was a nice touch but what you showed us lacks the presence we were looking for in our first Chart Topper."

"I'd have to agree," said the final judge. "Here's your chance to show us your technical skill and it's like you choked. Great song, but I think this wasn't the place in the contest for it."

Naymond stepped to the front of the stage. "Can I just say one thing, please?"

"Sure. Why not?" quipped the second judge. "No, we won't let you do your performance over, but maybe we'll take your excuse into consideration."

The trio laughed as Naymond stepped forward and strummed a series of chords lightly on his guitar. "I appreciate your comments, but I need to let you all and everybody else know that I'm dedicating tonight as an anniversary gift for my wife. No disrespect to you judges, but as long as *she* believes, nothing else matters. Thank you." He blew a kiss in her direction and walked offstage.

"Well, he picked the wrong time to be sentimental. That's too bad," sniped Judge Number One.

His sarcastic comment closed out the individual acts portion of the show. Lucky for Naymond, the average of scores from previous shows carried one-third of the final vote. Tonight's judging scores and audience vote counted for another one-third each.

Contestants piled onto the stage for one last group production number in which Naymond played keyboards, sang backup, and stood the audience back on its feet as he put Luther to shame on the last two lines and final refrain of the song.

Fallon joined the standing ovation that followed and begged God to let Naymond win. "I understand how I need to be, how I need to trust. If you can just let him have this, please."

The music ended, which meant the audience at home was being treated to a nice five-minute mix of beer, automobile, and discount vacation commercials. Some of them would ambush the kitchen in search of snacks, others would attend to duties they neglected while the show was on, and a few would call the toll-free number to cast their last votes for the first *Chart Toppers* star.

Meanwhile, contestants seemed to heave a collective sigh of relief. Whether they were happier that the song was over or that the show was near its end, Fallon couldn't tell. Some leaned forward, hands on knees, to catch their breath. Others strolled in small circles, hands on hips, taking in what could be their final moments of glory.

Naymond stood at the edge of the stage, drinking a bottle of water, staring into nowhere. Fallon knew exactly where he was.

Returning to this moment in time had to be even harder for him than it was for her. After all, in the life they lived last weekend, he'd already won. The pulse-pounding competition was behind him. Victory was his. Now . . .

Stagehands began barking orders, rounding up contestants and preparing to resume the show. They cleared the stage and lowered the curtains as the show's director reminded them that there were two minutes to curtain call. Slowly the group assembled itself in a single line in front of the curtain.

". . . in five, four, three, two, one," the director whispered. "We're on."

"Welcome back to the final show in the first season of *Chart Toppers*. Let's take a look back at the memories we've shared getting to know one another."

A video montage ran on the screen above the row of contestants. When it concluded, the announcer turned the show over to the judges and the show's accounting firm, which was busy tabulating phone votes and judges' scores.

"Are you ready?" the female judge asked the contestants, who replied with an ear-blasting, united "Yes!"

The second judge repeated the question to the audience and received the same answer.

An accounting firm rep stepped on stage and handed a gold, star-shaped envelope to Judge Number One. "Tonight's winner receives a recording contract with VIP Records, $25,000 cash and a guest appearance with us back here next year." He paused. "And the winner of the first-ever *Chart Toppers* competition is . . . Sofie Carter!"

Sofie Carter? Not Naymond?

How could it not be Naymond?

Fallon slumped into her seat, stunned and hurt. At best, she thought fate left them where they started, on the verge of celebrity. She and Naymond assumed he'd win and they'd spend the next nine months trying to avoid tabloids and divorce.

It didn't occur to either of them that he might lose.

The show's theme song began to play. Contestants, including Naymond, gathered around the winner. Hugs, kisses and questions flowed. Fallon wanted to run onstage and whisk her Naymond away from the heartbreak he must be feeling.

The music ended, house lights came up, and contestants scattered. Naymond hung back, watching the winner parade her trophy, take her publicity shots and utter the words he ought to be speaking: "I can't believe I won!"

Chapter Twelve

Fallon and Naymond strolled through the bustling Detroit Metro Airport without speaking. Their hand-in-hand attachment lacked enthusiasm and desire, and served mainly to keep them from getting pulled apart by the surging crowd. Rather than spend another night in the hotel—and increase their already escalating travel bill—they decided to fly standby and get out of Tinsel Town as fast as they could.

The silence stung. Fallon knew there was little she could do, but she didn't even know what else to say that might help Naymond feel better. She had already told him a thousand times that the judges missed the mark and something better must be waiting for him. And she told him it would all start with the wonderful song he sang just for her—the one he later mentioned he wrote in the Chicago airport as he waited for her to arrive.

Still, each time they walked through a doorway, a small part of her hoped they would step into the life they left at the Inn because here they were: still unfamous, carrying their own bags, and destined for coach.

The idea of returning to overtime at the hospital sickened her. Even though her patient roster of area athletes was more fun than most others on staff, she now knew how it felt to be on the receiving end of personal massages. In this instance, she didn't expect to enjoy giving more than receiving.

And Naymond still didn't have a job. Lawns across the area were littered with FOR SALE, LEASE TO OWN, and AUCTION signs. She couldn't remember the last time she helped him hammer a SOLD sign in someone's yard.

"What are we going to do, Naymond?" She asked as they walked through the airport.

"When I said that stuff about shoveling driveways or stuffing envelopes from home as a way to make some money, you know I was joking, right?"

"That was then."

"So you think I should give this up altogether?"

She stopped and made him look at her. "No, but, we said we'd pay attention to the things that are supposed to be breaking us apart. Financial strain, time away from each other, I'm sure all that was part of it." *Along with Eva*, she thought.

"I can't talk about this with you right now, Fallon." Naymond shook his hand, dropping hers, and walked ahead toward the escalator marked, BAGGAGE CLAIM. The moving stairs shuttled them downward and deposited them beside an overstuffed revolving carousel rotating luggage from their flight.

"Naymond, I'm not fighting you." She reclaimed his hand, hoping he understood what she'd finally realized. "I'm saying it's time to go for it."

"Wait here." He broke into half a grin, probably all he could muster in light of her slow-coming admission and their new reality. "I'll get our bags."

Being back in the Detroit airport reminded Fallon of her pre-glimpse departure. She reached into her tote and dug out the snow globe. This time, inside, there was a couple—she was no longer alone. And the Inn looked an awful lot like an oversized, snow-covered house—the kind she'd love to be headed to right now.

She sighed, holding it tight, as a commotion rose from the far end of the room. People began to cluster around a carousel. *Sounds like a skirmish over a look-alike suitcase*, Fallon speculated, and moved closer to the commotion.

"Miss DuCayne, over here, please," someone from the crowd shouted.

It was Trixie—*again*. What were the chances? Half-excited, hoping for answers for herself and an introduction for Naymond, Fallon returned to the carousel—where he'd located just one of their five bags—grabbed his hand and pulled him toward the singer.

"Excuse me," Fallon called through the clamor.

"That's the lady who caused all our trouble, isn't it?" Naymond halted.

"Too much coincidence. I know." Chance left them very empty-handed this weekend. Fallon dragged her reluctant husband forward, flagging Trixie down. "Come on. I want to hear her explanation."

She thought it was her waving that caught the singer's attention, but soon discovered that the woman had already spied them. Trixie pushed through the crowd, ignored Fallon, and confronted Naymond.

"What happened to you last night?" she asked, sounding more critical than the judges.

He looked at Fallon with a smile on his lips and defeat in his eyes. "Priorities."

"Good. You two figured out what matters. That's a hard lesson for some folk to learn." Trixie wagged her finger mama-style at Fallon, then looked hard at Naymond once more. "I tell you what—*I* like that song you did last night better than anything else you've done on the show all season. My daughter did, too. Hold on. Let me introduce you." Trixie turned around and called to a young woman buried within the crowd.

"I've got a good feeling about this, babe," Fallon whispered into Naymond's ear as Trixie awaited her guest. "Everything's going to work out. Watch."

He swung Fallon into his arms. "It did. You believe. That's all I could have asked for."

Brushing a stray strand of hair from her eyes, he strummed his fingers across her cheek, lifted her chin and kissed her.

Fallon felt herself tumbling through memories of their first embrace, the first time they'd made love, their first moments of marriage. Far more good times than trying times lay buried beneath the passion in his kiss. She clung to every second, sealing them in her heart for safekeeping before opening her eyes with a smile.

Movement at their side broke the spell. Naymond glanced toward Trixie and grinned. Fallon's gaze followed. She immediately recognized the woman at the singer's side.

"Come on over here, Tana," Trixie coaxed. "I got somebody I want you to meet."

By New Year's Day

by Phyllis Bourne Williams

For Dad, Mom & Liz.
And also for Byron, my real-life hero.

Chapter One

Devon Masters glanced sideways at his wife as he steered the SUV along the winding stretch of New Hampshire highway. She still wasn't speaking to him, and the stoic expression she'd worn since their flight left Miami this morning was firmly in place.

"You can't stay mad all weekend," he said, breaking the silence. "This is supposed to be a vacation, remember?"

Eva turned to him, her impassive façade giving way to a full-fledged frown. "A trip you sprung on me at the last minute, when you knew darn well we had plans for New Year's weekend."

Plans? Devon nearly laughed aloud. Their so-called plans were the same every weekend and the majority of evenings, he thought. *Babysitting.* Their daughter would drop by unannounced with her two kids in tow and make a hasty exit without them. His fingers tightened around the steering wheel. Their oldest wasn't the only one taking them for granted. Her sister and brother were just as bad.

Devon swallowed hard, forcing back down his throat the anger threatening to surface. He hadn't whisked Eva fifteen hundred miles away from their home and family to get into the same old argument.

After thirty years, four kids and two grandchildren together, their relationship should be solid. Instead, they squabbled constantly over their grown children, and even worse, they hadn't made love in months.

Now Devon was on a mission. He'd booked the weekend at the Snow Splendor Ski Lodge with one thing in mind: getting his marriage back on track. It didn't matter that neither of them skied, it was the seclusion they needed.

What better time than New Year's to resolve their disagreements and start fresh, he thought, looking through the windshield at the snow-covered landscape.

He flicked on the wipers to brush away the falling snowflakes. It was only flurries now, but the weather forecast promised more of the white stuff over the weekend.

"Snow's a big change of pace for us, huh?" Devon offered a not-so-smooth segue to a safer topic. He held his breath, hoping his wife would bite. The sound of his watch ticking off the seconds was deafening inside the vehicle's quiet cabin.

"It's beautiful alright," she finally said. "Our grands would love it."

Devon chuckled, imagining the kick their three- and one-year-old grandchildren would get out of seeing snow for the first time. "Yeah, they would. Thomas actually asked me to bring some back," he said, referring to the oldest.

"I imagine the baby would just want to eat it."

"There isn't much that girl won't put in her mouth," Devon laughed.

"Maybe we should have brought them along."

He reached across the armrest for Eva's gloved hand. "Next time," he said, squeezing it. "This weekend is ours."

She squeezed back. The tiny gesture infused him with hope for both the trip and the future of their marriage. For two people as much in love as they, there had to be a middle ground.

All he had to do was find it.

"Eva, I want this weekend to be a new start—"

A cell phone belted out a tune, cutting him off mid-sentence. Eva's, he thought, once again swallowing his frustration. Devon hadn't switched on his mobile, because for the next few days he was unavailable to everyone except Eva.

He glanced at his wife, who was busy clawing through her purse. The woman seated next to him, while still beautiful, looked older than her forty-nine years. Her brow was furrowed, and he noticed fine lines prematurely creasing her makeup-free, mocha skin. Though her shoulder-length hair was tucked beneath a hat, he knew it was pulled back into a bun or slapdash ponytail.

Devon wasn't sure when the feminine touches of lipstick and perfume had ceased being part of Eva's daily routine, or when she'd stopped going to the beauty salon.

In the year since he'd sold his successful construction business and began spending more time at home, he'd become aware of many things he'd missed that were going on under his own roof.

"Hi, honey," Eva said into the phone. "Is everything okay? Are the kids alright?"

It was their oldest daughter. Devon tightened his already firm grip on the steering wheel. What did Mallory want now, he wondered, silently cursing modern technology.

In the close confines of the SUV, it was impossible not to overhear Eva as well as their daughter on the other end of the line. Devon rubbed the knot forming at the base of his neck. Over a thousand miles away, and Mallory's demanding voice came through like she was sitting right next to them.

"I'm sorry, sweetheart," Eva said. "I know our leaving unexpectedly left you in a bind."

His wife listened calmly as their daughter continued to belabor the same point.

"Yes, I'm sure it's not easy locating a sitter at the last minute."

Eva's voice seemed to get smaller as Mallory heaped on the guilt. "But I didn't know we were leaving until yesterday. I was shocked, too. I'm really sorry, honey."

Devon placed both hands on the wheel, resisting the urge to snatch the cell phone from his wife and chuck it into a passing snowbank.

Eva flipped the phone closed. She sighed wearily as she sunk back into the leather passenger seat.

"I told you we should have rescheduled this trip. Poor Mallory is beside herself," she said. "Her boss is having his annual New Year's party this weekend, you know?"

Devon frowned. How could he not know? Mallory had been whining about it since they'd told her they would be away for the holiday. Not that she'd bothered asking them to look after the kids, as usual, she'd just assumed they would.

"Maybe she should skip it this year," he suggested. "It'll be good for the kids to spend a little time with their mother."

"But this party is critical to her career," Eva explained. "The senior partners from her law firm will be there, and there's bound to be shop talk."

"Hmmm." Devon pressed his lips together to keep from saying something that would surely lead to an argument. Their kids had Eva wrapped so tightly around their collective finger; nothing he could say would make a difference anyway.

If only he had spent more time at home instead of on his construction business, he thought. He would have figured out his wife had never really gotten over the fire that swept through their house years ago and nearly killed their young children. The passage of time had done little to move her beyond her guilt for not being at home.

In hindsight, he wished he had focused more on Eva instead of work and rebuilding their house. He should have helped her deal with her emotions before fear and guilt drove her to spoil and overprotect their kids.

Devon stole another peek at his wife. He was here now, and over the next few days he'd find a way to make her realize she had to let them go. For their sakes as well as hers.

He also intended to show her that in addition to being a wonderful mother and grandmother, she was a woman. A remarkable and still very desirable woman.

But right now her mind was still on their daughter.

"Mallory's worked hard to get ahead at work. She deserves our support."

"We've been nothing but supportive. Didn't we take out a second mortgage to pay for law school, so she wouldn't graduate with a mound of debt?"

He didn't bother mentioning they'd also given her and her husband the down payment on their five-bedroom McMansion in the suburbs.

Eva shook her head. "I'm not talking about money. I mean hands-on help with the kids."

"Have you ever thought we're a little too hands-on with *her* kids?"

"Oh for heaven's sake, Devon, they're our grandchildren."

"That's exactly it. Thomas and the baby are our grandchildren," he said. "They shouldn't be calling *you* Mama."

"How much longer to the lodge?" Eva asked. This time it was his wife who changed the subject, just like she always did when he punched holes in her argument.

Devon tapped the GPS screen in the rental's console

with his fingertip. "According to this, it should be on the other side of this hill. Tired?"

Eva yawned. "A little."

Devon couldn't blame her. They'd left their house early to make their morning flight. After four hours on a plane crammed with holiday travelers and another two on the road, she had to be exhausted.

Relief washed over Devon as the lodge came into view. The exterior appeared as impressive as the photos in the travel agency brochures. It was all rustic wood and sparkling glass, flanked by sky-high evergreens and topped by a snowcapped roof.

"This place looks like a snow globe come to life," Eva said.

A valet parking attendant, bundled in a parka, greeted them at the lodge entrance. Devon had barely put the SUV into park before the college-aged kid began yanking open doors and snatching luggage from the back.

"Welcome to Snow Splendor," the young man said through the scarf covering half his face.

Devon stuffed some bills into his palm and walked around to the passenger side. The door already open, he reached for his wife's hand and helped her down.

"We're going to have a great weekend—you'll see."

She pasted on a smile, but Devon knew her mind was still on Mallory and their grandchildren.

Devon told himself her lack of enthusiasm was just temporary. He and Eva were going to find their way back to each other this weekend, and he wasn't going to let anything or anyone stand in the way.

Not even his own children.

Warmth and the lingering scent of Christmas hit Eva the moment she trudged into the lodge's foyer.

Her eyes scanned the lobby as she stomped off the miniscule amount of snow clinging to her new boots on the welcome mat. Poinsettias, swags of garland and pine-cone-dotted wreaths filled the gaily-decorated room, while classical takes on holiday carols played in the background.

Yet the holiday spirit was lost on her.

She shouldn't be here. She should be back in Miami with her family, Eva thought. Mallory had sounded practically hysterical on the phone, and her granddaughter's wails in the background had nearly brought Eva to tears herself.

She yanked the wool hat off her head and smoothed any stray hairs back into her low ponytail. She should have never let Devon talk her into this trip.

What in the hell had she been thinking?

"A surprise getaway," Eva muttered. "More like an ambush."

Suddenly, she found herself swept into her husband's arms. Devon pointed to the sprig of mistletoe hanging above them before hauling her against him. He lowered his head and captured her mouth in a kiss.

His tongue was hot and demanding, surprisingly awakening a need buried inside her. Eva moaned low in her throat, fisted her fingers around the lapels of his coat and pulled him closer. She was still miffed, but her traitorous body hadn't gotten the message. It had been a long time since Devon kissed her like this, and God help her, she missed it.

"You two must be the Masters."

Devon broke off the kiss. His dark eyes bore down into hers, before he turned his attention to the interruption. Eva clung helplessly to him as backbone once again replaced her jelly of a spine.

A clerk clad in a red holiday sweater covered in reindeer appliqués smiled brightly at them from behind the front desk. With a head full of springy gray curls and rosy cheeks, the seventy-something woman looked like a storybook Mrs. Claus. The name "Beverly" was on her name tag.

"Hi, Beverly. I'm Devon and this is my wife, Eva."

"I can always spot the honeymooners." Beverly winked.

"But we're not . . ." Eva began, but the woman continued.

"I have the honeymoon suite all ready, just as you requested." She scanned Devon's credit card and handed them two slide-card keys. "Your luggage has already been placed in the suite. Congratulations!"

Eva felt her husband's arm slip around her waist, and he pulled her to his side. She shot him a don't-push-it look, which he all but ignored.

"Thank you, Beverly."

"Call me Bev," she said. "Oh, we're having a New Year's Eve party here at the lodge. I hope you two will join us."

"My bride and I will be there."

A satisfied smile played across Devon's mouth as they rode the elevator to the third floor. With the taste of him lingering on her lips, Eva couldn't decide whether to kiss him again or slap the smugness from his handsome face. If Devon thought she was going to melt in his arms every time he looked crossways at her, he had another think coming.

Devon had been increasingly difficult about their kids since he'd sold the business, and she didn't like it one bit. It was an issue they'd have to resolve before she allowed herself to be distracted by sex. No matter how much she missed it.

"Why did you lead her to believe we were newlyweds?"

The elevator chimed and the doors opened.

"I booked the honeymoon suite, so it was simply a natural assumption."

Eva caught her husband's profile out of the corner of her eye as they walked down the corridor. Despite his fifty-two years, Devon's face remained as lean and chiseled as it did on their wedding day. The manual labor involved with working in construction most of his life had kept his body the same way. A touch of gray at his temples was the man's only concession to middle age.

They stopped in front of double doors at the end of the hallway. A gold placard on one of the doors proclaimed it the honeymoon suite. Devon slid his card through the electronic lock and threw open the door.

Before she realized what was happening, Eva felt her feet leave the floor. Devon scooped her up effortlessly and carried her across the threshold.

"But we're not honeymooners," she protested weakly, pressing a hand to his solid chest.

"No, but we could be," he whispered against her ear. The timbre of his husky voice sent a shiver through her.

If only it were that easy, she thought as he lowered her to her feet.

Devon touched her arm. "Are you cold?"

"I'm okay."

"Are you sure? I can light the fireplace."

Eva shook her head and shrugged off her coat. Her husband had bought it for the trip, along with a wardrobe of clothes made of cold-resistant fabrics. She glanced around the room. If the crystal vases brimming with red roses and the bucket of champagne on ice hinted at romance, then the huge, four-poster bed dominating the room practically shouted it.

Eva chewed on her bottom lip as she stared longingly at it.

She and Devon hadn't made love in ages, not since she'd allowed their son to move in with them after his live-in girlfriend kicked him out.

The bed was a big, plush reminder of everything she was missing out on.

"Spectacular, isn't it?" he asked.

Eva's breath hitched. Could he have read her mind?

She turned around to see Devon staring out the window. It took a few moments for her to realize he was referring to the view.

She peered through the glass to watch the late afternoon sun start its decline behind the mountains. The delighted squeals of children sledding down a nearby hill pierced the air.

"Breathtaking," Eva agreed, taking it all in. Years ago, she would have whipped out her sketch pad and attempted to recapture the postcard-perfect winter scene on paper, but the artist in her had gone dormant long ago.

Nowadays, she was content teaching elementary school art and playing with her grandchildren.

"Thomas would love this," she said.

Devon shook his head and touched a gentle finger to her lips. "Not now."

Any other time the request would have come off like an order and started a fight. However, the underlying plea in his tone compelled her to comply.

Devon grasped her hand and led her to the sofa in front of the window. After they were seated, he lifted her feet from the floor and placed them in his lap. One at a time, he tugged off her heavy winter boots and dropped them to the hardwood floor.

"I'm sure your feet are glad to get out of those."

Eva eased her back down on the armrest and wiggled her toes in his lap. Slowly, working from her heel, he began massaging her foot.

"Ahhhh, that feels good," she said, yawning. "I could have my feet rubbed like this every night."

She yawned again. Her body slid farther down the armrest until she was practically lying down. She closed her drooping eyelids. Just for a moment, she thought, drifting off.

The plaintive wails of her granddaughter filled Eva's head.

She reached for the baby, but she was trapped in some kind of fog. Instead, she watched helplessly as the baby sat in her high chair, fat tears rolling down her chubby cheeks.

What was going on? Where was Mallory?

Eva spied the teenager her daughter sometimes hired to watch the kids kicked back on the living room sofa. The teen yapped away on her cell phone while rap videos blared in the background.

"Get off the damn phone!" Eva shouted over the noise.

The girl muted the television and pulled the cell phone from her ear. Eva heaved a relieved sigh. If she couldn't see to her granddaughter, at least she'd gotten the sitter back on the job.

The teen pulled herself off the sofa and looked toward the kitchen.

"Shut up!" she screamed at the baby. "Can't you see I'm on the phone?"

The baby sucked in a terrified breath, before letting out another ear-piercing howl.

Taking the television off mute, the teen put the phone back to her ear. "Brat," she said, rolling her eyes.

Fury ebbed to panic as Eva looked around for Thomas. Where was he? "Thomas!" She shouted his name, though no one seemed to hear her.

After several frightening moments that felt like hours, she spotted him playing in his room. He was so absorbed in his task, he didn't hear his sister's cries.

Eva looked closer. He was playing with a cigarette lighter. He flicked the lighter, but to Eva's relief it didn't ignite.

"Put that down! Thomas! Put the lighter down!"

He didn't hear her. She called out to that idiot of a babysitter. Nothing.

Thomas flicked the lighter again. This time it caught. Startled by the flame, he tossed it aside. The fire leapt from the carpeting to the curtains.

"Thomas!" Eva screamed.

Chapter Two

"Eva, wake up!"

Devon shook Eva's arm in another attempt to rouse her. Finally, she jolted awake. Perspiration and a look of sheer terror blanketed her features.

"Everything's okay," Devon said, kneeling beside the sofa. "You just had a bad dream."

From the way she'd tossed in her sleep, it must have been horrendous. He'd spent the last five minutes trying to wake her up.

"There was a fire. The kids were in danger. I tried, but I couldn't get to them," Eva babbled, holding a shaky hand to her chest.

Devon brushed his knuckles against the side of her face. He could feel her pulse beat frantically against her temple. "The kids are fine."

Eva nodded, not looking quite convinced.

Devon filled a glass from the bathroom tap. While he hated her much-needed rest disturbed by the dream, perhaps it had provided the opening he needed.

She reached for the water with trembling hands.

"I'll hold, you drink." Devon watched her swallow the entire contents of the glass in two gulps. "More?"

"No, I'm fine. Thanks."

He placed the empty glass on the end table and sat down beside her. "The fire wasn't your fault," he began.

"I know it was just a nightmare," Eva said.

"Not your dream," he said. "I mean the fire at our house." He felt her body stiffen next to him, and the tension between them ratcheted up a notch.

"That fire happened over twenty-five years ago. Why bring it up now?"

Devon placed a hand on his wife's jean-clad knee. "Because I think it's at the root of our problem with the kids. I believe it's why you knock yourself out doing any and everything for them. Now that I've been around more, I see you've never really gotten past what happened."

"So one year of retirement has turned you into an armchair psychologist?"

"Eva, honey. I want to talk, not fight," Devon said, hoping the conciliatory words were in time to stop the wall his wife was erecting between them.

"Our house caught fire with our children in it, and I wasn't there," she said softly.

"You have to stop beating yourself up over it." Devon lifted his hand from her knee and put his arm around her shoulder. "You made a twenty-minute trip to the grocery store, and you left them with a babysitter."

"A babysitter I hired who fled the house without them."

"How can that be your fault?"

Eva shrugged his arm from around her and looked around. "I don't want to talk about it anymore." She pushed off the sofa and walked across the room to her purse.

"What are you doing?" Devon asked

"Getting my phone. I need to check on things at home."

Damn, Devon silently cursed. The nightmare was bad enough. The last thing Eva needed was a second dose of Mallory's guilt tripping. "Come on, Eva. You just had a bad dream."

He glanced down at his watch. He'd made plans for tonight. If they didn't get ready soon, they'd miss their reservations.

"Why don't I call instead?" he volunteered. It was the perfect solution. He could reassure Eva and at the same time shield her from another one of Mallory's tirades. He loved his daughter, but she knew better than try to pull the same crap with him.

His offer came a second too late.

"Mallory, it's Mom. How's everything going?"

Eva exhaled with an audible whoosh and a smile came over her face, causing Devon to heave his own relieved sigh. Now if she'd just end the call before their daughter could start in on her.

Sure enough his wife's smile was short-lived, and familiar worry lines began to creep onto her forehead.

"It can't be as bad as all that," Eva said into the phone. "You're a brilliant lawyer. You won't be skipped over for promotion because of a silly party. No dear, I'm not just saying it because I'm your mother."

Gratefully, Devon wasn't subject to Mallory's side of the conversation this time. Eva looked over at him like she wanted to ask him something, but must have changed her mind.

"No, sweetheart," she said into the phone. "There's no chance of me and Daddy coming home early."

The sheer audacity of his daughter's request didn't surprise Devon. Mallory was a bold one, alright. Even as a child, she would ask them for things the others wouldn't dare.

Again, Devon regretted not putting an end to this nonsense months ago, when he discovered how bad things had become. He'd listened to Eva's pleas for him to be patient with their offspring. Now each day he got a little more fed up with their selfishness.

"Yes," Eva said, then paused. "I know you can't entrust your kids to just anybody."

Unable to stand by and listen to another word, Devon headed to the bathroom to change out of his travel clothes and dress for dinner.

He'd gone all-out to put together a memorable date for his wife. He hoped she'd let herself enjoy it.

Eva forced herself to push both her nightmare and conversations with Mallory to the back of her mind as she dressed for dinner.

Devon hadn't said much, but it didn't take a rocket scientist to figure out he was pissed. Again.

"What right does he have to be ticked anyway?" she grumbled as she tugged her new cashmere turtleneck over her head. Her husband had given her the green, tunic-length sweater last week for Christmas.

At the time, the gift had baffled her. It wasn't like she'd get much use out of it living in Miami. She'd simply chalked it up to men being clueless about gifts for the women in their lives.

She had no idea she'd be spending New Year's weekend in New Hampshire. Nor had she known the trouble it would stir up.

Still, she was here, and Devon was trying so hard. The least she could do was meet him halfway.

Besides, they hadn't been out to dinner for ages. Eva glanced at the bathroom mirror for a quick glimpse of herself in the ultrasoft sweater. She leaned in closer, surveying her reflection.

Dark circles battled with crow's feet for the space around her red-rimmed eyes, and her once luminous complexion looked tired and sallow.

"When did you turn into an old lady?" she whispered to the woman in the mirror.

Slipping off the rubber band holding her ponytail in place, she shook her head. Her dark hair, threaded with more strands of silver than she remembered, hung limp on her shoulders, making her regret blowing off her once-regular salon appointments.

Too bad she hadn't thought to bring along a curling iron. She smoothed her hair back with her hands and fashioned a bun at the nape of her neck. Hopefully, she'd find some makeup in her toiletries to perk up her face.

Eva rooted through the bag and smiled when she spotted her cosmetics kit. Whipping out the mascara first, she twisted open the tube only to discover a clumpy, black mess.

"You'll just have to make do with lipstick and a touch of blush," she told herself, tossing the rancid mascara in the trash can.

She pulled a dark berry blush from her makeup bag. One glance at the see-thru lid and she didn't have to open it. The contents had disintegrated into tiny chunks.

When was the last time she'd purchased makeup, she wondered, and couldn't remember. Nor could she recall when she'd last bothered applying it.

Eva threw the entire outdated kit in the trash. Between work, babysitting and helping the kids, she didn't have time to fuss with her appearance like she used to.

"Your husband loves you. It doesn't matter what you look like," she told her reflection. Then she tried to ignore the voice inside her that told her it did.

Devon watched a grin spread across Eva's lips.

"A horse-drawn sleigh!" she exclaimed, taking in the green sleigh trimmed in red.

Eva's delight warmed his insides, despite the frigid outdoor temperatures. Devon wished he could keep a smile on her face forever, but he'd settle for tonight. He had his wife to himself this evening, and he planned to make the most of it.

Before the driver could climb down from his seat to assist them, Devon placed a hand on each side of Eva's waist and hoisted her onto the sleigh. He climbed in beside her and together they spread the blanket left on the padded bench across their laps.

Satisfied they were seated, the driver tugged on the reins and the horse began a slow trot along a path flanked by tall trees and snowdrifts. Moonlight and a sky filled with sparkling stars illuminated the inky night.

"I always thought the closest I ever wanted to be to December up north was watching it on television," Eva said. "But this isn't so bad."

A gust of wind kicked up the fallen snow, sending it flying into their faces.

"Maybe I spoke too soon," she sputtered.

"You want to wear my hat?" Devon offered.

"Um . . . no thanks." She glanced up at his head and winced. Errant snowflakes clung to her long eyelashes. "It's not *that* cold."

Devon couldn't suppress a laugh at the comical expression on her face. His leather and faux fur hat, reminiscent of Rocky the Flying Squirrel's aviator helmet in the old *Bullwinkle* cartoons, wasn't his idea of high fashion either. However, it was all he could find while shopping for warm clothes on an eighty-degree afternoon in Miami.

"How about borrowing my scarf, then?"

Without waiting for an answer, he pulled the wool scarf from around his neck and draped it around hers. He dropped his arm around her shoulders and silently thanked the second wind gust that coaxed her deeper into his embrace.

"Better?" he asked.

"Much." Her warm breath caressed his jaw, sending a shot of pure lust through him.

It had been months since he'd made love to his wife, and he missed her like crazy. Through thirty years of marriage, his passion for her never waned. If anything, he found her familiar curves even sexier.

Tonight, he hoped to get reacquainted with them.

"Hungry?" she asked.

His gaze dropped over her. "Starved."

"So what's for dinner?" she asked innocently, unaware of the detour his thoughts had taken.

The driver picked up the pace, and the bells around the horse's neck jingled in time with the crunch of the animal's hooves through the snow.

"You'll see."

Twinkling lights from the village ahead pierced the darkness as they closed in on their destination. The travel agent who'd booked this trip for him said the tiny village boasted a variety of upscale shops and cozy eateries. She'd called it a quaint haven for out-of-towners minus the tackiness of a tourist trap.

"How about a hint?" Eva nudged his side with her elbow. "Just a little one."

"Alright. Alright," Devon relented. "I think you'll like it."

Eva rolled her eyes. "You call that a hint?"

"Too late now," he said.

The sleigh slowed to a stop, and Devon inclined his head toward a row of storefronts housed in colonial-style buildings. "We're here."

Despite the temperature, the village was abuzz with

people ducking in and out of stores and restaurants. Devon stepped down from the sleigh and helped Eva to the slush-covered sidewalk. Fairy lights sparkled from the barren trees lining the street, while smoke curled up from the chimneys, filling the air with an inviting, woodsy scent.

Eva's eyes widened. "This must be a fun spot, to attract so many people on such a chilly night."

Devon placed a guiding hand on Eva's back and walked into the Down To Earth restaurant on the corner. A blast of heat from the old-fashioned wood stove and savory smells from the kitchen greeted them.

The hostess seated them at a candlelit table near the window.

"Whatever's cooking smells delicious," Eva whispered across the table to him.

Devon watched her scan the menu. She hesitated a moment, before fixing her gaze on him. "This is a vegetarian restaurant?"

He nodded. "You've always been the one to accommodate my tastes; tonight I'm deferring to yours."

"But you never . . ." she began. Her vegetarian lifestyle was cause for lighthearted tiffs over the years.

"I know. I'm a meat-and-potatoes man." He repeated his oft-said mantra. "But I'm flexible."

Eva raised a brow. "Since when? You're the reason our children aren't vegetarians."

"Me?"

"Yes, you. The first full sentence out of their little mouths was, 'I want what Daddy's having.'"

Devon held up his hands in mock surrender. "Guilty as charged." He looked over the menu and frowned. "Now how about helping me choose something?"

They decided on cannelloni minestrone for starters. Beaming with pleasure, Eva ordered a squash-and-potato frittata for her entrée, while he opted for the eggplant cacciatore.

When their food arrived, Devon dug into it. He didn't know if it was because it tasted good or he was simply ravenous.

Then it occurred to him what made a meal with no meat pleasant. Other than her reference to them as children, Eva hadn't mentioned the kids. It was rare for him to sit down to a meal and not be inundated with what their offspring needed or wanted, he thought. Or even worse, get into a disagreement over it.

This evening they simply enjoyed each other's company.

After a dessert of strawberry tofu cheesecake, they headed back outside. The village's main thoroughfare continued to bustle with activity.

"Now that wasn't so bad, was it?" Eva asked.

"I was skeptical about the cheesecake, but . . ."

"Um . . . was that before or after you scarfed down your slice and half of mine?"

He put his arm around her and dropped a kiss on the tip of her nose. "Okay, you win. It was pretty good," he said as they walked toward the sleigh. "But remember this pumpkin turns back into a steak at midnight."

They both burst into laugher. Devon savored the happy sound. It had been a long time since they'd shared a laugh, almost as long as their dry spell in the bedroom. He hoped that tonight they'd put an end to the drought.

Spotting an outdoor vendor selling hot chocolate, Devon stopped. The perfect night for one of his favorite drinks.

He took a sip, peering at Eva over the rim of the steaming cup. The chocolate had satisfied one of his desires tonight. He yearned for the sweet, brown woman before him to satisfy the other.

"Are you sure you don't want one?" She'd shaken her

head when he asked the first time, but he could tell she was dying for a taste.

"No, I've already had a dessert," she said. "Anything with chocolate goes directly to my thick thighs."

"You thighs are perfect." *Especially, when they're bare and wrapped around my waist.* He grew hard at the thought.

She gnawed on her full bottom lip. An innocent gesture, but on her it came off as downright sexy.

"Stop trying to tempt me," she said with a laugh.

"Walk with me," he said, hoping the chilled night air would cool his libido.

Arm in arm, they strolled down the street, taking in the sights. A block later, Eva stopped in her tracks and pointed out one of the stores to him. "Let's take a peek in here."

"Granite State Haberdashery," Devon read the sign above the doorway. "I can't imagine what you'd want from this place." He rolled his eyes up toward his hat.

Eva wrinkled her nose.

"Come on." She tugged on his sleeve. "Consider it a fashion intervention."

Twenty minutes later, Devon walked out of the store wearing a stylish, flannel driving cap.

"Better?" He spun around to give his wife a full view.

"Much." She nodded her approval. It was just a little thing, but knowing he'd pleased her made him feel good.

"Well now that you've got me looking respectable again, there has to be something I can do for you."

"As a matter of fact, there is." Her gaze slid slowly down the length of him, before it came back to rest on his face. "You can take me to bed."

Chapter Three

"Let's get out of here."

Devon wasn't sure which one of them moved faster as they sprinted through the snow and across the street to the waiting sleigh.

All he knew was he could hardly wait to honor his wife's request.

The driver must have sensed their urgency as they scrambled aboard the sleigh, because he didn't waste any time getting started.

Neither did Devon.

Dispensing with the preliminaries, he joined his mouth to his wife's in a scorching kiss that made the frigid winter night feel like a heat wave in August.

Eva pulled him closer with a force that startled him. The aggressive move by his usually demure spouse set off a growl from deep in his throat, and he deepened the kiss.

When their lips parted, her gaze captured his. Not even the shadowy night could hide the passion sparkling in her eyes. They never left his face as she undid the buttons on his coat.

Eva slipped her hands inside it and splayed them against his chest. He drew in a sharp breath.

"I've missed touching you," she said. Her hands roamed up to his shoulders and around to his back.

"Then don't stop."

He kissed her again, sucking her tongue into his mouth.

She tasted sweet, like the ripe strawberries from tonight's dessert.

The wind whirled around them, but he didn't feel chilled. If anything, being outside kissing and touching Eva beneath the stars made him hotter.

It was all he could do not to strip off his sweater and the remaining layers of clothing barricading her soft hands from his eager flesh.

"Even after all these years, I still can't get enough of you," he whispered raggedly.

He blazed a slow trail of kisses from her earlobe down to the hollow of her throat, reveling in the sweet softness of her skin.

She moaned her approval, and in one swift motion, Devon pulled her onto his lap.

Eva straddled him with her hips. "The driver?" she whispered in his ear, as if she'd only now realized they weren't exactly alone.

Devon looked over her shoulder. "Has his eyes on the road."

She returned her gaze to him, and a wicked smile spread over her face. Just when he thought he couldn't get any harder he did.

Devon stifled a groan as she boldly began rocking her pelvis back and forth against his hardness. His erection strained against his zipper toward the apex of her thighs.

Eva's fingers dug into his shoulders, and he once again captured her lips in a slow, wet kiss.

Devon hoped she was prepared to hold on even tighter, because this was nothing compared to the ride he had in store for her when they made it to bed.

The sound of Eva's cell phone sliced through their passion-induced haze. He felt her go stiff in his arms, before she tore her mouth free.

"Ignore it," he whispered breathlessly against her lips.

"What if there's an emergency with one of the kids?"

"They're adults. They'll handle it."

The phone continued to ring. Frustration washed over him as she pushed her hands against his chest and pulled herself off his lap.

"Don't do this, Eva," he said, already missing her nearness.

"I have to."

She reached down for her purse and retrieved the ringing phone. She glanced at the Caller ID. "It's Ben," she said. "I'll just make sure he's okay, then we can pick up where we left off. Promise."

Her eyes pleaded with him for understanding he wasn't sure he could give.

Devon pressed his lips together hard as bitter disappointment overtook the desire pulsing through him just moments earlier. He'd brought Eva all the way to New England for time alone together, and it didn't make a damn bit of difference. They might as well be sitting at home in Miami.

Didn't anyone in his family realize the whole point of a weekend getaway was to get-the-hell-away?

"Hello, sweetheart," Eva said to their son. "Everything alright?"

She put her hand over her other ear to hear more clearly. Devon buttoned his coat. Her taking the call had pretty much killed the mood. And suddenly the late December night felt mighty cold.

At least he wasn't subject to his son's side of the conversation, he thought. After Ben's girlfriend had kicked him out of their apartment, Eva welcomed him home with open arms.

The girlfriend, who seemed like a nice young lady to

Devon, had accused Ben of treating the place like a pigsty and her like his personal maid. Now their twenty-four-year-old son was turning their house into a dump and hiding behind Eva's skirt anytime Devon got on him about it.

"Oh, I'm sorry, Ben," Eva said.

Her words stung Devon's ears. What was she apologizing to one of their kids for now, he wondered. If anything, they should be asking for their mother's forgiveness.

"I just got so busy with packing and preparing for the trip, I didn't get a chance to go to the grocery store."

Her voice, which had been hoarse with lust before the call, was guilty and sad. The drastic change made Devon want to strike out against anyone who caused her a moment of sadness or regret.

He closed his eyes, leaned his head back and pinched the bridge of his nose with his fingertips. Slowly, he began counting backward from ten. This entire trip was about coming together with his wife. Losing his temper with their son would only push her further away.

Nine.

"There are some frozen dinners in the freezer. Just pop one in the microwave," Eva said.

Eight.

Seven.

"Laundry. No, sorry. I didn't get a chance to do that either."

Six.

Five.

Four.

"I know that doesn't help you now, but . . ."

Devon had heard enough. Abandoning the futile countdown, he snatched the cell phone from his wife's hand.

"Ben!" he barked into the phone, interrupting his son midcomplaint.

Devon struggled to keep his cool as he spoke. "What is so important you had to interrupt your mother and me on the first vacation we've had in years?"

It was bad enough listening to Eva's side of the conversation. Actually hearing his son's complaints snapped the fragile threads of Devon's control.

"Pay attention, because I'm only going to say this once. Don't you ever ask your mother to waste time on some menial task."

There was silence on the other end of the line. Devon thought Ben had dropped the phone until he heard him breathing.

"Calm down, Devon." Eva reached for the phone. "You're making a big deal out of nothing."

Devon moved the phone to his opposite ear. He'd started this, and he was going to finish it. He was sick of their kids stressing Eva and running her ragged. It ended tonight, whether his wife liked it or not.

"You may treat your girlfriends like your personal servants, but I'll be damned if I'll allow you to continue to treat my wife like your maid," he said through gritted teeth. "Understand?"

"Yes, sir," came a timid voice.

"Good."

Months of built-up tension drained Devon's body. He'd probably blown his opportunity to make love to Eva tonight, but at least his need to set their offspring straight was being satisfied.

"You're not a kid anymore. You're a grown man with a college degree under his belt. Straighten up and start acting like it."

Devon finally passed the phone back to Eva. She called out their son's name, but he'd already hung up.

Wordlessly, Eva stared up at him. His satisfaction turned to sorrow as her expression slowly transformed from surprise to fury.

The sleigh slowed in front of the lodge. Before it could come to a complete stop, Eva was halfway to the entrance. Devon watched her push through the foyer doors and quickly cross the lobby.

His gaze panned out to the lodge. From the outside, it had all the trappings of a romantic winter hideaway.

The irony of the situation wasn't lost on him.

Just moments ago, he couldn't get his wife back to their room fast enough.

Now that they'd finally made it here, it didn't matter.

After three decades of marriage, Eva thought she knew her husband better than she knew herself.

Now she wasn't so sure.

The man she'd loved all of her adult life had morphed into a cold-hearted stranger. If she hadn't heard him with her own ears, she would have never thought Devon capable of such callousness. Especially toward his own son.

Stepping off the elevator, she strode down the long corridor toward their room. Each step stoked her anger. She threw open the suite door, and her eyes immediately fell upon the king-size bed she'd been so eager to get her husband into.

Apparently, the turndown maid had already made her rounds.

The white, downy comforter was pulled back to an inviting angle and a single red rose had been placed in the center of the sheets.

From the plump feather pillows to the European foil-wrapped chocolates, it was the perfect setting for a romantic night.

Memories of his chocolate-laced kisses flitted through her mind, and she licked her lips.

Appalled at the detour her thoughts had taken, she shook her head to banish them. What kind of woman lusted after a man who'd talked to her child so dreadfully?

Behind her she heard Devon close the door and his footfalls against the hardwood floor.

"Eva . . ." He touched his fingertips to her shoulders.

She whirled around, not giving him a chance to utter more than her name. "How could you talk to my son like that?" she hissed.

"Ben is my son, too. And our conversation tonight was long overdue."

Eva searched his familiar face for signs of the once doting father who'd been so kind and patient with the kids. Where was the man who had taught Mallory to ride a bike and Ben to tie his shoelaces?

"Our son is going through a rough patch in his personal life," Eva explained. "He came home to heal."

"Open your eyes, Eva," Devon said. "Our son came home for hot meals and twenty-four-hour maid service."

"Washing an extra load of clothes or setting an additional place at the dinner table won't kill us," she said.

He stared at her a moment, as if *she* was the one who didn't have a clue. "Are you so naïve that you can't see that Ben is taking advantage of you?"

She shook her head. "That's absurd."

"It's true," he said, pulling off his hat. He shrugged off his coat and hung it on the rack by the door. "And he's not the only one."

"Is this about Mallory calling earlier?"

"What it's about is Ben, Mallory and Veronica treating you like a lowly servant, available round-the-clock to do their bidding."

"But Veronica didn't call today," Eva said, wondering how their second child had got on his bad side.

Devon snorted. "It's just a matter of time, and trust me, when she does it'll be because she wants something from you."

"She might just call to say hi," Eva countered weakly.

Sadness crossed her husband's features. His chin dropped to his chest before he tilted it up to face her. He looked like he hated what he was about to say.

"When is the last time Mallory, Veronica or Ben called or stopped by just for a visit?" he asked, and immediately answered his own question. "Never. They *always* want something."

"But . . ." she began.

Devon cut her off. "Karen is the only one of our kids who comes over to check on us or calls to invite you out for lunch or a day at the mall."

Shame warmed her cheeks as she remembered Karen bringing her a tin of cookies from her favorite bakery last month as a treat. She'd allowed Mallory to take them because her oldest daughter had said she needed something special to bring to her sorority tea.

Eva walked slowly to the coatrack and hung her coat next to Devon's. "Can't you see the others just need us more right now?" she asked. "Sometimes helping them is inconvenient, but I'm their mother. I can't stand by and do nothing."

"Then you should understand why I can't continue to stand by and do nothing either."

Alarm shot through her at the steely determination in his tone. "What are talking about?" she asked, almost frightened to hear his answer.

"Ben and I will finish our talk when we get back to Miami. Next comes Mallory and then Veronica. The housekeeping, babysitting, begging for money and all the other crap they've been pulling is over," he said. "It won't be tolerated in the new year."

She gasped. "We're only giving them a hand . . ."

Devon sat on the edge of the bed and removed his boots. "Eva—"

"You love our children as much as I do. I know you do. Why are you doing this?"

Devon patted a space next to him on the bed for her to sit, but she purposely strode past him and seated herself on the sofa.

"Perhaps you were right earlier when you alluded to retirement turning me into an armchair psychologist," he said. "I've seen enough this past year to know you've let misplaced guilt turn our kids into tyrants."

The harshness of his statement hurt her heart. Her husband had basically called her a bad mother who raised a bunch of horrible kids.

"I'm a good mother," she protested through clenched teeth.

"Yes, you are," Devon said. "Now it's time for you to cut the apron strings and let go. For both our kids' sakes and yours."

Eva stared at her husband. "I can't abandon them, Devon."

He crossed the steps between the bed and the couch, then heaved a weary sigh. "It's obvious we're not going to resolve this tonight." He touched a gentle hand to her cheek, sending a shiver all the way to her toes. "Let's just go to bed."

She pulled back as if she'd been burned. She was angry with him, but furious at the way her heart turned somersaults when he touched her.

"Things will look better in the morning," he said.

The notion he could sleep after vowing to unload on Mallory and Veronica the way he had on Ben this evening infuriated her.

"I'm sleeping on the couch tonight," she declared, "and every night until you come to your senses. And if you haven't by the time we get home, I'll move into one of the kid's old rooms."

One look at Devon's crestfallen face made her want to take it back, but pride wouldn't let her.

He opened his mouth to say something, then clamped it shut.

"Suit yourself," he said finally.

Eva pushed off the couch and walked over to the bed. She snatched one of the pillows, tossed it onto the sofa and plopped down next to it. Unfortunately, a television was purposely left out of the honeymoon suite, so she'd have to make do reading a magazine left on the end table.

The room was quiet, except for the sound of her occasionally turning a page. She heard the rustle of Devon pulling his sweater over his head and taking off the shirt beneath it.

Earlier tonight she'd anticipated being the one to strip off his clothes. They'd been married for decades, yet it had been a while since she'd seen her husband's bare chest.

Between her job and chasing after their grandkids most evenings, they fell asleep as soon as their heads hit the pillow. Or they'd get into an argument and end up retreating to opposite sides of the bed.

She peeked at him from the corner of her eye. She had to admit, Devon Masters wasn't merely fine for a man his age. He was damned fine for a man of *any* age.

Barefoot and with his back to her, he emptied his pants pockets of his wallet and keys. It gave her a chance to look at him unnoticed. The shoulders she'd clung to earlier were as broad as she remembered, and her fingers itched to touch his well-muscled back and arms.

Closing her eyes briefly, she tried to summon her anger. However, her brain wouldn't kick into gear. Instead it silently screamed for him to turn around so she could get a glimpse of his still-flat abs.

Then Eva heard his pants unzip and watched them, along with his underwear, drop to the floor.

A gasp escaped her lips before she could stop it. His butt was as enticing as the rest of him. He stepped out of his clothes and turned around.

Her throat went dry at the sight of him in his full glory.

"What are you doing?" Her voice sounded raspy to her own ears.

"Going to bed," he said, matter-of-factly.

"Didn't you bring a robe or pajamas or something?"

"I didn't think I'd need them." He held up his arms. "Besides, there isn't anything here you haven't seen already."

Her eyes remained riveted. What began as a stolen glance had turned into a full-fledged ogle. She couldn't look away, not even when his body stirred to attention under the intensity of her gaze.

Devon's eyes issued an unspoken invitation as he slipped into the huge, four-poster bed.

Eva bit down on her bottom lip. Looking at him was like staring at the last pint of chocolate ice cream in the grocery store freezer after enduring months of dieting hell.

"Go 'head," a tiny voice urged in the back of her head. "One little taste won't hurt."

Fortunately, or maybe unfortunately, the common sense she'd earlier summoned decided to finally make an appearance.

Eva tried not to think about what she was missing tonight as she switched off the lamp on the table beside her. She stretched out on the sofa, closed her eyes and prayed for the oblivion of sleep.

Chapter Four

Eva finally dozed off at four A.M.

Devon knew because he'd lain awake all night listening to her toss on the sofa, and then finally to the rhythmic sound of her deep breathing.

He'd given up on getting any sleep himself around five. So he quietly showered and dressed.

Now he sat on a chair near the sofa looking down at his sleeping wife, wondering how last night could have gone so wrong?

Their date had started out great. It made him believe bringing her here to escape their problems had indeed been a good idea. Then their son's call confirmed those problems were not in Miami but with them.

If only he could do what Eva wanted, he thought. Just sit back and watch her continue to beat herself up over something that wasn't her fault.

Devon reached out his hand to smooth an errant lock of hair from her sleeping face, then pulled it back. As much as he wanted to see her happy, he knew he couldn't ignore their issue. Not anymore.

Eva stirred and her eyes slowly opened. For a split second, they seemed to brighten at seeing him, but just as quickly he saw them cloud over with memories of last night's fight.

The word *sorry* sat on the tip of his tongue, but he wouldn't lie to her. While the fact he'd hurt her filled him with remorse, he wasn't sorry for what he'd said to Ben. He'd meant every word.

"Morning," he said, breaking the silence.

"G'morning," she muttered groggily, stretching her arms over her head. He could almost hear the muscles in her neck and back groan in protest.

She sat up and pivoted until her feet touched the floor. Her elbows on her knees, she leaned forward and dropped her head into her hands.

His wife wasn't great at mornings in the best of circumstances. He imagined waking up in a strange place after a night on an uncomfortable sofa made this one even worse for her.

He stood, walked over to where she was sitting and held out his hand. She stared at it a moment before grasping it and allowing him to pull her into a standing position.

She came up a little faster than he anticipated and bumped into his chest. Instinctively, Devon put his hands on her arms to steady her.

It was all he could do not to touch his lips to her forehead and kiss the memories away. Then gently caress her until the sadness lifted from her pretty face. And finally, lay her on that huge bed, which had been so lonely without her, and make love to her until she couldn't tell where her body left off and his began.

Instead, he let her go.

Eva stumbled off to the bathroom and moments later he heard the shower. When she emerged clad in her worn terry robe, he handed her a cup of hot coffee he'd brought from the cart in the lobby.

"Thanks," she said, immediately taking a big gulp. He watched her close her eyes briefly, as she did every morning, to savor the first sip. She sighed and opened them, turning her attention to him.

"We need to talk, don't we?"

Eva's question was hesitant. He knew it was because she wasn't sure there was anything left to be said. Like him, she wasn't sorry, but also she hated the arguments and awful tension they left behind.

He glanced down at his watch. "We don't have time right now. You have an appointment at the lodge spa." He shrugged. "I made it back when I booked the trip."

She shook her head. "I don't know. After last night, a spa day seems frivolous."

"That's why I insist you go," he said. "I want you to do something frivolous."

Chapter Five

Eva read the sign above the doorway to the lodge's spa tearoom.

"We take that sign seriously around here," said the blonde, pink-smocked attendant with matching pink lip gloss and nails. "We want our guests to leave the outside world behind once they step into our relaxation tearoom."

After yesterday's reality check in the bathroom mirror, putting herself in the spa's hands didn't seem like such a bad idea, Eva thought. Worries of Devon sending her here because he too had noticed how frumpy she'd grown crossed her mind, but she decided to take the sign's advice.

She adjusted the belt on the fluffy, white spa robe and stepped into the tearoom.

Soft lighting, plants and the melodious tinkle of harp strings greeted her on the other side. The soothing atmosphere in the lavender-infused room made her feel like she had indeed walked out of her life and into a trouble-free Shangri-la.

Other robe-clad women and a few men lounged about awaiting treatments. Meanwhile, an array of teas and fresh fruit were spread out on a buffet in the corner for sampling.

After pouring herself a cup of Earl Grey tea and adding

a sprig of grapes to the rim of the saucer, Eva took a seat on a chaise, leaned back and allowed the harp music to wash over her.

"School teacher, right?" asked a woman curled up in a nearby oversized chair. Her hair was a striking shade of gray and shorn in a spiky cut.

"Is it that obvious?" Eva replied.

"Air of authority, ramrod straight posture, tiny wrinkle between your eyes from scowling." The woman, whose flawless skin belied her silver hair, hoisted a delicate china teacup in camaraderie before taking a sip. "As my students would say, it takes one to know one."

Eva laughed, instantly taking a liking to her.

"Guilty as charged. I teach art."

"I'm a French teacher." The woman set her tea on the table separating their chairs. "By the way, I'm Katie."

"Enchanté. Je m'appelle Eva."

"Ahhhh, parlez-vous francais?"

"Je parle un peu," Eva said with a chuckle. "Very little. Just what I can remember from decades-old college classes, back when my master plan was to take the Parisian art scene by storm."

The statement popped out of her mouth so easily. Yet she hadn't thought about Paris or, for that matter, her own artist goal in years. She blew lightly on her still steaming tea before venturing a taste. Long-forgotten memories of spending hours in her studio sketching and painting came flooding back to the forefront of her mind.

She recalled the early days of her marriage, when she would start painting the moment Devon left for work in the mornings and greet him in the evenings covered in paint spatters and smelling of turpentine. Back then she would get so engrossed in her work, she'd lose all track of time.

"You still paint?" Katie asked.

"No, that's ancient history," Eva said, feeling an expected pang of longing. She brushed it off by changing the subject. "So, Katie, what brings a nice schoolteacher like you to a ski resort in the middle of nowhere for the holiday?"

"Actually, I live in a town five miles from here on the other side of the village," she said. "One of the parents gave me a spa gift certificate for Christmas. What about you?"

"My husband surprised me with this trip. We're from Miami."

Katie raised a brow. "Doesn't sound like it's a pleasant surprise."

"I feel bad about abandoning my kids and grandchildren," she said glumly. "What about you, married? Kids?"

Katie stared down at her tea. "Widowed. I have a son and a daughter, both grown. One lives in Texas and the other in California."

Eva's heart went out to her. She couldn't imagine life without Devon or with her kids scattered across the country. She wouldn't know what to do with herself.

"You must miss them terribly."

"And there isn't a day that passes I don't miss my husband. Fred was my best friend," Katie said sadly.

"I'm sorry," Eva offered. "Have you thought about moving near one of your children?"

Katie looked at her as if she'd grown a third eyeball in the center of her forehead.

"God, no," she said, waving her hand. "Don't get me wrong, I love when they visit and vice versa. But having them around was like another full-time job."

Eva's eyes widened as Katie continued.

"It was always, 'Mom, I need this' or 'Mom, can you do that.' From the time I got off work until the time I went to bed, I was busy running errands and doing favors," she said. "They were grown, mind you, and as demanding as toddlers."

Eva absently reached for another grape. "But as a mom don't you feel obligated to help, no matter how old they are?"

"I do," Katie said, "if they need something."

The woman's conflicting statements puzzled Eva. "But you just said—"

"Eva, dear, there's a big difference between them truly *needing* me and them *wanting* me to be their combination housekeeper, nanny and ATM machine."

Eva sat motionless as Katie's comments sunk in. For the first time, doubt trickled into her mind. Her new acquaintance's philosophy sounded an awful lot like Devon's. Could her husband have a point? Was she in the wrong?

"What about preserving a sense of family?" Before Katie could speak, Eva rushed an apology. "I hope my inquiry doesn't come off as condescending. I'm not questioning your love for your children. I only hope for some—understanding."

Katie smiled. "If you mean my relationship with them, yes, it's shifted, but for the better," she said. "It took me a while to come to grips with it, but the job of parenting them is over. We're all adults."

"But you're still their mother."

"Now I'm their mother and their friend." Katie's blue eyes bore into Eva's like somehow the woman knew what she'd been going through.

What had began as friendly chitchat had left Eva more troubled. At least before she'd been positive Devon was wrong.

Now she wasn't so sure.

"So what's your resolution for the upcoming year?" Katie's voice broke into her thoughts.

Saving my marriage, Eva said to herself. "I haven't really thought about it," she said aloud. "What about you? What do you want in the new year?"

"Actually, I've already laid the groundwork for my resolution." Katie's eyes practically sparkled. "I'm taking early retirement at the end of the school year," she said. "In the fall, I start cooking classes at Le Cordon Bleu in Paris."

"Oh, Katie. How exciting!"

"It's what I've always wanted to do, but I was too scared."

Eva couldn't help admire her new friend for following her dream. "I envy you."

"Well then, you'll have to come for a visit. Perhaps you can rediscover your inner artist?"

Eva chewed at her bottom lip as she contemplated the comment. Katie had caught her off guard and dredged up long-forgotten aspirations. Was there an artist still inside her, she wondered.

"Nowadays, I'm really busy with my grandchildren," Eva said.

"Mrs. Masters?"

Eva looked up at a redhead dressed in the spa's pink uniform.

"I'm Rhonda, your masseuse. If you'll follow me, we'll get started."

Placing her other hand over Katie's, Eva smiled. "It was nice talking to you," she said. "Good luck in Paris."

"Happy New Year, Eva."

"The same to you."

"Eva, before you go, I want to tell you my New Year's resolution."

"I thought it was to go to cooking school in Paris?"

Katie shook her head. "No, it was to finally do something just for me."

Whoever started the myth that snow was soft hadn't spent two hours falling on their butt in it, Devon thought.

"Mr. Masters, remember to flex your legs," the snowboarding instructor said, "and your upper body should be facing the same direction as your front foot."

If anything, Devon wanted to use his foot to kick his own behind, but it was already sore from falling. In fact, there wasn't a square inch of him that wasn't begging for mercy.

Ignoring the protests of his body, he slowly pulled himself to his feet. *You're over fifty, man, you should have known better*, he silently scolded himself.

What on earth had possessed him to schedule a snowboarding lesson anyway? When he booked it last month, he thought it would be fun to try out a new sport while Eva was at the spa. He was in decent shape, and it looked so easy on ESPN.

He'd have been better off trying to catch up on the sleep he'd missed last night or kicked back by one of the lodge's many fireplaces nursing a hot toddy, he thought.

But sleeping or sitting alone would have only given him more time to replay yesterday's events. He looked downhill at the lodge as his thoughts once again drifted to Eva. He wondered if she was enjoying the spa and hoped her morning of pampering had softened her heart toward him.

"You ready to give it another go?" asked the instructor, who didn't look much older than Thomas.

Devon nodded. Moving with the agility of a ninety-year-old, he clamped his back foot onto his board.

He heaved a sigh of relief when it didn't immediately begin sliding away, like it had the last five times.

"Okay, good. Now give yourself a wiggle to set off, like I showed you."

Devon's board glided a total of two inches before he hit the ground again, hard.

The instructor gave him a pitying look. "Maybe you've had enough for one day," he said.

Devon removed the rented snowboard from his feet before he stood up and took off his goggles. "I think you're right."

A half hour later, he was stepping out of a hot shower that had pelted a good deal of the soreness from his muscles. He rotated his shoulder. Only a mild twinge. Then again, he hadn't fallen on his shoulder.

He exited the bathroom with only a towel wrapped around his waist, to pull clean underwear from his suitcase. The door to the room opened, and Eva walked in.

After thirty years of marriage, his wife walking in when he wasn't dressed shouldn't have felt awkward, but it did.

He stared at her, momentarily taken aback. The woman before him looked like a fresh, updated version of his wife. Her mocha complexion was radiant, and he had to stop himself from running his hands through the shiny mane of hair falling onto her shoulders in gorgeous dark waves.

Devon allowed his gaze to slide downward. Her fingernails were painted red, and the salon flip-flops on her feet revealed toenails painted the same sultry shade.

"You look pretty." His mature voice sounded like that of a boy picking up his junior prom date.

"Thanks," Eva said.

Her focus dropped to the towel wrapped around his waist. "I know you didn't bring pajamas, but you did pack clothes for this trip," she said, the corner of her mouth quirked upwards in a hint of a smile.

They shared a clumsy laugh, before he changed into a light gray sweater and a pair of charcoal slacks.

"I figured we could grab lunch at the restaurant downstairs," he said. "We need to discuss last night, and where our relationship goes from here."

Chapter Six

Eva felt like a death row inmate on the way to the electric chair instead of a diner about to have lunch.

She'd known since this morning she and Devon were going to try to talk things out again. However, this afternoon she saw something different in the depths of her husband's dark brown eyes. Something she couldn't quite identify, a resoluteness, maybe.

It made her wonder if Devon hadn't reached the end of his rope with both her and their family. Perhaps he'd come to the conclusion they weren't worth the aggravation, and his life would be simpler without them.

Although the lodge's restaurant was busy with the lunch crowd, they managed to snag a table by a window offering a panoramic view of the slopes. Eva stared at the skiers whooshing down them and frolicking in the snow and wished she and Devon's holiday was as carefree.

A waiter came by with menus, but she didn't need one. "Just coffee," she said.

Her appetite had vanished, and she silently prayed her marriage wasn't about to disappear along with it.

Thirty years was a long time, but she'd known couples together even longer calling it quits. For instance, the Davidsons, who lived two doors down from them, had divorced after forty-four years of marriage.

Eva chewed the inside of her lip as she fought to rein in her runaway thoughts. Images of bumping into

Mr. Davidson six months ago when she'd taken Thomas to the pediatrician's office flooded her mind. The senior citizen sat in the waiting room, with his young girlfriend and their new baby, wearing a huge dentured grin.

Devon ordered a burger and fries and paused until the waiter left. "I thought this trip would help us sort this out, but so far it hasn't."

Eva stared down at the crisp, linen tablecloth and waited for her husband to break her heart. They'd been hopelessly deadlocked over the same issues for a long time.

Too long.

"So what I think we should do . . ."

The waiter placed Eva's coffee on the table.

"Your lunch will be up momentarily, sir," he said.

Devon nodded and turned his attention back to her. "I propose we call a truce for the rest of the year."

Relief hit Eva first, followed by confusion. "But New Year's Eve is tomorrow."

"Exactly," Devon said with a nod. "And it's the first time we've been away together in years." He waved his hand toward the window. "It's beautiful here, don't you want to enjoy it?"

"Didn't we try that yesterday?" she asked, not quite following him.

"That's where the truce comes in. Let's temporarily table any discussion about the kids until we're back in Miami next year," he said, as if the notion was a stroke of genius. "Meanwhile, we relax and explore what the resort has to offer."

His idea sounded fine in principle, but Eva wasn't so sure about the reality of it.

"What if one of the kids calls up again?" she said, bringing up one of the land mines that could potentially blow any truce to bits. She wasn't trying to be uncooperative, just realistic. "I'm uncomfortable cutting off my cell phone."

She braced herself for Devon to get upset and tell her to just forget the whole thing. Instead, he reached across the table for her hand.

"I'm willing to compromise," he said. "If they call and I find myself getting angry over your conversation, I'll walk it off."

The waiter brought Devon's food, and her husband released her hand. Devon immediately popped two fries into his mouth.

"So what do you think?" he asked before reaching for more fries.

It certainly wouldn't work long-term, and there was something odd about them avoiding the topic of their own children. On the other hand, it was only for a little more than a day.

"Okay, we'll try it."

"Great," he said. "From now until the end of the year, we'll just concern ourselves with the here and now. And cramming in as much fun as we can stand."

She gave a bright smile. "I like the sound of that."

Devon frowned.

"Did I say something wrong?"

"No, I forgot something. I'll be back."

Eva helped herself to a few fries and a pickle from his plate, while she waited. Her appetite having returned with a vengeance, she signaled the waiter and ordered a salad. She was about to dig into it when Devon returned, holding what appeared to be a Christmas present.

"This is for you." He placed a box, wrapped in tattered holiday paper, on the table. "It's a belated Christmas present."

"But you already gave me my gift," she said.

Devon sat down. "No, I got this for you last year."

Overcome with curiosity, Eva pushed aside her salad and began ripping away the paper. She hesitated a moment, savoring the anticipation, before opening the slightly dented box.

"Devon," she whispered, lifting a metal tin filled with an assortment of charcoal sketching pencils and two thick sketch pads from the box.

Her earlier conversation with Katie flashed through her mind. How did her husband know she'd been thinking about her long-lost art, she wondered. Then it occurred to her Devon had purchased the supplies over a year ago.

He couldn't have known.

"I realize it's been a long time, but sketching and painting used to mean so much to you," he said. "I figured you might have a little time up here. You know, more than at home."

She opened the tin and ran her hand over the pencils. "I love it." She tore her gaze away from the precious pencils and pads to face him. "Why did you wait so long to give it to me?"

He shrugged. "You always said when the kids were grown you were going to quit teaching. Remember, you were going to paint while we traveled the world." His voice took on a wistful tone. "Nowadays you're so preoccupied, I wasn't sure if you'd changed your mind or simply lost interest."

At the moment, Eva wasn't sure herself. Her thoughts and emotions were in chaos.

When she arrived here yesterday, all she wanted to do was go home. Her kids and grandchildren were foremost in her mind. Now she looked forward to enjoying their mini-vacation in earnest and tinkering around with her new gift.

"Happy?" Devon asked.

Before she could answer, her cell phone rang. She hesitated a moment before retrieving it from her purse. She glanced at the Caller ID.

"It's Veronica."

They both stared awkwardly at the ringing phone as if they were afraid to test the strength of their fragile treaty.

"Go ahead, answer it," Devon heard himself say aloud, knowing deep down it was the last thing he wanted her to do.

He hated feeling that way, because he truly adored their Veronica. A "daddy's girl" from the moment they brought her home from the hospital, she was sweet, calm and levelheaded.

At least she used to be.

Her recent engagement had turned her into the bride from hell. It was like she walked into Superman's phone booth a mild-mannered accountant and came out a raving lunatic.

The wedding, or, as Veronica called it, "my moment on the red carpet" was over nine months away. However, every detail sent their daughter into a hysterical fit that Eva held audience to.

Devon watched his wife blow out a breath as she flipped open the phone.

"Hi, Roni."

Devon wasn't sure what Veronica was saying, but if the outraged shrieks coming from the phone to his side of the table were any indication, it wasn't good.

Eva's eyes widened. "Oh, dear."

Devon picked at one of his now-cold fries. Whatever was going on with Veronica and no matter how Eva reacted to it, he would remain calm, he vowed. He was not going to let it ruin his vow to her.

Eva held the phone away from her ear a moment and looked up at him. "Veronica and Joan got into a huge fight, and now Joan refuses to be her maid of honor," Eva whispered to him.

Devon pasted what he hoped passed for a concerned look on his face. Their daughter and their next-door neighbors' daughter, Joan, had been best friends since kindergarten. They'd always had little squabbles, but they never lasted long.

To Devon, it didn't seem like a big deal.

The waiter cleared their plates and left the check.

"Well, honey, to the untrained eye orange and tangerine might look the same," Eva said in what he recognized as her diplomatic schoolteacher tone. "And it probably isn't Joan's best color."

Devon watched his wife wince at the sound of their daughter's protests coming loudly through the phone.

"No, I don't think you're trying to make her look like a big pumpkin."

This time Devon felt his eyes go wide, and he stifled a laugh. The thought of redheaded, freckle-faced Joan in an orange dress brought pumpkins to his mind too.

"I know orange—eh, I mean tangerine is your favorite color."

The noise from Eva's phone sounded an awful lot like the squawks of the off-screen adults in a *Peanuts* cartoon.

"Yes, I realize that you're the bride and it's supposed to be your day."

Squawk.

"I'm sure Joan didn't mean to say you purposely picked

unflattering bridesmaid dresses. She loves you. She's your best friend."

Squawk.

"Honey, I don't think it's a good idea for me to get involved."

Squawk.

"No, I wasn't trying to make you cry. Please don't cry."

Devon took Eva's tone as his cue to get out of there. Besides, it sounded like she was going to wind up playing referee for Veronica and Joan.

He paid the check and left the restaurant. Spotting Bev as he crossed the lobby, he walked over to the front desk.

She greeted him with her always-present smile. Today, she wore a blue sweater with large, white snowflake appliqués.

"How are you and your new bride enjoying your stay with us?"

"Just fine," he said. "Bev, I need your help."

Her halo of gray curls bounced as she nodded for him to continue.

"Where's the most romantic spot around here?" he asked. "I'd like to take my wife someplace off the beaten path."

Bev's eyes narrowed in thought, then brightened. "Well, where I have in mind is popular in the fall with the leaf peepers. Personally, I think it's more romantic at this time of year."

Devon leaned across the counter as Bev filled him in.

"I don't know, Bev," he said, stroking his chin. "She's not exactly the outdoors type."

Devon had little more than a day to make this weekend special for his wife. He couldn't afford any wrong moves.

"Once you get there it'll be worth it," Bev said. "Trust me."

"Okay," Devon nodded, putting their afternoon in Bev's hands. They were finalizing the details when Eva walked up.

He'd expected to see the stress from dealing with their daughter on her face, but was pleasantly surprised. Her brow was free of worry lines, and she was actually smiling.

"You okay?" he asked hesitantly.

"Fine."

"And Veronica?"

She looped her arm through his. "I managed to calm her down without having to mediate between her and Joan." She looked at Bev and back to him again. "So what are you two up to?"

"That's for us to know—" Devon began.

"—and you to find out," Bev finished for him with a wink.

Chapter Seven

Eva's curiosity was peaked—right up until the moment Devon handed her a pair of snowshoes.

"I feel like a clown." She hoisted one foot in the air before letting it plop to the snow-covered ground with a crunch.

When her husband had said he'd planned the perfect nonskier afternoon, she'd envisioned sipping champagne in a hot tub or checking out the village shops.

She hadn't expected to spend the last half hour hiking.

Devon Masters had been married to her long enough to know she wasn't an outdoors girl. For her, getting back to nature meant picking up carrots from the organic section of the grocery store.

Devon sidled over to her. Leaving room for their oversized footgear, he dropped a kiss on the tip of her nose. "You look adorable."

Eva had on so many layers under her parka, she knew she looked more like the chubby, biscuit doughboy than a supermodel.

"Yeah, right," she said. "I'll bet you say that to all the women you convince to hang out with you in the frozen tundra."

Devon rested his foot on a boulder and tilted his face to the afternoon sky. "You have to admit, it's a beautiful day," he said.

Shielding her eyes with her hand, she craned her neck to

follow his gaze. The sun shone high in the sky, but its far-away rays didn't provide any heat. Instead they bounced off the snow and bathed the afternoon in dazzling sunshine.

Eva's eyes fell to her husband. The same sun high-lighted Devon's most attractive features. She could see the flecks of toffee in his brown eyes and the burnished red tones just beneath the surface of his mahogany skin.

Though out of his element in the winter setting, he cast an aura of power that brought to mind an Artic explorer standing victorious at the top of a conquered mountain.

Eva's throat went dry with desire, and she swallowed, hard.

"Yes," she said, her voice barely a whisper. "Beautiful."

"Well, we'd better get going." He pulled his foot off the rock, adjusted the pack on his back and placed a gloved hand on her arm.

A zing of awareness penetrated her clothing where he touched her and her toes curled inside her boots.

Eva's mind flashed to their sleigh ride. Devon could have stripped her naked, laid her on that bench and had her right there—even with the driver watching. Her teeth sunk into her bottom lip. Who was she kidding? He could have her right here. Right now.

All he had to do was ask.

Her husband's voice interrupted the illicit scene play-ing out in her head. "You look flushed. Are you sure you're okay?" he asked.

She cleared her throat as if she could wipe away the vivid images of her husband trailing kisses from the sweet spot behind her ear down to her collarbone.

"I'm fine," she said.

He removed a glove and touched the back of his hand to her forehead. "You don't feel hot."

Oh, but I am, she thought.

"It shouldn't be much farther," he said, oblivious to her wayward thoughts.

They continued their trek through the snow. Eva's feet had adjusted to the snowshoes, enabling her to keep pace with her husband's longer stride.

"Look. Over there." She tugged Devon's coat and pointed out a deer with its young fawn. The mother grazed on a bush while its child ate off a lower-sitting shrub.

The foraging deer spotted them and moved closer to the fawn. "She thinks she needs to protect it from us," Devon observed.

"That's what mothers do," Eva said, feeling a kindred spirit with the animal. "They protect their babies."

Her husband took her gloved hand in his, before bringing it to his mouth. He closed his eyes and kissed it. When his eyes opened, they were filled with what appeared to be understanding.

Eva's heart split open with love for him.

Hand in hand, they left the deer to their meal. They continued walking until Devon stopped at a snow-covered table. Before Eva could wonder why it was sitting in the middle of nowhere, he cleared the snow off the tabletop with a swipe of his arm. He pulled the two chairs from beneath the table and brushed the snow off them, too.

Eva stood by, quietly speculating on what her husband had up his sleeve. She watched him shrug the pack off his back and set it on one of the chairs. He pulled a white linen tablecloth from the bag and covered the round, wooden table. Then he produced a bottle of wine and two glasses.

Next, he held out one of the chairs for her, then sat in the one beside it. She looked out at the mountains surrounding them. They were covered with snow and dotted with evergreens and barren trees. Without the hoards of vacationers swarming around with skis, snowboards and sleds, they looked majestic and peaceful.

Devon poured them each a glass of wine. He lifted his glass and she touched hers to it with a soft clink.

The wine, fruity with a hint of vanilla, warmed her insides.

"It's a local wine," Devon filled her in. "Made with blueberries grown right here in New Hampshire."

Having removed his snowshoes, Devon put his boots on the table and leaned back in his chair. He reached into his pocket and pulled out two foil-wrapped chocolates. He handed one to her.

"From your pillow last night," he said.

She put the bite of candy on her tongue and closed her mouth over the treat. The velvety, sweet chocolate was the perfect complement to the local wine.

"The view of the mountains is amazing. I have to admit it was worth the walk." She scanned the horizon and took another sip of wine. "The company's pretty amazing, too."

"This is what I wanted for you, for us, you know?" Her husband's deep voice softened.

"What, the trip or the view?"

"No, for us," Devon said. "I sold the business so we could spend time together like this."

Surprised, Eva put her wineglass on the table and turned her full attention to her husband. "But I thought you sold it because they made an incredible offer."

Devon shook his head. "The figure was eye-popping, but money isn't the reason I accepted," he said. "I saw it as an opportunity for us to get to know one another again."

Eva tried to follow, but he'd lost her. She'd been with Devon nearly all of her adult life. He knew her better than anyone.

"We've been married three decades, we're together every day," she said.

"No, we're present every day, and like two business partners, we discuss our joint holdings. Our conversations revolve around finances, the house, car repairs or the kids."

Devon took his boots off the table and leaned forward. He gently placed his hand over her heart, and Eva covered it with her smaller one.

"We never talk about *us* anymore," he said.

Embarrassed, she said, "I didn't realize . . ."

"I love our family, but I'm more than ready to embrace our empty nest. We need to rediscover ourselves as a couple," he said. "I want us to travel the world, sleep naked and make love in the middle of the afternoon."

Eva breathed a half sigh, half swoon. It sounded so perfect. Why hadn't she thought of it herself? She squeezed his hand. "We have plenty of time to do those things."

"I'm over fifty, and we have the opportunity. The time is now."

She dropped her hand to her lap, unsure of how to reply to her husband's words, which still hung in the chilly air.

"Well, I'm sure you're ready to head back to the lodge and get out of the cold," he finally said.

Eva hesitated. Despite the cold, she wasn't ready for their date to end. "Not yet. There's something I'd like to do first."

Devon's raised an inquiring brow.

"I want to build a snowman."

"A snowman?" His eyes narrowed. "Do you even know how to build a snowman?"

"No," she said with a shrug. "But between the both of us we'll figure it out."

Eva felt as giddy as a kid Thomas's age as she surveyed

the clearing for the perfect spot to build her very first snowman.

"How about over here?" Devon said.

She considered it a moment, before frowning and shaking her head. "I want him to have a good view of the mountains," she said. "How about over there?"

"It's a snowman, Eva, not a tourist."

She rolled her eyes skyward and heaved an exaggerated sigh. "Okay, let's compromise." She walked to the mid-point between the spots they'd chosen.

Dropping to her knees, she began gathering snow in a pile, like a poker winner collecting his pot. Once she'd pulled together a big enough mound, she figured she'd start shaping it into a ball.

Devon came up carrying a soccer ball-size chunk of snow. She looked up at him.

"Is that for the middle?"

"No, the base."

"I'm already working on the base."

Devon shook his head. "That's not the way to do it. We'll roll my ball through the snow. It'll pick up more snow as we roll it." He paused. "Make sense?"

Eva thought about it a moment. "No, it doesn't."

"But it's more efficient than what you're doing."

"Then maybe you should work on your own more efficient snowman."

"Maybe I will. That way I'll have time to enjoy another glass of wine while you dillydally around with that." He looked down at the pile of snow that would eventually form the base of her perfect snowman.

Eva caught the smirk on his face, just before he turned away.

* * *

Thwack!

He should have never turned his back on her, Devon thought. He whirled around, only to be slammed by a second snowball. This one, lacking the dead-on aim of the first—which landed in the center of his back—grazed his shoulder.

Devon looked down at his wife, who was lifting yet another snow missile over her shoulder. She looked like a quarterback about to launch a Hail Mary pass.

"You don't want to do that."

His wife's eyes flicked to the snowball and back to him. "I think I do," she said mischievously.

He took one slow step toward her. "I'd advise you to drop it." He lowered his voice an octave. "Now."

She raised a perfectly arched brow. "That sounds like a threat." Her tone was teasing. "I don't take well to being threatened, Mr. Masters."

"Put the snowball down, Eva. Make it easy on yourself."

"Okay."

"Just like that?"

"Yep." Still kneeling, she held the snowball out in front of her and let it drop to the ground.

Unease settled over him. It wasn't like Eva to give up so easy, and it really wasn't like her to do what she was told. Then again, she had to know there was no way she could beat him in a snowball fight. She'd just saved herself from the embarrassment of defeat.

"Now wipe that smug look off your face, and let's get out of here," she said.

"What about your snowman?"

She patted her mound of snow. "Maybe another time."

"I'll gather up our things." He looked up at the sky. Clouds had overtaken the sun from earlier that afternoon and snowflakes were drifting toward the ground.

"How about helping me up first?" She extended her hand.

Devon leaned over and grasped her hand.

He spotted the wicked gleam in her eye a second too late. She yanked his arm. The unexpected pull knocked him off balance, and he tumbled face-first into her mound of snow.

Spitting snow out of his mouth, he looked up to see her scooting backward crab-walk style with a huge grin on her face.

"Oh, no you don't." Devon's arm shot out and grabbed her boot, dragging her toward him.

"Nooooo," she squealed, then giggled. "I didn't mean to do it. I'm sorry!"

"No, you aren't, but you're going to be," he growled, stifling the urge to laugh along with her.

The next thing he knew, she was lying beneath him, looking as lovely as she did the day they married. Time melted away as he stared into her big, brown eyes. It was as if he was holding her for the very first time.

Devon brushed his lips against hers. He'd only meant it as a simple peck. Then she gasped. And he knew he had to have more.

He kissed her again. If the first kiss was tentative and tender, then this one was hard and demanding. She tasted faintly of blueberries and chocolate. Holding her tightly in his arms, he rolled over so she was on top of him, never taking his mouth from hers.

When they finally came up for air, she moaned softly and he fought the urge to kiss her all over again.

There was so much he wanted to say to her right now. He wanted to tell her how desperately he missed holding her like this, touching and kissing her. And no disagreement was worth their not making love for such a long time.

But the snow was falling harder now, and they needed to head back to the lodge before it covered their path.

A blast of blessed heat greeted them when they walked into the lodge.

"Are you sure you don't want to keep the footwear?" he asked Eva as they stood on a mat, stomping the remaining snow from their boots. "I'm sure the rental shop would be willing to sell them to us. After all, don't they say a girl can never have enough shoes?"

Laughing, his wife shook her head. "I'll pass, but I want you to hang on to this generous, shoe-buying mood the next time we're in Macy's."

Devon spotted Beverly behind the front desk. Holding Eva's hand, he walked over, intending to thank her for her help. The expression on her face when she looked up stopped him cold.

Instead of a smile, her lips were pressed into a thin line. "Mr. and Mrs. Masters, I'm afraid there's a problem," she said nervously.

Devon felt his gut clench at the word *problem*. He'd thought he had a reprieve from them until the clock struck twelve tomorrow night.

"I'm afraid the heater in your room is on the blink," she said. "Maintenance won't be able to fix it until after the holiday."

Devon released a breath he hadn't realized he'd been holding. The honeymoon suite was nice, but it wasn't as if he was attached to it. Another room, even minus the space of the suite and fantastic view, would be fine by him. He just wanted to be alone with his wife.

"Where are you moving us?" he asked.

Bev averted her eyes to avoid his gaze. "That's just it. We're booked solid for the holiday. There aren't any vacancies."

"Oh my," Eva said, her eyes troubled.

Devon squeezed her hand. "Don't worry. We'll find someplace else. I believe I saw a hotel in the village."

"They're booked, too," Beverly said. "I've been on the phone making calls for hours. There isn't a room available at a hotel, inn or lodge within a hundred-mile radius of here."

"I don't understand," Eva said. "Isn't the building centrally heated? It feels warm to me."

Beverly nodded. "We've been renovating a bit at a time during the off-season. The section you're staying in isn't on central heat yet."

Devon couldn't believe what he was hearing, and from the look of alarm on her face, neither did Eva.

"What are we going to do?" she asked.

Devon pulled back his coat sleeve and looked at his watch, trying to calculate how much time he could shave off the two and a half hour drive to the airport in Manchester. "We'll catch a flight back to Miami tonight."

Bev shook her head slowly, and his gut clenched tighter. "The airport is closed. Manchester's already got over a foot of snow today and it's still coming down," she said. "The storm that slammed them is heading our way."

Devon felt like he was trying to pull himself out of quicksand. Every move just pulled him deeper into the quagmire.

"So what are our options—camping out in the lobby?"

"Well, you could stay in your room," Bev offered.

"But it's ten degrees outside," Eva said.

The desk clerk held up her hands in a hear-me-out gesture. "Only the heater isn't working. The hot water, electricity and fireplace are just fine," she said. "We've already taken the liberty of starting the fire and bringing up extra logs."

Devon looked at his wife as he weighed the option.

"It'll give you honeymooners some privacy," she said.

He felt Eva squeeze his hand.

"We'll stay in our room," Eva said, making the decision for them. She looked up at him. "It'll be fine."

Devon nodded. "Okay. We'll change out of this snow gear, then come back down to the restaurant for dinner."

He heard Bev clear her throat.

"Please don't tell me the restaurant is closed," he said.

"Oh, no. The chef prepared a special picnic hamper to make up for inconveniencing you," she said. "I'll have it sent up to your room."

"Thank you, Beverly," Eva said graciously.

This time the front desk clerk smiled full out. "It's the least we can do. After all, you only get one honeymoon," she said, then added, "If you're lucky."

Chapter Eight

"Why do you continue to let everyone here believe we're newlyweds?" Eva asked, after her husband shut the door to their room.

Her stomach growled at the delicious smells coming from the picnic basket as Devon set it on the table in front of the sofa. A thermos of hot coffee and extra blankets had been included in the bellman's delivery.

Fortunately, the fireplace had generated enough heat for them to shed their parkas and exchange their high-tech snow pants for jeans, but a slight chill remained so they opted to leave on their scarves and sweaters.

Devon shrugged. "They're all so happy for us I don't have the heart to tell them otherwise."

"Newlyweds." Eva rolled her eyes heavenward and shook her head.

"Seeing as though you're so abhorred, I'm sure you don't want any of these honeymooner goodies." Devon screwed the lid off the thermos and held it under her nose.

Eva inhaled the rich, French roast. "I'll find a way to get over it while you pour the coffee."

She pulled two sandwiches from the hamper. She peeled back the wax paper, revealing roast beef and cheddar for Devon and roasted vegetable for herself. Both sandwiches were on thick slabs of homemade bread spread with stone-ground mustard.

Too famished for politeness, she dug into hers immediately. "Hungry?" Devon said, taking a seat beside her on the sofa.

She nodded and continued chewing, savoring the hearty flavors of red pepper and eggplant. "Whipping a big guy like you in a snowball fight gives a woman an appetite."

"You did not whip me." Devon picked up his sandwich. "I got sucked into helping you up, and then you yanked my arm."

"You must have tripped."

Devon laughed; the deep, rich sound sent a ripple of joy through her. It felt good to joke with him again, without worrying about their next argument about the kids.

The kids. Eva hadn't thought about them or even her grandchildren in hours. Nor did she feel the familiar pangs of guilt.

At this very moment, all she felt was happiness.

They polished off the sandwiches and the accompanying sides of salad, cheese and fruit.

"There's cake in here," Devon said, looking through the basket.

Eva yawned. "No thanks, I'm stuffed."

"And tired," he said. "Go ahead and get ready for bed. I'll clear everything away."

"Okay." She put her fist to her mouth to stifle another yawn and shuffled off to the bathroom. It was a good twenty degrees cooler in the bathroom, so she quickly slipped into her pajamas and covered them with her cardigan. Slippers and two pairs of thick socks replaced her boots.

When she emerged, she spied Devon adding another log to the fire. She grabbed a pillow from the bed, one of the extra blankets and spread them out on the couch.

"What are you doing?" Devon frowned.

"Going to bed."

"That's not the bed."

"For me it is. I told you last night . . ."

She watched him cross the room in two long strides. "I thought we'd called a truce."

"We did, but . . ."

He rubbed a hand over his short-cropped hair. "How about we both sleep on the bed, and I promise to keep my hands to myself."

Eva shook her head. "Your promise doesn't matter."

"In all these years together, I've never lied to you."

"It's not that." She averted her eyes.

Devon touched a finger to her chin and gently lifted it until she met his gaze.

"Then what is it?"

"If we both get into that bed"—she took in a shaky breath and slowly released it—"*I* won't be able to keep my hands off *you*."

Wordlessly, he walked her backward until the backs of her thighs bumped the bed. He slowly slid his finger from her chin down her neck, not stopping until he reached the dip between her breasts. Then using the same finger, he gently pushed her onto the bed.

"Show me," he said.

Panty-melting desire pooled at the juncture between her thighs at his husky request. She reached up, clamped her fingers around his sweater and pulled.

Her eyes met his darker pair. More love than she'd ever seen shone back at her. His large hand was gentle and achingly tender as it smoothed away a lock of hair that had fallen in her face.

"It's been so long for us," he whispered. His powerful erection pressed against her stomach, the heat of it penetrating her clothes. "I don't want to hurt you."

His concern for her brought it all back. Months of

going to bed angry, each of them hugging the opposite side of their king-size mattress. Nights of lying awake denying her body's plea to defect to his side of the bed and surrender to her passion.

Now everything she wanted was right before her and nothing was going to stop her from taking it.

"I don't want to hurt you, either."

A wicked gleam flashed in his eyes, and he captured her mouth in a kiss almost savage in its intensity. He thrust his tongue into her mouth, as his hand moved to her breast. Her nipple hardened instantly, straining against the layers of fabric separating it from his hand and the sweet anticipation of his mouth.

Eva clutched his broad shoulders, before her fingertips roamed down his back to his waist. There she jerked the hem of his sweater and the two shirts beneath it from his waistband.

She tore her lips from his, sacrificing the contact with his mouth for the greater reward of his nude body against hers.

"Take it off," she said, in a voice that came out in a breathless pant.

Coming up to his knees, he tugged the three garments over his head.

Her eyes dropped to his crotch. His impressive erection surged forward against his zipper, sending out a silent invitation.

Unable to resist, she ran her palm over it. Her husband drew in a sharp breath and desire flamed in his dark eyes.

"Pants, too," she commanded.

Seemingly oblivious to the chill in the air, he eagerly complied.

When he returned to the bed completely naked, her hands were all over him. They moved of their own accord, greedily exploring his chest, back and still-firm butt.

He kissed her again, and she felt herself grow damp as his hardness ground against her. So caught up in the delicious sensation of his bare skin she didn't notice he'd stripped her of her clothing until he covered her nipple with his mouth.

Pure pleasure shot through her all the way down to her core as he licked and sucked both breasts. His hand ventured down to her thighs, and she spread them wide. He pushed a finger inside her and Eva bucked so hard she thought she'd come off the bed.

"You're so wet," he whispered raggedly as he stroked her with his fingers.

Part of her didn't want him to stop. The rest of her craved more. Placing a hand against each side of his face, she raised his head to meet her gaze.

"Make love to me, Devon."

Lifting her hips, he entered her with one, smooth thrust. She clung to him and it was all she could do not to scream out his name as he moved inside her with the familiarity of a life-long lover. One who knew what she liked and was willing to give it to her hard and fast.

Again and again.

Eva arched her back to meet his pace. Each pounding stroke sent tingles through her body as it freed it from its love-starved grave.

Her walls tightened around him as her orgasm rumbled through her like a runaway freight train. Seconds later, she heard Devon moan low in his throat as he found his own release.

"I'll always love you," he said.

And like her body before it, her heart melted for him.

Rolling over, Devon did the same thing he'd done every morning for the last thirty years: reached out for his wife.

Nothing.

He peeled open his eyes to find her side of the bed empty. He sat up with a jerk, relief washing over him when he spotted her.

Eva sat on the sofa, wrapped in the fluffy white robe she'd bought at the spa. Her head was bent over her new sketch pad, while her pencil scratched furiously against the paper. She paused only occasionally to peer through the window.

She was so deep in concentration she hadn't even noticed he'd awakened. Devon leaned back on his elbows. He remained silent, not wanting to intrude. He hoped their kids would do the same and her cell phone would remain blessedly silent.

Eva deserved this time to herself, and he enjoyed having the luxury of simply watching her.

His wife never looked even more beautiful to him. Her glossy, dark hair was loose around her shoulders, providing the perfect frame for her mocha-colored face. Even at a distance he could see her lips were swollen from a night of his kisses.

Finally, she turned toward the bed. When she realized he was awake, she dropped her pencil.

"Don't stop," he said.

"What? This?" She looked down at the sketch pad.

"It's been a long time since I've seen you lose yourself in your artwork."

She cradled the pad to her chest. "I didn't know how much I'd missed it until this morning," she said. "I woke up thinking about your gift. It seemed to call out to me— if that makes any sense?"

"It does. You used to say it all the time when we were first married."

She chewed nervously on her bottom lip, and he could

tell she had something on her mind. "Actually, this trip has opened my eyes to a few things," she said. "And I owe you an apology."

Devon didn't know what she was sorry for, but as far as he was concerned his wife had done enough apologizing this weekend. "You don't owe me anything."

Eva shook her head. "No, let me finish," she said. "I took a good look at myself in the mirror the other night, and I realized how badly I'd let myself slide."

Devon opened his mouth to stop her, but she held up a silencing hand. "I'm sorry for neglecting both you and myself," she said. "Thank you for this trip, the spa day, and most of all for reminding me that despite all of my other roles in life, I'm still a woman."

"You're welcome," Devon replied.

Eva put down the sketch pad and walked over to the bed. Devon leaned his back against the headboard and pulled her down into his embrace. He grappled over whether to say something that could potentially break their fragile peace, and then he decided to take the risk.

"Eva, you don't owe me or the kids any apologies, but somehow you have to learn how to forgive yourself."

One look at her face told him she understood exactly where he was headed. "You are a fantastic mother. That fire wasn't anyone's fault; there was an electrical short in the stove. You couldn't have known the babysitter would panic and leave the kids."

"I know. Logically, I know you're right, but . . ."

"Eva, you ran into that burning house and rescued our babies," he said. "Don't squander your life being a martyr for our children when you're really a hero."

He felt her stiffen in his arms. "I thought we'd tabled discussions like this until next year."

Devon kissed the top of her head. He held her tight,

deciding not to push any further and risk losing the ground they'd gained last night. He wanted to make the most of the little time they had before the clock struck midnight and their troubles returned with a vengeance.

"So when did you fix it?" Eva's voice broke into thoughts.

"Fix what?"

"The heater. When I woke up this morning, the fire had died out but the heat was going full blast," she said. "I figured you got up sometime during the night and repaired it."

Devon looked over at the heater and it was indeed working perfectly.

"I wasn't thinking about the heater or the fireplace last night," he said. "You were putting out more heat than both of them combined."

He nuzzled her neck and she giggled.

"Well, what do you want to do today?" She asked. "It snowed all night. You interested in snowshoeing again?"

"I know you've turned into a winter sport enthusiast," he said. "But if you don't mind, I'll pass."

His body stirred as her hand slid lazily up and down his chest.

"Then how about some breakfast?" she asked. "I can order up room service. I'm sure you're starved after last night's performance."

"You know what I'd like?" He grasped her hand and moved it lower. He watched her eyes widen and a smile spread across her lips. "An encore."

Chapter Nine

If only he could stop the clock. Devon glanced down at his watch. The second hand seemed to spin around the dial at warp speed.

All too soon midnight would strike, ending the year and the truce.

Tension knotted the back of his neck, but he didn't try to rub it away. The past day and a half with his wife had been spectacular, both in and out of bed. However, they hadn't resolved anything. All they'd done was temporarily push their issues aside.

Somehow he had to figure out a way to make the magic they found here at the lodge get them through the reality waiting at home.

"So how do I look?" Eva twirled around, giving him a view of her holiday finery.

Devon wasn't in the mood for the lodge's New Year's Eve party, but he couldn't spoil the night for his wife. Who knew how many more nights they'd enjoy before one of their kids started ordering her around and he got angry?

"You're stunning," he said.

His compliment was an understatement. Eva wore a short, cream-colored cocktail dress that both hugged and flattered her curves. Her hair was swept into an updo, highlighting the delicate features of her face. Draped around her arms was a sheer, silver wrap that matched her purse and strappy high heels.

He took in her jewelry tonight and wondered if she'd selected the pieces on purpose. The pearl choker he'd given her the day Mallory was born encircled her neck. On her wrist she wore the diamond bracelet he gave her the night Veronica made her entry into the world, and the diamond studs he'd presented her with after Ben's birth adorned her ears. He glanced down at her hand and, as he expected, the emerald ring for Karen flashed up at him.

"You seem distracted. Is everything okay?" she asked.

Devon pasted a smile on his face and said all the right things to reassure her. Then he pulled her against him and kissed her. He'd only meant to buss her cheek, but the light, floral fragrance of her new perfume drew him in, turning the simple peck into something more.

When they came up for air, she wiped her red lipstick off his face. "I thought we were supposed to save the kisses for midnight." She winked. "If you keep kissing me like that, we'll never make it to the party."

Exactly, he thought. If it were up to him they wouldn't leave their room tonight. However, Eva looked so pretty and she was looking forward to it.

The party was already going full swing when they arrived after ten. A live band banged out seventies hits, while a dozen or so couples danced along.

"Look at how festive everything looks," Eva said, gazing around the ballroom.

The Christmas decorations had been replaced with silver and blue steamers and banners welcoming 2009.

"We haven't been to a party in ages." Eva practically squealed with excitement. "We're going to have so much fun."

He smiled down at her, and this time it was genuine. Despite his dreading the problems lurking in the new year, he loved seeing her so happy.

"Well, hello there," Bev said. Her springy gray curls bounced as she walked toward them. Tonight, she wore a simple but elegant green dress.

A gray-haired man was beside her. "This is my husband, Sam," she said. "Sam, these are our resident honeymooners, Devon and Eva Masters."

Devon shook Sam's extended hand as they completed the introductions.

"You look lovely, Mrs. Masters," Bev said.

"So do you," Eva said.

"No theme sweater today?" Devon asked. In the few days he'd known Bev, he'd grown accustomed to seeing her practically covered in appliqués.

Bev and Sam exchanged a look. "Well, I've kind of retired them . . ." Her voice trailed off.

"Our daughter keeps buying her those oddball sweaters and Bev here feels obligated to wear them," Sam said.

"She means well," Bev said. "Her taste has always been a bit—"

"Awful!" Sam finished for her.

Devon looked at Eva and saw she too was stifling a laugh.

"Anyhow, you've seen the last of those sweaters," Sam said. "Bev's New Year's resolution is to stop wearing them."

"But what about your daughter?" Eva asked.

Sam shrugged. "If she loves them so much, let *her* wear 'em."

Sam tugged at Bev's hand. "Let's dance."

After the older couple parted, Devon looked at Eva. "Would you like some champagne?"

She shook her head. "No, I think I'd like to dance, too."

Devon grimaced. They both knew he wasn't much of a dancer, but he didn't want to disappoint his wife.

He took her in his arms just as the band slowed down

the pace; he was grateful he could get by with simply holding her and swaying.

"Devon, I can't begin to tell you how wonderful this weekend has been," she said, slipping her arms around his neck.

Her gratitude warmed him, and he pulled her even closer. For the first time that night he let himself feel hopeful about the upcoming year.

A ringing sound immediately dashed those hopes. Eva dropped her arms. She opened her small purse and the ringing got louder. Of course, it was her phone.

"It's Mallory," she said.

Reluctantly, he dropped his arms from around her waist and mentally prepared to walk her off the dance floor. He prayed whatever their daughter wanted wouldn't destroy their entire evening.

Eva placed a restraining hand on his chest. With her other hand, she flipped open her phone.

"Hi, sweetheart."

She paused.

"Yes, that's music you hear. Daddy and I are at a party."

There was another pause, and Devon watched his wife's expression change.

"Well, you're an adult now. I'm sure you'll handle it."

Devon felt his jaw nearly hit the floor when Eva bid their daughter good night. He continued to stand there slack-jawed, unable to believe what he'd heard. Then Eva turned her phone off, flipped it closed and dropped it in his jacket pocket.

"So are you ready to resume our dance?" She touched her hand to his chin to close his mouth.

"I . . . I can't believe what I just saw and heard," he said.

"It's my resolution for the New Year."

"Are you sure about this?" He patted his jacket pocket. "What if there's an emergency?"

Eva looked up at him, her face serious. "Then our kids will work it out. That's what grown-ups do."

He pulled her back into his arms and nuzzled her neck. He placed a light kiss on the sweet spot behind her ear and felt her shiver. "Come upstairs with me, and I'll show you something else grown-ups do."

His wife nodded.

And with a kiss, the Masters welcomed a new year.

MARJORIE M. LIU

THE LAST TWILIGHT

A *Dirk & Steele* Novel

A WOMAN IN JEOPARDY

Doctor Rikki Kinn is one of the world's best virus hunters. It's for that reason she's in the Congo, working for the CDC. But when mercenaries attempt to take her life to prevent her from investigating a new and deadly plague, her boss calls in a favor from an old friend—the only one who can help.

A PRINCE IN EXILE

Against his better judgment, Amiri has been asked to return to his homeland by his colleagues in Dirk & Steele—men who are friends and brothers, who like himself are more than human. He must protect a woman who is the target of murderers, who has unwittingly involved herself in a conflict that threatens not only the lives of millions, but Amiri's own soul...and his heart.

ISBN 13: 978-0-8439-5767-9

Leslie Langtry

"Mixing a deadly sense of humor and plenty of sexy sizzle, Leslie Langtry creates a brilliantly original, laughter-rich mix of contemporary romance and suspense."
—*The Chicago Tribune*

Stand By Your Hitman

A Greatest Hits romance

Missi Bombay invents things—fatal flowers, Jell-O bullets, stroke-inducing panty hose and other ways to kill a target without leaving any kind of evidence. She's a great asset to her family of assassins. The one thing she can't invent, though, is a love life. Unfortunately, her mom has decided to handle that for her. Next thing Missi knows, she's packed off to Costa Rica for a wild reality show where she's paired with Lex, the hottest contestant on TV. Too bad she also has to scope out a potential victim. But the job becomes tougher when someone starts sabotaging the show...and love-of-her-life Lex thinks she's the culprit!

ISBN 13: 978-0-8439-6037-2

SARAH ABBOT

Destiny Bay

Someone is watching…someone who knows what Abrielle Lancaster wants to know: what caused her mother to leave the tiny, picturesque St. Cecilia Island a broken woman.

Abby has fallen in love with the island's dangerous beauty, with its quirky customs and warm-hearted inhabitants. But most of all, she's fallen in love with enigmatic, charismatic Ryan Brannigan, the one man who has every reason in the world to hate her.

Is he the one who's been lurking outside her bedroom window in the dark? Is he the one who's painstakingly plotted every move to recreate a relationship so twisted and terrifying it will never, ever die?

ISBN 13: 978-0-505-52744-5

"Carpe Scrotum. *Seize Life by the Testicles.*"
—Electra-Djerroldina

Knight's Fork

The Queen Consort of the Volnoth needs a sperm donor, and only one green-eyed god has the right stuff. Little does she know she has pinned all her hopes on the crown jewels of the fabled Royal Saurian Djinn. Not only is he the son of her greatest enemy, but he has taken a vow of chastity.

The Saurian Knight is caught between a problem father who has all the moral integrity of a Mafia Don, and a married Princess who would stop at nothing to have his seed in her belly. No matter which way he turns, he's "forked."

Taking the wrong lover…in the wrong place, at the wrong time…is dangerous. And when the High and Mighty intervene, it can be fatal. Can true love and a pure White Knight's virtue triumph, when society loves a right royal scandal?

Rowena Cherry

ISBN 13: 978-0-505-52740-0

For centuries they have walked among us—vampires, shape-shifters, the Celtic Sidhe, demons, and other magical beings. Their battle to reign supreme is constant, but one force holds them in check, a race of powerful woarriors known as the

IMMORTALS

The USA Today *Bestselling Series Continues*

Immortals: THE REDEEMING
September 2008

Immortals: THE CROSSING
Coming October 2008

Immortals: THE HAUNTING
Coming November 2008

Immortals: THE RECKONING
Coming Spring 2009

Molly Anderson is built to survive.

RAZOR GIRL

It's been six years since she and her family escaped into a bunker, led by her conspiracy theorist father and his fore-knowledge of a plot to bring about the apocalypse. But her father's precautions didn't stop there.

Molly is faster, stronger, and her ocular implants and razor-tipped nails set her apart. Apart, when—venturing alone out of the bunker and into a plague ravaged, monster-ridden wilderness—what Molly needs most is togetherness.

Chase Griffin, a friend from her past, is her best bet. But while he and others have miraculously survived, the kind boy has become a tormented man. Together, these remnants of humanity must journey to the one place Molly's father believed all civilization would be reborn: the Magic Kingdom, where everyone knows it's a small world after all.

MARIANNE MANCUSI

ISBN 13: 978-0-505-52780-6

TRIPLE EXPOSURE

"[Thompson] more than holds her own in territory blazed by Tami Hoag and Tess Gerritsen."

—Publishers Weekly

COLLEEN THOMPSON

Better than anyone, photographer Rachel Carson knows the camera can lie. That's how lurid altered photos of her appeared on the Internet, starting a downward spiral that ended with her shooting a nineteen-year-old stalker in self-defense. Fleeing the press and the threats of an un-identified female caller, she retreats to her remote home-town in the Texas desert. In Marfa, where mysterious lights hover in the night sky, folks are used to the unexplainable, and a person's secrets are off-limits. But recluse Zeke Pike takes that philosophy even further than Rachel herself. In her viewfinder Zeke's male sensuality is highlighted, his unexpressed longing for human contact revealed. Through a soft-focus lens, she sees a future for them beyond their red-hot affair, never guessing their relationship will expose the lovers to more danger than either can imagine.

ISBN 13: 978-0-8439-6143-0

✂ ☐ YES!

Sign me up for the Love Spell Book Club and send my
FREE BOOKS! If I choose to stay in the club, I will pay only
$8.50* each month, a savings of $6.48!

NAME: _____

ADDRESS: _____

TELEPHONE: _____

EMAIL: _____

☐ I want to pay by credit card.

☐ VISA   ☐ MasterCard   ☐ DISCOVER

ACCOUNT #: _____

EXPIRATION DATE: _____

SIGNATURE: _____

Mail this page along with $2.00 shipping and handling to:
Love Spell Book Club
PO Box 6640
Wayne, PA 19087
Or fax (must include credit card information) to:
610-995-9274
You can also sign up online at **www.dorchesterpub.com**.
*Plus $2.00 for shipping. Offer open to residents of the U.S. and Canada only. Canadian
residents please call 1-800-481-9191 for pricing information.
If under 18, a parent or guardian must sign. Terms, prices and conditions subject to
change. Subscription subject to acceptance. Dorchester Publishing reserves the right to
reject any order or cancel any subscription.